Don Girvan graduated from Georgia State University, where he edited the award-winning *Georgia State Signal* newspaper during his senior year. He also established a community paper called *Plantation Times* in Atlanta. After graduation, he was commissioned Second Lieutenant Armor serving as a Tank Platoon Leader, Armored Cavalry Troop Commander, and Aide to the Commanding General U.S. Army Alaska, Information Officer for Yukon Command, publishing the award-winning *Yukon Sentinel*. His last assignment was Editor of the *Bayonet* at Fort Benning. He was awarded the Army Commendation Medal and decided, upon leaving the Army as a Captain, that he preferred a career in chemical manufacturing with Celanese Corp. After six jobs with Celanese, he founded ProTeam Products, manufacturing a commercially successful line of swimming pool chemicals in the USA and Europe. He holds five U.S. chemical patents and a number of foreign patents. Don retired, following the acquisition of ProTeam by Haviland Consumer Products, and lives with his wife and best friend, Patty, in a home that they built on the St. Johns River near St. Augustine, Florida.

To the greatest generation.

Don Girvan

BROADSIDE

AUSTIN MACAULEY PUBLISHERS™

LONDON • CAMBRIDGE • NEW YORK • SHARJAH

Ordering Information:
Quantity sales: special discounts are available on quantity purchases by corporations, associations, and others. For details, contact the publisher at the address below.

Publisher's Cataloging-in-Publication data
Girvan, Don
Broadside

ISBN 9781643783352 (Paperback)
ISBN 9781643783369 (Hardback)
ISBN 9781645367499 (ePub e-book)

Library of Congress Control Number: 2019907906

The main category of the book — FICTION / Romance / Military

www.austinmacauley.com/us

First Published (2019)
Austin Macauley Publishers LLC
40 Wall Street, 28th Floor
New York, NY 10005
USA

mail-usa@austinmacauley.com
+1 (646) 5125767

My wonderful wife, Patty, deserves five stars for encouragement and six stars for patience with my feeble computer skills. She was thrilled when four publishers offered a contract for my first book and helped me choose the best.

Commander Kevin Owens USN (RET), my friend of twenty-five years, knew that an army guy was writing a navy story, so he helped me with little words, big pictures, and expert proofing.

Dr. Bryan Hickox, my movie producer friend, advised, after going over the story outline, that this would be a very expensive movie to make, and I should do it as a novel. I would then have a better chance negotiating movie rights.

Monika Forrest, a dear friend of twenty-eight years, was three years old and alone with her mother when the Red Army captured Berlin. She received a solid education learning English beginning in the fifth grade. As a young woman, she was hired by the U.S. Army and met her soldier husband who was from Texas. I have been fortunate to spend hours with Monika's mother learning what it was really like and for Monika proofing the second German story line.

Leon Holbrook Esq. and William Horne Esq. both proofed the legal part of the story and offered encouragement when the early chapters were taking shape.

This original historical fiction story describes the life of Homer Harris in America before World War II, and the challenges faced by a young man coping with difficult events. He is helped by many good people and overcomes evil. His experience at the U.S. Naval Academy prepares him for a decisive role in the Merchant Marine and the U.S. Navy during the Second World War. Well-known military and political figures are combined with fictional persons in America, Australia, Great Britain, and Germany. Two fine young women appreciate his faith, character, kindness, and courage. One will become his bride.

Chapter 1
Formative Years

Homer Harris was born at the Newton New Jersey Hospital on November 1, 1921 to Mildred and Bob Harris. Bob received the Medal of Honor during the Great War for saving his submarine that dove with the main induction valve stuck open. He placed his leg into the intake and nearly died before the crew spotted a warning light and re-surfaced. After the Great War, Bob returned to Sparta, New Jersey, and went to work in sales with New York Metropolitan Life Insurance Company. Bob and Mildred were married on June 1st, 1920, at the Sparta First Presbyterian Church. Mildred, known to her friends as Mil, graduated from the St. Barnabas School of Nursing. Mil and Bob had been in love since their freshman year at Sparta High School.

During the next 17 years, Bob Harris became one of the top insurance salesmen and, using both Mil and Bob's income, they bought their dream home on Manitoe Island in the middle of Lake Mohawk. The Island had 31 houses served by a one-lane wooden bridge. The Harris home was built by the same builder who built a similar English Tudor for Charles and Ann Morrow Lindbergh following the loss of their baby.

The Lake Mohawk Country Club was a real estate development of the Arthur D. Crane Company, with very high security. The spring fed lake had nine miles of shoreline. There were three guard houses manned 24/7 by shotgun-armed, off-duty local police, or New Jersey State Patrol officers. The security plan was created by General Norman, Schwarzkopf's father. The development had a beautiful nine-hole golf course with a separate club house, and 21 miles of private roads. If you lived at Lake Mohawk, you had arrived. Many of the neighbors were New York multi-millionaires who wanted a safe, casual place to raise their families, and did not want the fast lifestyle on Long Island. The Harris Family did not make it to even the bottom of the social register, but at Lake Mohawk that didn't matter.

Homer and his best friend, Hans Schmidt, were partners in a 100-customer *New Jersey Herald* paper route, and saved their profits to buy a 13 ft. Penn

Yan Swift runabout boat with a 22 horsepower, rope-start Evinrude outboard motor that was kept in the Harris boat house, because the Schmidt family did not have a lakefront home. In 1920, the Schmidt family immigrated to the USA following the Great War, and Hans's dad became a home builder, while Frida Schmidt designed and sold custom wedding dresses. She was a wonderful cook. The Schmidt family spoke German at home and Homer began to pick up the language.

During the ninth grade at Sparta High School, Homer elected to take German for two reasons. First, he already had a head start with his vocabulary, and second, his teacher, Christine Costello, was a beautiful Italian blond widow from Northern Italy. Mrs. Costello had graduated from the University of Florence with a master's degree in languages. Italy was on the allied side during the Great War, and when her husband was killed in the Alps during an attack led by Erwin Rommel, she decided to immigrate to America. She had a cousin in New York who sponsored her, and economic conditions in Europe were dismal after the war. She became the much-loved language teacher at Sparta High.

During the 10th and 11th grade, Homer developed a strong interest in shortwave radio. The small den off their kitchen was turned into the radio room. For Christmas in 1936 Homer opened a package with a 10 band Zenith Transoceanic receiver radio and immediately attached the 100-foot long antennae that had given his old Farnsworth AM radio the ability to pick up clear channel stations all over the USA. A whole new world emerged. The BBC, Radio Berlin, Dusseldorf, and Hamburg came in clear as a bell on the evening of December 25th. Listening to the German stations helped Homer with his vocabulary, however Mrs. Costello cautioned him to not believe the propaganda. During late January, Bob Harris and Hans' dad, Manfred Schmidt, drilled the ice behind the Harris boat house to ensure safe skating and helped the boys clear a 50-by-100-foot rink. All four seasons at Lake Mohawk were fun.

As the crow flies, Lake Mohawk was exactly 50 miles from Manhattan, but it seemed like a different country. Both Homer and Hans were making very good grades at one of the top academic high schools in New Jersey. In early October Hans' dad, who Americanized his name to Fred, took both boys and Homer's chocolate Labrador retriever Buddy duck hunting down on the Jersey Shore. Buddy had never been duck hunting, but he brought every downed duck back through ice cold water and heavy weeds. His tail never stopped wagging, as if to say, "this is what I was born to do."

On December 1, 1937 a fancy special delivery envelope was delivered to the heavy, oak-carved front door of the Harris home, and was signed for by

11

Homer. When Mildred Harris came home, she noticed that it was addressed to Mr. and Mrs. Robert Harris, and so she opened it.

President Arthur Haviland
Cordially extends an invitation
to Mr. and Mrs. Robert Harris to attend
the 50th annual New York Metropolitan Life
Awards Banquet and Christmas celebration
at the Waldorf Astoria on Wednesday December 22
from 6:00 p.m. to 10 p.m. in the Grand Ballroom.
Black Tie
Please RSVP

When Bob Harris drove up in his new grey Nash Ambassador, Mil met him in the driveway with the invitation, saying "We've never been invited to this before."

Bob gave her a kiss and said, "Honey, I sold a lot of policies."

"I will have to go shopping for a dress, and you will need to get a tux."
In the past the New York Metropolitan Life company newsletter described the gala affair, the bonus checks, paid life insurance and special recognition awards.

"Being invited probably means that we are going to get something from the company."

Homer had never seen his mother so excited about an invitation. Mil scheduled off work at the Newton Hospital, had her hair done at the Sparta Beauty Parlor, and made sure Bob's tux fit properly. They said goodbye to Homer and pulled out of the driveway at 3 p.m., which would give them plenty of time in case they had a flat tire.

December 22nd was the long-awaited opening of the Lincoln Tunnel, connecting Route 3 in New Jersey with midtown Manhattan. Bob pulled the Nash up to the sign that said Waldorf Astoria Valet Parking, gave his keys to the attendant, and received a check stub. Mil and Bob walked through the heavy brass front doors of the Waldorf at exactly 5 p.m. according to the big round clock by the café off the lobby. Mil had never been to the Waldorf, and started looking around just like a tourist from Atlanta.

Bob held her hand and said, "lets' go in the café and have a cup of coffee before this thing gets started."

At exactly 6 p.m., the doors to the Grand Ballroom opened and the crowd started moving to a large seating chart, then to a receiving line with President Arthur Haviland, Mrs. Victoria Chase Haviland, William T. Sherman the third,

Vice President of sales, Mr. and Mrs. Orville Olsen Vice President of Finance and Actuarial Science, and Mr. and Mrs. John Leone the new Vice President Comptroller.

Everyone in the line said kind words about Bob and his importance to New York Metropolitan Life and complimented Mil's dress. When they reached the seating chart, they were surprised to see that they were at the far-left side of the head table. Mil was seated next to the Vice President of Sales, who preferred that his friends call him Billy. Billy was not a direct descendant of the General, but he was a legitimate second cousin. After the 5-course dinner was served, Arthur Haviland stood with a toast to another successful year and to the people that made New York Metropolitan Life the fastest-growing insurance company in America, according to Fortune Magazine.

"As a second toast please raise your glass to Bob Harris, our 1937 Salesman of the Year and our Medal of Honor winner, who has grown with our company ever since he left the Navy just 18 short years ago." There was a rousing round of applause, and Mil started to tear up with pride. Arthur Haviland went on to say "In addition to this bonus check for ten thousand dollars, I am proud to present a fully paid up New York Metropolitan Life one-million-dollar whole life double indemnity policy in effect immediately, with his lovely wife Mildred and son Homer Harris as beneficiaries. Of course, Bob can change the beneficiaries and put me on the policy if he should choose." There was a round of laughter that shifted to applause. "Now, Billy Sherman would like to tell you about Bob Harris."

Following some glowing remarks Billy asked Bob Harris to say a few words. Bob stood, turned to Mil and asked her to stand alongside and placed his arm around her shoulder. "I am honored beyond words and would not be here without the support from my dear wife. I would like to thank our staff for their untiring back up support and our President Arthur Haviland for keeping our company solvent and strong during some very difficult economic times."

There was a round of applause and then Arthur Haviland said, "perhaps the orchestra will play some dancing music while we enjoy dessert."

At 9:45 p.m., the lights were brought up and everyone began their goodbyes. When Mil and Bob walked out the front door of the Waldorf, their Nash Ambassador was parked directly behind Arthur Haviland's black Cadillac. Mil thanked Victoria and Arthur Haviland for a wonderful evening.

Victoria kissed Mil on the cheek then said, "I hope we see more of you and Bob."

Bob shook the President's hand and said, "I will never forget this honor."

Arthur Haviland said, "Bob, the honor is mine…have a safe trip home."

The valet assisted Mil as she entered the Nash and Bob handed him a dollar bill. The motor was quietly running, and Bob released the emergency brake, pushed the left clutch pedal to the floor, and pulled the shift lever toward him and down into first gear. After the Cadillac pulled away, he added gas and slowly released the clutch and the Nash pulled smoothly out on the northbound lane of Park Avenue.

Bob found an area where he could make a U-turn and head south to signs at 39th street leading traffic to the Lincoln Tunnel.

Chapter 2
Oh No!

The 50-cent toll was collected inbound toward Manhattan but there was no toll going west. Traffic entered the 8,216-foot-long, brightly lit tunnel with white tile walls. Green lights were suspended on the right lane ceiling and red lights on the other side of the two-lane traffic. There was a large sign on both sides of the tunnel entrance stating, "NO EXPLOSIVES OR BULK PETROLEUM PRODUCTS ALLOWED."

Traffic was moving at 30 miles per hour until the road started climbing toward the exit on the New Jersey side, and then brake lights came on and Bob pulled the Nash to a dead stop behind a Mayflower moving truck. A split second later, the Nash was struck in the rear with great force by a large truck, and then a second impact was caused by a cement truck striking a propane gas truck that first hit the Nash. Bob looked in his rear-view mirror and saw a huge fireball. The Nash had been pushed into the moving truck, and there was no way to pull into the opposite lane. Mil and Bob had only a few seconds to live when the Nash was completely engulfed in flames and their gas tank exploded. In less than five minutes, a massive sprinkler system started dumping thousands of gallons of Hudson River water into the tunnel, but it was too late.

After it got dark, Homer went in the kitchen to feed Buddy and warm a pot of homemade vegetable soup that his mother had left for him in the refrigerator. After finishing his homework, he put on his earphones and started scanning the globe. His first clear signal came in from the BBC, with their 12 p.m. Greenwich Time London Calling program. The big story was about the December 21st California premier of Disney's *Snow White and the Seven Dwarfs,* which would soon be premiered in London. After listening to four German stations, he let Buddy out for the night and got comfortable on the leather couch in the radio room.

At 7 a.m. on December 23, Buddy started pushing against Homer who was sound asleep on the couch. Buddy rarely barked unless it was something important, so when a loud bark went straight into Homer's ear he jumped up and followed Buddy to the front door. Two cars were pulling up to the parking area on the other side of the low rock wall, just off the road. Homer turned on the front door porch light and saw that two men were getting out of what looked like a Ford police car, and another man was getting out of a Packard. As they approached the door Homer recognized Dr. Porter, who was pastor of the Sparta Presbyterian Church.

Homer greeted them at his open front door and said, "Dr. Porter, and gentlemen, please come in."

"Homer, this is Police Chief David Earl and Detective Don Delay."

"Is something wrong?"

"Well, yes," Chief Earl said. Dr. Porter moved to the living room and was followed by the policemen and Homer.

Dr. Porter said "God sometimes calls us to heaven when it is least expected. Last night your mother and father were killed in a terrible accident in the Lincoln Tunnel on their way home."

Homer dropped to the floor with shock and began grasping for breath between cries. "How could this happen…They never hurt anybody…Are you sure it was my mom and dad?"

Detective Delay said, "When we leave, I'm going straight to the Lincoln Tunnel and I will report back when I can verify what has happened."

"Can I go with you?" Homer asked.

Chief Earl said, "No Homer…they will only admit police personnel, but I have authorized a wrecker to bring your dad's car to our impound lot, and if we find that your mom and dad were in the car their remains will be cared for by the Arlington Funeral Home then the Presbyterian Church."

Dr. Porter put his arms around Homer. "I will stay with you and we will pray to God for the strength and faith to help you through your loss."

Homer struggled to pull himself together. After the police left, Capt. and Mrs. Lindbergh came across the road to see what was wrong.

They were followed by Fred and Freda Schmidt, who heard a report on the early WOR morning news. It was Hans turn to throw the morning *New Jersey Herald* paper route so when he arrived at the Harris home it was crowded with friends and neighbors offering sympathy. During the afternoon Freda Schmidt made coffee and sandwiches and a variety of food started arriving. Chief David Earl returned and asked Dr. Porter and Homer to join him in the radio room away from the crowd.

"Homer, I am so sorry to say that we verified the loss of your parents. I'm sure Dr. Porter will help with arrangements. I'm sorry but I need to ask you Homer, where do you intend to stay?"

"This is my home…my dog Buddy is with me and I need to graduate from high school. I don't have anywhere else to go."

"Unfortunately, there is a state law that a person under 18 years of age cannot occupy a residence without adult supervision. We checked your driver's license record and you are only 17, so perhaps Dr. Porter can arrange a suitable adult to move in with you at least until you turn 18."

"That will be done," said Dr. Porter.

The last visitor on Saturday evening was Mrs. Christine Costello.

Chapter 3

Reconstruction

After a warm hug, Homer asked Mrs. Costello if she was going to renew her lease. Homer and some students had discussed helping her move closer to school. Homer explained that he needed adult supervision to remain in his home, and Mrs. Costello could stay for free. He would pay for the food and all other expenses. Homer knew that he could fulfill this promise because his mother had placed his name on her home checking account.

"You would have the master bedroom and bath."

Without hesitation, Christine Costello said, "I would be glad to move here for you. I hope you realize that I will be as tough on you as I have been in school. You are actually doing me a favor Homer, because this is a beautiful place to live and I would never have been able to afford a home on the island. Now, to keep things legal we should talk with Dr. Porter and make sure he has no objection. Then I will go home and get some things and be back in about an hour. We can make arrangements to put my furniture in storage and get some help moving next week."

At 9 a.m. Friday morning, the phone rang, and it was Arthur Haviland, President of New York Metropolitan Life insurance company.

"Homer, my wife and I would like to drive out to your home today to pay our condolences, or we could come on the 27th, after Christmas. On second thought, it would be good if you could have your dad's Attorney or CPA attend, because we will also have some important things to discuss. If 2 p.m. on the 27th would be okay, will you call to confirm?"

"Yes, Sir."

"Is there anything that we can do for you right now? You know your dad was an outstanding member of our company, and he is deeply missed."

"I'm doing pretty well Sir, and thank you for calling."

On Monday, December 27th, at 1 p.m. Attorney Lawrence Cohen and CPA Sam Cornelius arrived and offered condolences to Homer. Both had been highly regarded by Bob Harris, and Homer felt comfortable with them.

Mrs. Costello came in the living room and was introduced by Homer. She suggested they could have the meeting in the large dining room facing the lake and had coffee and cookies on the table along with school note pads. At 2 p.m., a large, black, chauffeur-driven Cadillac pulled up in front. Three distinguished men wearing black overcoats and homburg hats came to the front door. Homer and Buddy greeted them, and Arthur Haviland shook hands with Homer and introduced Arthur Olsen, the V.P. of Finance, and John Leone, the Comptroller. Then Homer introduced Lawrence Cohen as his dad's attorney, and Sam Cornelius as the family CPA.

Mr. Haviland said, "The reason for this meeting is to let you know, Homer, that your dad will not be forgotten and to cover insurance matters that will secure your future. I would like Mr. Olsen to describe the policies that are in force, beginning with the oldest in force moving the most recent."

Olsen began with policy number NYML32189, a 20-year term life policy on your mother with a value of $500,000, however it had a double indemnity clause in case of violent death which added another $500,000. NYMLW number 12,389 is a whole life $1,000,000 double indemnity policy, purchased by your dad, insuring your dad. On December 22nd, during our awards banquet, your dad was awarded Salesman of the Year and given a $10,000 bonus check that we are certain was destroyed, so the check has been re issued in your name."

Arthur Haviland handed the check to Homer.

"Your dad was also awarded a fully paid, whole-life double indemnity policy #NYMLW25132 at the banquet, for $1,000,000 effective immediately in force. Now I'll turn the meeting over to Mr. Leone, our Comptroller."

Leone began by saying, "Your dad was a strong believer in New York Metropolitan Life and the concept of being prepared with life insurance. We will prepare beneficiary checks totaling $5,000,000, and will need to know if you want them sent directly to your bank or we could set up an annuity with a $100,000 annual lifetime pay out."

Homer looked at Mr. Cornelius and Mr. Cohen then after a pause responded by saying, "Thank you gentlemen for your kind words and your financial support. I think rather than make a quick decision, it would be good if Mr. Cornelius and Mr. Cohen can give me guidance, because this is truly a large amount of money. Then we can get back to you with an informed answer. Thank you so much."

The group shook hands and Arthur Haviland told Homer, "Please feel free to call me if there is anything we can do for you."

After the delegation from New York Metropolitan Life said their goodbyes, Homer, Sam Cornelius and Larry Cohen went back to the dining room and Mrs. Costello brought in a fresh pot of coffee.

Although she wasn't in the room, Homer thought she may have heard some of the conversation, so he said, "Why don't you get an extra cup and join us, because I would appreciate your comments."

Sam Cornelius began the conversation by saying, "We need to come up with some suggestions for investing this large sum of money. My first reaction to the suggested $100,000 annual annuity is that it would only provide a 2% return, and tie up all of your capital. While $100,000 sounds like a lot of money, inflation can diminish the value over time. Also, you would be putting all of your eggs in one basket. Even though it is unlikely that this very sound company would go under, remember what happened in 1929. I think we should consider setting up five investment baskets with long term growth in mind."

Larry Cohen said, "That is exactly what I think is best for Homer. In basket number 1, I would propose allocating $500,000 for extraordinary growth potential with some risk but very high reward. These funds could be used as market opportunities presented themselves. The first common stock that I would buy is the Loft Candy Company."

Sam Cornelius interrupted and said, "Who the hell is the Loft Candy Company?"

Larry Cohen said "I've been accumulating this stock for nine months, because they are going to change their name to Pepsi-Cola and the shares have gone from 10 cents to 25 cents. Their business plan is to follow Coca-Cola, setting up franchise bottlers with a 12 oz. cola that is a little sweeter than Coke and twice as much for your money. They have a long list of bottlers signed up and will be making their announcement in 3 months. This will not give much time to start buying without creating a rush that will drive up the share price. I would try to purchase $100,000 before the share price doubles. My guess is that we will probably reach 200,000 shares. Whatever remains could be placed in Standard Oil, DuPont and Boeing. In the second basket, I would accumulate $500,000 in common stock for U.S. Steel, General Motors, and 3 railroads The Southern, Pennsylvania, and the L&N because they are paying a 3% dividend and are serving growth areas. My third $500,000 bucket would be preferred stock in New York Metropolitan Life, The Hartford, and Travelers. Their preferred stock will average 4% dividends and offer some growth, not as much as the common stock, but with less downside risk. My fourth basket would diversify $500,000 into electric power companies that pay a good dividend. Georgia Power, Alabama Power Florida Power, and Light and Con Edison. They will average 4.5% dividend and have some appreciation. My fifth

$500,000 basket would include AT&T, IBM, General Electric, and CBS radio. If my math is right, this this will leave $2,900,000 deposited in a solid bank like Chase-Manhattan to invest over time."

Sam Cornelius said, "Over time we can invest more in the winners and sell the weak performers. To do this right Homer it will take time and diligence and I would propose a monthly fee of $1,000 per month to each of our firms. You will approve all stock trades and all accounts will be in your name with a brokerage firm like J.P. Morgan or Meryl Lynch."

Homer took a deep breath. He turned toward Mrs. Costello and said, "Well, it doesn't look like we will have any trouble making ends meet. Let's move forward with this plan, and let me thank you for your friendship over many years."

Larry Cohen said, "Homer, this will give you more income and diversification. I would recommend that I draft an agreement describing what we intend to do on your behalf. I would suggest that the Cornelius firm continue to keep your financial records and prepare checks and deposits and submit records for an annual outside audit firm."

"Mr. Cohen and Mr. Cornelius, if my dad was here, he would vote yes. I can't thank you enough for your support."

After they said goodbye Homer turned to Mrs. Costello and asked, "What do you think?"

She said, "Your dad was a good judge of intelligence and integrity, so I believe that your CPA and your attorney will do their best to look out for you."

Homer smiled and said, "I agree. By the way I wanted to get you a Christmas present, so when I looked at your 1926 Plymouth which is falling apart, I decided that we should pick out a new Ford, Chevrolet or Plymouth. We should buy it from one of the large dealers near the city so the locals will not know that I had anything to do with the purchase and start rumors."

The next day they settled on a 1937 Ford Deluxe woody station wagon and got a $75.00 trade in for the old Plymouth.

When school started after the Christmas vacation, only one teacher asked about the new Ford.

Mrs. Costello said, "I've been saving for a long time."

Chapter 4
Evil in Germany

Dusseldorf, Germany, April 1, 1933

Abraham Goldberg had served in the Great War, and was awarded the Iron Cross for staying behind enemy lines and repairing a radio so his cut off unit could call in Artillery fire and retake a critical position at Verdun. After the war in 1920, he opened a radio repair shop in Dusseldorf. In 1930, he brought his older son David into the business, and they began to sell and repair radios. The business was called Welt Radio (World Radio) and developed a strong customer base among the elite class even though the economy was having great problems due to huge reparation payments demanded by France and England.

David's younger brother Moses started working in the repair shop after school in 1935, and became highly skilled. On the evening of April 1, 1938, the Goldberg family sat at their dining table and said their prayers.

Abraham said "Mother and Sarah, I do not want you to be upset about what we need to discuss. Today Hitler has proclaimed a boycott of Jewish shops. This could cause us to lose our business. He has also proclaimed in many speeches that Jews are not Germans. This turn of events makes it necessary for our family to plan a new course of action. I have contacted our cousin, Rabbi Solomon Goldberg in Chicago, and he has arranged visas for David and Moses to use an American State Department regulation that will allow them to bring money into the country to start a business and immediately get green cards. We have buried in our basement vault a little over $300,000 dollars in gold. We will need to send half of our savings, so our boys can get started with a good location, an inventory of German AM and shortwave radios, and a well-equipped repair shop. We will also need to sell American brands, like Philco, Farnsworth, Zenith, and RCA. This needs to be done very soon, because the Nazi dictatorship is going to impose travel restrictions for Jews."

"David and Moses, pack a light bag as if you were going on a short holiday and take the morning train to Lisbon. In five days, the SS Brazil will sail for

Rio De Janeiro and you can catch a Pan American flight to Miami then on to Chicago."

Ruth Goldberg broke into tears, and Sarah said, "Papa, why do we need to move so soon?"

Abraham put his arm around his daughter and said, "You and your mother will need to work full time at Welt Radio and be prepared to leave at a minute's notice, if the evil that is going on in Berlin and Munich spreads to Dusseldorf. Should we have to run for our lives, we can go over the mountains through France to Spain and then Portugal. It may be difficult, but we can join our boys in America, and we will have a good business there.

Lisbon, Portugal, April 6, 1938

Moses and David were shown to second class cabin 306 on the port side of the SS Brazil. The cabin had one porthole and two above and below bunk beds. There was a small desk with one straight metal chair. The bathroom was so small you could hardly turn around and the shower head would only spray a mist of water. David had shaved his dark beard and Moses began going through their luggage to remove anything that might identify them as Jewish.

David said, "that's a good idea, but what about Goldberg on our passports?"

Moses looked up and said "we just won't wave our passports or visas around and try to avoid conversations with other passengers. We don't know if there are any Nazis on the ship."

After a lifeboat drill, a daily newsletter was found on the desk back in their cabin saying that dinner would be served in the first-class dining salon and the second class dining room at 1900 hours, and a chime would ring 15 minutes before dinner. The newsletter was printed in Portuguese, Spanish, French, German and English. The first-class salon had an assigned seating chart, but second class was open seating.

The sea was calm, and the SS Brazil only experienced a gentle roll that did not upset anyone for dinner. David and Moses found a corner table for six, that had three older ladies and a teenage boy already seated. They were speaking Portuguese so very little polite conversation was necessary.

There were two dinner entree choices on the menu. David had broiled chicken and Moses had meat loaf with gravy and both had a salad and green beans. Chocolate cake was served with coffee for dessert. Beer and wine were available for an extra charge but David and Moses were saving every penny. All passengers were allowed in the smoke-filled casino however David and Moses chose the library, and brought books back to their cabin.

Breakfast and lunch were uneventful, but dinner on the third day of the 10 day trip caused some concern, when a well- dressed blond man in his late 30's or early 40's moved quickly across the dining room to take a seat at a table for 4 with David and Moses. One seat was left vacant. He opened the conversation in English and David and Moses introduced themselves just as David and Mo in English. After they made their dinner selections, the inevitable "where are you from?" and "where are you going?" questions started.

David took the lead and kept the answers short. They were radio repairmen from Dusseldorf on a holiday trip to Brazil.

"Well, I thought your English was not your first language," and then he switched to German. "I'm Heinrich Richter and will be attached to our embassy in Buenos Aires after a short stay in Rio.

Richter tried many probing questions and was given short vague answers. Just before leaving Richter said, "I saw you up in the library. Perhaps we can schedule a card game up there."

Moses thought, "Sure, we'll go out of our way to do that," but instead said, "Enjoy your cruise."

Then Richter got up and said, "Heil Hitler!"

So, David and Moses got up and said reluctantly, "Heil Hitler."

Upon returning to their cabin, Moses said, "This is one guy we should avoid. I nearly choked when I had to say 'Heil Hitler.'"

David said, "Yeah…he's probably sending a radiogram about us to the Gestapo right now."

"I didn't tell him our last name, did you, David?"

No but he probably has our cabin number or could get it from the Purser.

"We should avoid him but if he becomes more of a problem David, I'm for throwing him overboard. I have my athletic sock with a pound of coins to use as a blackjack."

Richter told the German ship's doctor, "Those two are Jew fairies. We can deal with them when they get back to Germany."

Rio de Janeiro, April 16, 1938

David and Moses passed a sigh of relief when they disembarked carrying their own luggage. They had no problem with customs, because they were being transported to the Pan American Clipper Terminal where they would be processed by American Customs before boarding the 5 p.m. Clipper to Miami with their prepaid tickets from Rabbi Solomon Goldberg.

Rabbi Goldberg would be repaid as soon as they arrived in Chicago. The big four-engine Boeing flying boat was moored to a floating dock, with the flight crew assisting passengers to their large comfortable seats. Prior to takeoff, the attractive stewardesses, who were also registered nurses demonstrated the use of their seat belts and May West inflatable life jackets, and then served a choice of Coca-Cola, coffee, tea, water with ice, or white wine. David and Moses both chose Coca-Cola.

The Radial engines mounted on the wing just forward of the passenger cabin began revving up and they could feel the plane begin rocking like a boat. The engine noise became so loud that you could not hear the waves pounding on the hull as they gathered speed. After what seemed like a long run down the harbor heading due south, the aircraft broke free from the water and gained speed. After reaching about 500 feet the flying boat made a 180-degree turn heading north.

Neither David nor Moses had been in an airplane before and, here they were in the most advanced passenger plane in the world. As the Clipper turned north, they passed over Rio and then many farms and ranches then nothing but jungle and rivers. They were seated on the port side and stayed glued to the window looking at white clouds and a beautiful sunset. The flight crew turned on the cabin lights and began serving dinner.

Moses turned to David and said, "I'll never forget this trip!"

After the dinner trays were cleared the flight crew distributed pillows and blankets and helped David and Moses recline their seats.

They were both asleep in a few minutes. At 6 a.m. the cabin lights were turned on and coffee and orange juice were served, along with warm towels. As the blankets and pillows were collected, the flight crew announced that they would be landing in Caracas for refueling in one hour. The passengers entered the terminal from a floating dock and were served a full American-style breakfast.

David remarked "I can't believe all of the food."

After breakfast, they went to the men's room and were given a toothbrush and a small tube of Colgate toothpaste, then came back to the newspaper stand and bought a copy of the last evening *Miami Herald*. Exactly two hours after landing the clipper took off for Miami, Florida. At 5:30 p.m. the clipper started descending and the passengers could see tall buildings and Biscayne Bay.

Moses turned to David and said, "Thank God we are in America. I just wish Sarah and our parents were with us."

Their flight to Atlanta on Eastern Air Lines connected with Chicago and Southern to Midway airport. Both flights were good, but not as nice as the clipper. Rabbi Goldberg met David and Moses at the airport and, after dinner and conversation about the situation in Germany, they began planning for the opening of World Radio in America.

Chapter 5
From out of Nowhere

Sparta, New Jersey, January 25, 1938

Homer Harris settled into his routine at Sparta High School and continued improving his point average. Homer was invited to dinner with the Lindbergs, Schmidts, Dr. and Mrs. Porter, and several other families from the Presbyterian Church. Having Mrs. Costello stay with him was a pleasure.

One evening, she asked Homer if it would be okay to invite her cousin, who was a teacher in New York, out for a weekend.

Homer said, "We can pick her up at the Dover Train Station."

That Saturday evening Homer took Rosa Dragonetti, who sponsored Christine Costello, to their favorite pub restaurant called Krogh's, which was in the Plaza at Lake Mohawk. At dinner, Homer started talking about college, and was encouraged by Mrs. Costello.

Life wasn't like it used to be with his mom and dad alive, but it was settling down. Homer attended Presbyterian services, and Christine Costello went to services at Don Bosco Catholic College in Newton, NJ. They fell into a pattern of meeting after church for an early dinner at one of many great restaurants away from Sparta. The favorite was Sammy's Old Cider Mill in Mendham, NJ. Sammy's was a speakeasy during prohibition years. They only served two items, either steak or lobster, and took your order at the door. You were then sent downstairs, to a bar with slot machines, pinball, a rifle range and pool tables.

Homer picked up two bottles of Coca-Cola, and a guy at the bar said, "Aren't you a little young to be going out with that blonde?"

Homer replied by saying "That's my aunt, and she is married."

He heard, "Harris!" called by the bartender. When you were called for dinner, it was waiting for you on the table.

Money was coming into the accounts set up by Sam Cornelius faster than Homer could imagine. He even thought about taking the Schmidt Family, and Mrs. Costello, on a cruise, but didn't want to leave Buddy. Then, a travel agent in Sparta told him that Cunard Line had kennels and for an extra charge you could take your dog. Now this idea, for the summer of 1938, was a possibility.

On Saturday, April 25, 1938, that possibility was dashed when a process server knocked on the front door and handed Mrs. Costello an official Order to Show Cause for why Homer Harris, a minor child, should not be placed under the guardianship of his blood relative uncle, Benjamin Harris, of Roswell Georgia. Homer had heard his father mention a younger brother Ben, who was constantly in trouble. After Ben joined the army before finishing high school, he was never heard from again. That was all Homer could remember his dad saying.

Homer immediately called Larry Cohen and read the document over the phone.

"As your attorney, I've got to tell you, Homer; this could be serious. What do you know about this Uncle Ben?"

"Not much except my dad had no use for him."

"We are going to need to find out everything we can about this Benjamin Harris, and then answer this Order to Show Cause. He has engaged a local Sussex County attorney in Newton, so I will begin checking on him. Can you check the date of issue and see if we have ten days to respond?"

"Mr. Cohen, It was issued on Friday April 24, and it says that we must answer by May 4th."

"Homer, I would assume that you are not ready to pack up and move to Georgia, so we will need to get busy. I will come out to your house on Sunday afternoon and pick up the court order. Will you be home?"

"Yes Sir, and thank you."

Larry Cohen called his friend David Shore with the Pinkerton Detective Agency in New York City on Monday morning, and explained the situation.

Shore's reaction was, "Sounds like this could be an attempt to take over your client's money. We'll find out all about this Ben Harris.

I'll contact our Atlanta Office and make sure they put a rush on it."

Larry Cohen received a direct call from the Pinkerton Atlanta office on Tuesday afternoon.

The Agent said, "I am reading from the report and a written copy is being forwarded by Air Mail to you. It reads as follows: Benjamin Harris is a 41-year-old white male resident of Cherokee County, Georgia near the town of Roswell. He operates a 400-acre cattle farm that was willed to his wife, Virginia, by her father Earl Mills. They have one son, 12 years old. Benjamin Harris was drafted into the U.S. Army as a private during The Great War, served at Camp Gordon Georgia, and was discharged after the war. Harris met his wife while in the Army, and married Virginia Mills one day after his discharge. He held a number of low-level jobs, finally being hired by her father, Earl Mills, for farm work. He does not have a criminal record. It is our opinion that the farm is providing a small income and that the family is struggling to make ends meet. Please advise if further information is needed."

Larry Cohen scratched his head, put his feet on his desk, and thought, 'This doesn't tell us much. A follow up with the Pinkerton's could tell us if Ben Harris is in debt, if he is a drinker, if he attends church, if his neighbors respect him, but not why there has been no contact for over 20 years with his brother. I wonder how he found out about his brother's death…probably a newspaper story. I'll tell the Pinkerton's to keep digging."

Larry Cohen had a number of fellow classmate friends at Rutgers Law School who were practicing in Northern New Jersey. A series of phone calls started to develop a pattern regarding Judge Andrew McCracken and John Killeran, the attorney representing Benjamin Harris. When McCracken rendered a judgement on a family law case represented by Killeran, eighteen out of eighteen times, Killeran won the case.

Cohen filed a request for a change of venue, moving the case out of Newton, and the request was promptly denied. On May 15, 1938, Court was called to order and Judge Andrew McCracken called on Attorney John Killeran to open the case.

Killeran told the Court that Benjamin Harris was the only living blood relative of the minor child Homer Harris and as such had the welfare of his nephew as his first priority. He explained that Benjamin Harris was married and that his loving wife Virginia and their twelve-year-old son looked forward to having Homer Harris live with them in their Christian home.

"Homer Harris will be able to live on their beautiful farm and attend Roswell High School for his senior year." Killeran pointed out that the only people who were supervising Homer were getting paid. "Homer now has an attorney who is here today and will be fighting to keep his clients checks coming, and an accountant who may not be managing the Harris estate in the best interest of the minor child."

Killeran then called Christine Costello to the witness stand, and remarked that this very attractive blonde woman is living with Homer Harris, and may have been taking more than a supervisory interest in him and the estate.

When he asked, "How many times have you slept with Homer?" Larry Cohen stood up and objected to this demining and unfounded question. The objection was overruled.

Mrs. Costello looked at Killeran and said, "You have a dirty, evil mind. I am a State certified secondary level teacher and I was asked by Homer and Dr. Porter, who is pastor of the First Presbyterian Church, to move to his home because New Jersey state law requires an adult in residence if a minor is under eighteen. I am a practicing Catholic and a widow with high morals. Homer has been one of my best students, and I felt great sorrow when his parents, who I have met at teacher conferences, were so abruptly taken from him. And for your information, Mr. Attorney, I am not sleeping with any of my students. I have an impeccable record. You can verify that with my Principal, Mr. Adams, and anyone on the school board."

"No further questions."

The audience believed Mrs. Costello and saw that Attorney Killeran was out of line and abusive.

The first witness that Larry Cohen called was Benjamin Harris. "Mr. Harris, as a loving uncle, can you explain why today, here in court, is the first time you have actually met your nephew Homer Harris? The information that I have is that you have been staying at the hotel in Newton since April 15, and have made no effort to see your nephew, and Newton is only ten or so miles from Sparta."

Ben Harris looked over at his lawyer and said, "I didn't want to get in an argument with him, and my lawyer said I should wait until we were in court."

"What is your educational background, Mr. Harris?"

Harris replied, "Well, I joined the Army before I finished high school."

The lawyer continued, "Do you have any other education?"

Harris again replied, "Only the school of hard knocks and some farming seminars at the feed and seed company."

"Who keeps track of your finances and pays your bills at your farm?"

"My wife, Virginia, she graduated from high school."

"How is your farm doing?"

"We are getting by okay."

"If you force Homer to move to your farm what are your future plans for him?

"I guess he'll go to high school and work on the farm."

"What about after high school?"

"Well there is always a lot to do on the farm."

"Have you discussed what Homer would like to do after high school?"

"No"

"No further questions."

Sam Cornelius was called to the stand to explain what was being done for Homer's investments.

"In the past four months, dividends paid to Homer's account were in excess of $33,000 and his investments have increased by 1.5%. These accounts are held in trust for Homer Harris, and no other person can buy or sell assets without his approval. All accounts are being audited by Price Waterhouse CPA's. My firm is keeping records and preparing checks for Homer to sign for living expenses."

Killeran rose to his feet and asked, "how much are you charging your minor client for these services?"

"The annual fee is $12,000."

"No further Questions."

A list of 10 character witnesses was called supporting Homer as a very responsible seventeen year old with an excellent school record.

After six witnesses Judge McCracken said, "Is council for Benjamin Harris willing to stipulate that the remaining witnesses will be saying the same thing about this minor?"

"We would, Your Honor." After closing arguments by both attorneys, Judge McCracken announced that a ruling would be given at 9 am the next day.

Larry Cohen thought to himself, "The fix is in."

That evening, Sam Cornelius and Larry Cohen took Homer to dinner and told him an appeal would follow if they lost the case.

Homer asked, "If we lose, does this mean that I will be made to go to Georgia Mr. Cohen?"

"That is a possibility, but we will do everything to keep that from happening. If we can stall for seven months, you will be eighteen and your uncle will not have the same case that he has now."

Chapter 6
What Now?

On May 22, 1938 Benjamin Harris was named Guardian of Homer Harris. He was also given full decision power over the Harris estate. The judgement also stated that the minor, Homer Harris, will accompany his Uncle Benjamin Harris to Georgia within one week.

On the afternoon of May 22nd, Ben Harris came to Homer's house and was greeted by Mrs. Costello. "May I come in? I want to talk with Homer."

"He is doing his homework, so have a seat and I will get him for you."

When Homer came in, Mrs. Costello was right behind him, and took a seat in a chair next to Homer.

"Ma'am, do you mind if I have a private conversation with my nephew?"

"That is up to Homer, but after the way your attorney treated me I think I should stay."

"Uncle, I want Mrs. Costello to stay."

"Well if that's the way you want it, I'll just say my piece to Homer. I have Railroad Tickets on May 26th, so you will need to get packed up so you can be picked up at 8 a.m. If you are not on the train, it will get messy with the court. Homer, I want you to get to know your Aunt Virginia and your Cousin Sandy. You will have a good family in Georgia, and I will be a looking out after you."

"Uncle, I don't need looking out after. It seems to me that, at seventeen years old, I am better educated than you are!"

"Well the court didn't agree with you, and I don't need no smart remarks from you. You will like being on the farm and you can go to Roswell High School."

"Uncle, did you get tickets for my dog, Buddy? I am not going without him."

"No, but we can take him in the baggage car. See, everything will work out." Then he looked at Mrs. Costello and said, "You will need to be out by the end of the week."

After his uncle left, Homer called Larry Cohen and asked about the appeal. His answer was not good. "We have the appeal on file but the appeal court has a four month backlog, so you will need to go to Georgia or be in violation of a court order."

"I have several questions. First, does Mrs. Costello have to be out by the end of the week?"

"Yes, or they will call the sheriff and have her evicted."

"Second, can we write her a check for moving expenses and for a rental deposit?"

"Yes, but Sam Cornelius will need to move fast before the accounts are frozen."

"Third, can Mr. Cornelius write a check for your services and his for the whole year, because I know I will need your help when I am down in Georgia?"

"Yes, but you need to call him right now and have the checks written and cashed right away."

"Fourth, what about the house? When I'm gone and Mrs. Costello is out by Friday, what happens next?"

"Your uncle or his representative will take possession because it is part of the estate. He could sell the house with or without the contents or rent it. Homer, I will have two men and a large moving truck out to your house in the morning and you can load up anything that you would like to have me put in storage for you. They can also help Mrs. Costello move."

"Fifth, there are things that I would like the Schmidts to have, such as my mom's Ford touring car and the boat that I can't take with me. Is this okay?"

"Go ahead and give away whatever you want to, but be sure to send the title with the Ford."

"It's going to be a busy four days, but Buddy and I will be ready to go on May 26th at 8 a.m. Thank you so much for your help!"

"Homer, Sam Cornelius and I will do everything we can to make this right. We were your dad's friends, and now yours. This thing has become personal. Your uncle is trying to appropriate your estate because you are a minor, and in my opinion he is too dumb to manage even his own checking account. You will need to hang in there and make the best of the next few months."

At 1 p.m. on May 26th, the Pennsylvania Railroad left Newark for Washington DC. Buddy was in the baggage car and Homer and his uncle sat silently in the front seat of the passenger car. When the conductor came by to take tickets, Homer asked if he could ride with his dog in the baggage car.

"When we make our next stop in Morristown, I will take you up to the baggage car and arrange it with the baggage attendant."

"Thank you, Sir!"

When they reached Washington, Homer made a similar request to the Southern Railroad conductor, and was back in the baggage car with Buddy and a very nice baggage attendant.

After the Dixie Flyer pulled away, Tom Cotton asked Homer, "Did you get some supper before you came up here?"

"Well no Sir, but I'm okay. I do have dog food for Buddy in my trunk over there, and I see you have given him water, so he will be fine."

"Well, my wife packs me much more than I can eat, so if you would like a ham and cheese sandwich, I'd be glad to share"

"If you are sure you have enough, your offer sounds good. Thank you!"

After dinner, Homer asked if it would be OK to let Buddy retrieve some tennis balls that he could roll down the car, and Tom said, "Go ahead, that is a beautiful chocolate Labrador retriever who probably needs exercise."

After fifty retrieves, Homer got his duffel bag to use as a pillow and Buddy curled up with him. When the Dixie Flyer pulled into Atlanta, the first stop was at Brookwood Station on the north side on Peachtree Street.

Tom said, "I'll bet Buddy needs to water the grass, so if you want to take him out on a leash, we will pull out in 15 minutes for Terminal Station downtown, where there ain't no grass."

When they reached Terminal Station, Homer met his uncle on the platform.

Uncle Ben said, "My truck is over yonder at the parking storage, so you can get a baggage porter with a cart to move your stuff out front and I'll come by to pick you up."

Homer sat out front for over an hour according to his dad's fine Hamilton watch and finally Uncle Ben walked up and asked Homer if he could borrow 10 dollars because he did not have enough to pay the parking fee. Homer took his left shoe off and pulled a 10-dollar bill from the toe and handed it to Uncle Ben.

"I will be right back."

Homer thought, 'What a dumbass, he probably spent his money on drinks in the club car.'

In about 30 more minutes, Uncle Ben rolled up in a 1929 Model A pickup truck.

Homer said, "I'll ride in the back so I can hold on to Buddy."

Homer got his first look at Atlanta looking backward down Peachtree Road, dodging street cars on the way to Buckhead, where they turned left on Roswell Road. The Ford had difficulty climbing hills, and when they got to the north side of the Roswell Bridge over the Chattahoochee River and started climbing the Model A needed second gear to make it into Roswell.

33

They passed two squares with statues surrounded by flowers, beautiful antebellum mansions and pre-war churches. The locals called it the War of Yankee Aggression. General Sherman used Roswell as his Headquarters and only burned one building that was manufacturing Confederate Uniforms. Finally, Uncle Ben turned off Roswell Road on Cox Road which was dirt. After a short distance they came to a stop in front of a modest farmhouse and he blew the horn. A tall, thin woman and a twelve-year-old boy came running out to meet Homer and his uncle.

Virginia Harris greeted Homer with a hug and said, "Sandy and I are so glad to have you here."

Homer said, "Thank you, Aunt Virginia."

Homer shook hands with Sandy, a nice looking blond boy with freckles. He noticed Sandy's hand was rough and calloused from working on the farm.

Sandy said, "is that your dog in the back of our truck?"

Homer called, "Come here, Buddy," and as he jumped out of the truck, a large Pit Bull, that was chained to a tree on the side of the front porch, slipped out of his leather collar and ran straight for Buddy. It attacked him with powerful jaws around his neck, crushing his windpipe and killing Buddy before Homer could get to him.

The Pit Bull kept chewing on Buddy, and Homer went to his duffel bag and found his dad's 1911 A-1 45 caliber automatic. He shoved the magazine into the loading position, pulled the slide back chambering a round, walked over to the Pit Bull, and shot him through the top of his ugly head.

After a pause he pulled Buddy away from the Pit Bull and walked slowly toward his uncle with the 45 pointing toward the ground.

"Now Homer, don't you do anything stupid. We shore didn't know this would happen."

Homer looked Uncle Ben directly in the eye and said, "You dumbass! Bring me a shovel right now!"

Aunt Virginia and Sandy said, "We are so sorry. We should never have kept that dog, but Ben wanted him to scare off intruders."

Homer unloaded the 45 and placed it under his belt behind his back.

When Uncle Ben returned with the shovel Homer grabbed it out of his hands and said, "Leave me alone, I am going to bury Buddy"

"Ain't you going to bury both of them?"

"Hell NO!"

Homer went back to Buddy with tears in his eyes, picked him up and carried him over to a large shade tree then went to his duffel bag and wrapped him in his Sparta High School award jacket before placing him at least four foot down into the grave that he dug. After covering the grave with a mound of dirt, Homer sat alongside and tried to pull himself together.

It was beginning to get dark when Aunt Virginia came to Homer and put her arm around him. "I fixed the family a welcome home fried chicken dinner, and kept your plate in the warming oven. Please come in and I will take you to your bedroom, and you can have your supper in there if you want to be alone. I know you are hurting and this was a terrible thing to happen when you just got here, or at any time. So please come in with me."

Homer had dinner in his bedroom. At breakfast, everybody apologized, and Homer made up his mind to make the best of being on the Harris Farm.

During the summer, Homer performed many chores around the farm. He mowed hay with the old John Deere tractor and changed the spark plugs and plug wires on the Model A pickup. He ordered a new carburetor from Roswell Ford and adjusted the timing until the engine sounded eager to rev up.

He spent most evenings on his shortwave radio, but being this far south many Spanish-speaking stations filled the airwaves. On a good night, when the atmospherics were favorable, he could get news from the BBC and pick up a strong station from Berlin. The news from the BBC about Germany and Hitler was beginning to sound grim.

Chapter 7
Summer in Roswell

In July, the buying started when Uncle Ben had delivered a new 1938 Ford three-quarter-ton pickup. He also bought Aunt Virginia a new 1938 Ford convertible. Homer thought to himself, 'I guess I know who paid for this.'

Next was a new large John Deere tractor, with every attachment that they made. A contractor was engaged to renovate the farmhouse with a new roof, a modern electric kitchen, a large screened porch off the kitchen, new windows, a forced air oil burning furnace with ductwork that replaced the individual room propane gas heaters, and a separate garage for the new truck and car.

Aunt Virginia told Ben that he should give Homer the title to the Model A as a good will gesture, so he can get back and forth to school. After breakfast, Homer thanked his uncle for the title to the 1929 Model A, and went into Roswell to the Motor Vehicle office to transfer the title. His next stop was the U.S. Post office in Roswell, where he rented post office box 101 and paid for a year up front. Now Homer could communicate with Larry Cohen, Sam Cornelius, the Schmidt family, and Mrs. Costello without having his mail intercepted by Uncle Ben.

Homer then drove his Ford truck to Roswell High School and asked to meet with the principal, Mr. Culpepper. Homer brought his sealed transcript from Sparta High. After welcoming Homer and asking him to have a seat, Mr. Culpepper opened the transcript and spent five minutes studying the contents.

Mr. Culpepper put the transcript package on his desk, smiled at Homer, and said, "You will do very well here at Roswell High School bringing in a 3.8 average and having most of your difficult courses behind you. Even though you did not finish a few days of your junior year, you have more than enough credits to be a senior. School starts on September first at eight in the morning and most classes are over by one in the afternoon. Many of your fellow students work in the afternoon and do their homework at night. By the way, we have a football team and a really good basketball team. I see that your basketball team won the North Jersey championship last year. What position did you play?"

Homer felt good about Mr. Culpepper and told him that he was a forward and had the team high point score.

"Well, I hope you go out for our basketball team; they are the Roswell Hornets. We won the class-A Fulton County championship last year, but we have lost our top scoring forward due to graduation."

Homer thanked Mr. Culpepper for his time and asked about his class schedule.

"They will be out by August first."

Homer thanked Mr. Culpepper again and said, "I'm looking forward to my senior year."

They shook hands and Homer left with a smile on his face.

When Homer returned to the farm Uncle Ben was all excited and told Aunt Virginia, Sandy and Homer that his offer for 1,000 acres of prime cleared bottom land running along the Coosa River, tying into their current fence line, had been accepted for only $300.00 per acre.

"This will be good for all of us 'cuz we can add 400 head to the 100 head that we have now and really make some money."

Homer thought, 'there goes $300,000 dollars,' but didn't say anything.

When school started Homer had American history taught by the football and basketball coach Mr. Toast. He had chemistry II that was going to be taught by a new teacher, Mr. Bells. Geometry was being taught by the assistant principal, Mr. Langford and his last class was English taught by Mr. Israel Iseman.

Initially the students called Homer the Yankee but after a few days together he became Homer. The teacher he liked the most was Mr. Iseman. He was excellent!

The only dud was Mr. Bells. Bells was a heavy smoker, and five minutes after class started he would tell the class to read so many pages, and he would leave the classroom lab for 30 minutes, and pop back in for 5 more minutes. He would then demonstrate a chemical reaction that could be done by a five-year-old, then leave for another 20-minute smoke break. The class named him Tinkerbell when they realized that they were not going to learn anything for a full year.

Homer took the lead with a plan to get rid of Mr. Bells, and presented the idea for class approval who gave a 100% yes vote, with sworn secrecy. Then, when Tinkerbell left the class for his 30-minute break, the black window shades were be pulled down to darken the room, then they filled the eight sinks half way full of water, dropped a turned on Bunsen burner to the bottom of the sink and then lit the gas so it would flame on top of the water and make the room look like it was on fire when Tinkerbell returned from his smoke break.

The door opened, and Tinkerbell let out a high-pitched scream and ran to the end of the hall and pulled the fire alarm alerting the Roswell Fire Department.

Mr. Culpepper, Mr. Toast, and Mr. Langford met Tinkerbell with handheld fire extinguishers in the hallway by the fire alarm. Bells was incoherent with panic.

Mr. Culpepper said, "Where are your students?"

Bell replied, "they are in the lab and some were laying on the floor."

Culpepper glared at Bells and Coach Toast said, "You idiot—you didn't go back to your lab to try to rescue anybody!"

"I was afraid."

The firemen were coming down the hall when Mr. Culpepper dragged Bells through the lab door and found the shades up, the sinks drained, and the Bunsen burners sitting on the countertop. The students quietly reading their chemistry books. Mr. Langford advised the firemen that it was a false alarm and thanked them for arriving so quickly.

Mr. Langford returned to the lab as the next class was starting and told the students that it was a false alarm caused by Mr. Bells. Mr. Culpepper and Coach Toast dragged Bells into the principal's office and listened to him babble about the fire and how scared he was. Mr. Culpepper called the Roswell Police Chief and had Mr. Bells transported to Crawford Long Hospital in Atlanta for evaluation.

It was decided that Bells would benefit from a stay at the Milledgeville State Mental Hospital. The excellent chemistry teacher who had just retired, Mrs. Appleby, agreed to return for the balance of the school year.

Penelope "Penny" Ponder was in the chemistry class and became friends with Homer. Homer didn't know that Penny was a neighbor, living three miles nearer Roswell, until he was invited to stop by the Ponder's place to see her horses after she had learned he had experience riding at a stable in New Jersey.

On his way back to the Harris farm, Homer located an impressive entrance off the main road. The Ponder home was almost one mile beyond the entrance just over a gentle hill. The property was enclosed by white board fences and the house was huge with white columns. Homer thought to himself, 'The Ponders must be rich.'

This was not a bad guess. Penny's father, Douglas Ponder, was the Treasurer of the Coca-Cola Company. He lost Penny's mother to cancer two years earlier, and devoted much more time than he had used in the past for Penny. They were very close.

When Homer pulled the Model A up to the elaborate barn, Penny and her dad came out to greet him. They talked about horses and when Mr. Ponder asked Homer if he could ride. He volunteered that he had worked part time at Hunter Barn Riding School in Sparta, NJ.

Penny asked Homer "What did you do? Clean stalls?"

Homer admitted that he had cleaned his share of stalls, but he was a trainer. He would take thoroughbreds that were to slow to make it at the area racetracks, and turn them into successful hunters for sale or use at the school.

This got Mr. Ponders attention, and he said, "You will have to come ride with us maybe this weekend. In fact, I have one three-year-old standard bred mare that has been difficult, and possibly you could straighten Hennessey's Babe out. We will ride for fun on Saturday if you can make it, however, if you begin a training program I will insist on paying you $5.00 an hour for three sessions of two hours each per week."

Homer asked Mr. Ponder to describe the Babe's bad habits. He said, "She rears up at the drop of a hat and I'm afraid she will go all the way over and crush a rider."

On Saturday Homer arrived in blue jeans. Penny was dressed for a horse show and Mr. Ponder was wearing Jodhpurs, shiny black boots, and a hunt jacket. Homer felt out of place.

"Let's go in the tack room, and Penny can help you pick out a saddle and bridle for the Babe."

Homer spotted a German Stubben top-of-the-line forward seat saddle with deep knee rolls. He said, "this one looks good."

Mr. Ponder replied, "A good choice. My Stubben is already on my horse, the dapple grey tied next to Penny's bay gelding."

After the saddle was tightly secured by the girth and the rubber Pelham bridle was in place Homer mounted the Babe. In less than a minute the Babe reared up and Homer did an emergency dismount, throwing both arms around the Babe's neck and swung to the ground.

He asked Mr. Ponder to hold the rains while he went over to the Model A and picked up a large 150-watt lightbulb that he had prepared by drilling a hole in the base and filling it with mild soapy water.

Penny said, "What is that for?"

"You'll see the next time the Babe decides to try to throw me off."

Homer remounted and just as they entered the outdoor ring, the Babe reared up again, and Homer leaned forward and struck the buckle on the bridle between the Babe's ears, shattering the light bulb.

Immediately the Babe came down on her front knees as if she was praying, and Homer dismounted and brought a bucket of water and cleared the soap from the Babe's eyes. He then pulled the reins up and brought the 17-hand tall beautiful black mare to her feet and re-mounted. They rode for two hours and the Babe never tried to rear up again.

The Ponders were amazed, and asked, "What happened?"

"When the light bulb broke the Babe thought she was bleeding and going blind and she decided that rearing up was a bad thing to do."

Uncle Ben gave Homer some flack about taking so much time away from the farm and spending it with those stuck up rich folks. Homer did not respond.

After several weeks the Babe was clearing fences with ease and becoming a fine hunter. Mr. Ponder asked Homer if he would like to take the Babe into the open jumper class at the big Chastain Park spring horse show.

"Penny will be showing in the thoroughbred hunter class."

Homer responded with a big grin and said, "I wouldn't be surprised if the Babe doesn't win."

Homer's friendship with the Ponders continued to grow.

Mr. Iseman, Homer's English teacher, developed a trusting relationship that allowed Homer to explain everything that had happened to him since his parents were killed.

Mr. Iseman listened intently, asked some questions, and finally said, "This uncle of yours has committed fraud, misappropriation, and downright theft and should be hauled into court. I have some connections in the Jewish community in Atlanta, and we will find you a lawyer that will make this right."

Homer asked Mr. Ponder if he had any knowledge of the Spaulding Law firm in Atlanta recommended, by Mr. Iseman, and was told that they are the best in the south.

"The Spaulding Corporate Group has been on retainer with the Coca-Cola Company for many years."

After learning details, Mr. Ponder said, "Ned MacNeely is a dear friend and one of the top Spaulding litigators."

By coincidence, Mr. Iseman had excellent references on Mr. MacNeely.

Mr. Iseman asked Homer what his plans were after graduation and Homer said "I would like to go to college."

"Have you ever thought about going to West Point or the Naval Academy? You know, as the son of a Medal of Honor recipient, you will have a priority for acceptance."

Penny Ponder had told her father about her excellent English teacher, and Douglas Ponder decided to host a meeting with Ned MacNeely, Mr. Iseman, and Homer. The meeting was held at the Ponder home on November first, Homer's eighteenth birthday.

Homer and Israel Iseman were introduced to Ned MacNeely, who explained that he had been given an overview from Doug Ponder, however he wanted to hear the details from Homer.

After an hour filled with many questions, MacNeely said, "Homer, as a senior partner in the Spalding Law Firm, I will assure you that we will take your case and we will win.

During the conference, Homer said, "I just don't believe that my uncle is smart enough to do what he has done without someone telling him what to do."

Doug Ponder said, "I don't either. He surely had help from someone who was familiar with family law.

MacNeely said, "there is one lawyer with an office in Roswell who has a reputation for shady deals, so with court subpoenas we can find out from his bank if your uncle has paid for his services. It may be that this lawyer read the newspaper articles and connected the dots enough to determine if Benjamin Harris was the brother of your deceased father. We will find out! "

Homer passed Larry Cohen's and Sam Cornelius contact information to MacNeely. Doug Ponder suggested a phone call right now, from Homer to Larry Cohen, to give his permission to cooperate on his behalf with the Spaulding Law firm. Homer had the home and office phone numbers memorized. However, since this was Saturday, they called Larry Cohen's home, Hemlock 5899 in New Jersey.

Ned MacNeely introduced himself and then handed the phone to Homer. Following the call, MacNeely told the group, "We have a very capable attorney in New Jersey who really cares about Homer."

Mr. Iseman had remained silent. "Gentlemen, there are some considerations for Homer's safety. If something happened to Homer, the uncle would probably get the estate through probate. Also, Homer and I have begun the application process to the U.S. Naval Academy using my home mailing address. He is making excellent grades at Roswell High School and will need to complete his senior year. His chances of acceptance are excellent, plus his dad's Medal of Honor gives Homer a priority. My suggestion would be to have all of the legal work ready to pull the trigger on Homer's day of departure when school is out on May 29th."

The group looked at each other and said, "This is an excellent plan; however, secrecy is a must."

Homer drove back to the farm with a feeling of confidence and appreciation for the men that were in his corner and had his back.

Chapter 8
Anxiety on the Rhine

Chicago, April 1, 1939

David and Moses Goldberg established World Radio with a prime location on Wacker Drive downtown. With the trouble in Europe, high-quality shortwave radios were in high demand. Their customers wanted to hear direct news from the BBC and other world capitals.

World Radio immediately became very profitable.

David and Moses's father, Abraham Goldberg, had developed a code system that could allow the family to communicate by mail, saying things that were dull and boring, but actually had different meaning. Welt Radio was under frequent Nazi surveillance, and their beautiful home on Rotterdamer Strasse, on the east side of the Rhine River, was also being watched. The taxes on their business and home were doubled in 1938. Abraham told his sons in code that he was unsure if they would be safe much longer.

David wrote in code to his father, urging them to get out now. Abraham responded saying that the travel restrictions were in place for Jews, and he wasn't sure that they could escape. Friends were disappearing and many Synagogues were being vandalized or burned. The situation was more violent to the east of Dusseldorf. Abraham had been handling the export of German radios to World Radio in Chicago; however, the supply was drying up because the Luftwaffe, Krieg's Marine, and the Army were expanding rapidly and had first priority on communication equipment.

Ruth and Sara Goldberg spent most of their working hours in the repair department of Welt Radio, which became the most profitable part of the business. At the dinner table, the Goldberg family prayed to God for protection from evil and asked for forgiveness because they stopped attending services, even on high holy days, to keep a low profile.

Chapter 9
Escape to Annapolis

Roswell, Georgia, May 21, 1939

One week before graduation on May 28, 1939, Homer and the group had a final meeting at the Ponder home.

Just as they had suspected, the crooked attorney in Roswell, Cornell Killeran, was a cousin of John Killeran in Sparta, New Jersey. They also developed evidence through the Pinkerton Detective Agency that Judge Andrew McCracken was paid indirectly by Benjamin Harris and attorneys John and Cornell Killeran. The payoff for the decision was Homer's Manitou Island home at Lake Mohawk. The judge paid $5,000 for a beautiful English Tudor waterfront property that cost $65,000 to build, and had a current appraised value of $100,000.

Larry Cohen and Ned MacNeely made a decision to go for disbarment of John and Cornell Killeran, with permanent loss of their law licenses. Judge Andrew McCracken would be removed from the bench, lose his law license, and be made the central figure of a nasty scandal that will be extensively covered by all of the major newspapers. Financial Judgements would be secured against the attorneys and the Judge that would keep them broke for years.

Benjamin Harris would be forced to sell or turn over everything that he has bought with money from Homer's estate, and surrender approximately $3,500,000 in cash, which is earning less than 1% interest at his Bank in Roswell. With some luck, they might recover a little over $4,000,000.

Homer made one request to his attorneys. "Aunt Virginia inherited the farm on Cox Road from her father and I don't want to hurt her. She was kind to me, and has a thirteen-year-old son, who is a boy that disserves a good future. I want her to keep the Ford convertible that was purchased last year. My uncle spent quite a lot of money modernizing Aunt Virginia's house, but I can't see a way to recover anything without a judgment against her property, and I don't want to do that."

Douglas Ponder thought, "What a solid young man."

Homer said, "I want to thank you gentlemen for standing by me. Mr. Iseman and I have a departure plan for May 29th that I would like to run by you to see if we need to change anything. I will contact you when I arrive at Annapolis. We may not see each other for a while, so thank you, from the bottom of my heart. I am most appreciative for all that you have done."

At 4 a.m. the next morning Homer got up, put his clothes on, left a letter addressed to his Aunt Virginia on his pillow and quietly went to the bathroom then slipped out the door with his duffel bag. He had parked the Model A on a slight hill so he could roll down Cox Road about 500 yards before starting the engine and turning on the lights.

Homer's first stop was the Roswell Post Office, where he was pleased to find three letters in his mailbox. He decided to put them in his duffel bag and read them on the train. The next stop was Mr. Iseman's house.

Homer pulled the Model A down the driveway, and parked behind the house so it could not be seen from the road. He was met at the back kitchen door by Mr. and Mrs. Iseman.

"You are right on time, Homer," Mrs. Iseman said. "You need to have your breakfast." She hugged him. "It's all ready, except for your eggs."

After a hearty breakfast followed by a second cup of black coffee, Mr. Iseman said, "it's time to go. Here is your packet of information from the Naval Academy, a sealed copy of your high school transcript, and the government T.R. transportation request so you can get your train tickets."

Homer reached in his back pocket "I have something for you."

He handed Mr. Iseman the pink slip, which was the Georgia title for the Model A. "I want you to have this. It is a really good-running little pickup truck. I would suggest either having it painted, trade it in, or hide it in your garage until everything is finished with my uncle. I don't know what he would do if he saw you with it."

"We'll take my Studebaker to Terminal Station."

At 7 a.m., Aunt Virginia called Homer for breakfast, and when he didn't answer, she went to his bedroom where she found his letter.

Dear Aunt Virginia,

When you find this letter, I will be on my way to the U.S. Naval Academy at Annapolis, Maryland. I regret that I have to leave without saying goodbye to you and Sandy, but avoiding a nasty scene with Uncle Ben is best for both you and me. I want you to know that you and Sandy have grown very dear to me. When I arrived on the first day this feeling would never have crossed my mind, however your kindness showed me that there was still good in the world and your wonderful meals made me appreciate you even more. You are a truly great cook and a fine mother. Please know that I have grown to love you and Sandy. I want you to keep your Ford convertible, and I hope Sandy will enjoy my shortwave radio as much as I have. There will be some legally difficult times coming for Uncle Ben. I want you to know that I do not hold you responsible for his actions, and will do what I can to protect you and Sandy.

Your Nephew,

Homer

Tears came to Aunt Virginia's eyes.

Terminal Station, Atlanta, May 29, 1939, 9:55 a.m.

Homer shook hands and hugged Mr. Iseman just before boarding the Southern Railroad north-bound Dixie Flier for Washington. At 10 a.m., the whistle blew, and the Conductor yelled, "All aboard."

After they were rolling, Homer asked the conductor if Tom Cotton was the baggage man on this trip.

The answer was, "Yes, how do you know Tom?"

"Well, it is a long story, but I was hoping to order lunch and have it with Tom in the baggage car."

"I'll check with Tom, and if he says okay, then it's okay with me."

When they reached Savannah, Homer and a waiter boarded the baggage car with steak sandwiches for lunch. Tom remembered their trip together about a year ago, and asked about that beautiful chocolate Labrador retriever. Homer told Tom the condensed version of the past year leaving out the legal situation.

When they reached Charlotte, Homer said, "I've been awake all last night, so I would not over-sleep and miss my departure at 4 a.m. I have to report to the Naval Academy when I arrive, so I better go back to my car and get some sleep. It has been great seeing you, Tom. I hope we can do this again."

"So do I, Homer. Good Luck with school."

When Homer settled down in his comfortable reclining seat he realized,

"Oh my gosh! I forgot the letters."

He untied his duffel bag and opened the first letter from Larry Cohen.

Dear Homer,

The coordination with your Georgia lawyer, Ned MacNeely, is going very well. As you know we won the appeal and Judge McCracken and John Killeran are both under investigation by the Attorney General and the New Jersey Bar Association. The Killeran cousins are knee deep in this conspiracy, and the Spaulding Law firm in Georgia has Cornell Killeran ready to be indicted by

45

the State of Georgia Attorney General. We will secure at least one million in judgments against them, and of course they won't have the funds, so from now on when they gain assets we will take them. I have no sympathy for these scoundrels! Good luck and best wishes for the Naval Academy. Let me know when you get a mailing address.

Your family friend,
Larry

The second letter was from Christine Costello

Dear Homer,
I hope your departure went well. I admire you for sticking it out and making top grades at Roswell High. I'm sure that the Naval Academy will be pleased with your grades from Sparta and Roswell. Things have settled down at school, and I have a nice apartment that is part of a large house over on the east shore of the lake. I guess you have heard that your friend Hans has been accepted at Rutgers and will begin his freshman year this fall. I am sorry to say that that nasty judge has purchased your house, and the word around is that it was a shady deal. I hope you get some vacation time, or leave, or liberty or whatever they call it so that you can come to Sparta for a visit. I continue to enjoy my Ford station wagon. It is running like new, and I can pick you up at the Dover train station. The Ford was a very kind thing that you did for me.
Thank you again.

Best wishes,
Christine

Homer saved the third letter from Hans for last

Dear former business partner,
I hope you are safely on your way to Annapolis. It is quite an honor to get into West Point or the Naval Academy. I have been accepted at Rutgers and will have an Army ROTC commission. If we both finish at the same time, you will be an Ensign and I'll be a Second Lieutenant. We will both be 0-1's.
Now to the juicy part: That crooked rotten judge bought your house, and according to the public records at the tax office only paid $5,000. We had 100 customers that knew both of us, and they all live around the judge. None of them will speak to the judge or his fat wife. Then things started to happen when he bought a new Chris Craft with a 95-horsepower motor and started showing

46

off up and down the lake. When he tied it up in your boathouse, he failed to notice that the cooling water intake had come lose and his new boat filled with water and sank to the bottom. It was still tied up inside the boathouse for over a week before the judge discovered that it was under water. He called the police and wanted to file charges against the neighborhood.

Then the best is yet to come! On a very dark Sunday night, somebody opened the water meter box and turned off the water meter. When the judge awoke, he couldn't flush his toilet, brush his teeth, or make a pot of coffee. He called the water company, and when the repairman opened the meter box, it was filled with rock-hard cement. The judge went into a rage when he was asked why he filled the meter with cement. Was it to prevent the meter from being read so he wouldn't get a bill? Some neighbors, including me, walked over to listen to his rant and threats to jail everyone that had a hand in this. It really made him mad when everybody laughed at him. The judge and his wife moved into the hotel in Newton until the water company could run a new line. They weren't in a hurry!

The best is still yet to come. Do you remember the glass gage on the side of the boiler in your basement? You had to keep the water level for the boiler between the up and down lines. Well, the judge forgot about needing water in the boiler, and left the oil-fired heat gun burning and BOOM. The boiler exploded and blew out all of the ground floor windows. The fireplace collapsed in the living room and the floor on the fireplace side was a foot higher than the side by the kitchen. When the judge and his wife arrived, they both swore and yelled at everyone who heard the noise and came over to see what was wrong. The judge called the Sparta police. The police brought a heating engineer who filed a report saying that the homeowner should have turned off the heat gun until the water was repaired and therefore was negligent. Mrs. MacCracken yelled at her husband, "if you don't sell this house and move back to Newton, I will file divorce papers."

Now, I have a question. Would you object if my dad bought your house and repaired the damage so we could then sell our house and live on the water?
Regards,
Hans

Homer went to the club car and got some paper and an envelope, and wrote a quick note to Hans.

Dear former business partner,

I would be happy if your dad can steal the house. I actually tried to give the house to your family before I got hauled off to Georgia, but was unable to legally. Congratulations on Rutgers! When we both get settled, we can write.

Go Navy Beat Army,
Homer

    Homer had dinner in the dining car and then covered up with a blanket for a four-hour nap passing through Richmond.

    The conductor came through the car, waking passengers and saying, "We have a short stop in Fredericksburg then Washington in an hour."

Chapter 10
Get on the Gray Navy Bus

Homer got off the train and climbed the long stairs with his duffel bag on his shoulder, up to the main Washington terminal. The first thing he saw was a grey-haired Navy petty officer holding a large sign, saying 'U.S. Naval Academy.'

He approached the petty officer and said, "Sir, I have orders to report to the Academy."

The petty officer looked at Homer and said, "Let's get something straight, Sonny. I ain't no Sir! I work for a living. You call commissioned officers Sir. Go out front and get on the first of four gray Navy busses where you find an empty seat. When it is full you will have a scenic, forty-mile ride to Annapolis."

Homer said, "Thank you Sir… Oops. I'm sorry. I mean, just thank you."

Annapolis, May 30, 1938

After a one-hour morning ride with twenty-six young men that he had never met, Homer Harris observed the Shore Patrol wave the Navy bus driver through the main gate to the U.S. Naval Academy.

They were met by a Navy Chief and assigned to their permanent quarters. There were three future-Midshipmen assigned to a bedroom with one up and down bunk and one lower bunk. The first room that they entered was the study room, with three desks and wood straight chairs.

The three guys who were assigned at random looked at each other and said, almost in unison, "I guess introductions are in order."

"I'm Homer Harris, from New Jersey, before a year in Georgia."

A short, overweight guy said, "I'm Jim Coriello, from Pennsylvania." He gave Homer a smile and a firm handshake.

The third roommate shook hands with Homer and Jim and said "Y'all, I'm Charles Forrest from Clute Texas." Charles was wearing his best boots and jeans that made him look taller than six foot two. "It's nice meetin' you."

Homer said, "If they leave us together for four years, we will really get to know each other."

Then the door banged open and a third year Midshipmen, a sophomore, barged into the room and said, "What are you ladies doing standing around? You are supposed to be drawing uniforms right now! Get your asses out the door and follow me, at double time, to supply."

The roommates were issued uniforms, bedding, towels, and so much other stuff they could hardly see where they were going on the way back to their quarters in Bancroft Hall. They decided that they should first make their beds. That sounded like a good idea, until the same third year Midshipmen arrived and told the roommates that he had never seen worse made beds. Then he pulled all of the sheets and blankets down in a pile on the floor.

"When I come back, I want to bounce a quarter off your tight blankets." Then he handed them a uniform instruction sheet, pointing to a class A uniform and said, "Get in this uniform just like the picture says, and fall out in front of Bancroft in thirty minutes. At 1100 hours, I will be taking you to the main gym for your United States Uniformed Services Oath of Office. You will be sworn in by our Superintendent, Vice Admiral Westfield. For you civilians, that is three stars. Now, if any of you children want to go home to Momma, now is the time. After you are sworn in, the Navy owns you."

590 of America's finest young men stood at attention when Admiral Westfield said, "Raise your right hand and repeat after me: I (your name) do solemnly swear that I will support and defend the Constitution of the United States against all enemies, foreign and domestic; that I will bear true faith and allegiance to the same; that I take this obligation freely, without any mental reservation or purpose of evasion; and that I will and faithfully discharge the duties of the office that I am about to enter. So help me God."

"Midshipmen, welcome to the finest Navy in the world—The United States Navy—During the next four years, you, the class of 1942, will be educated to be officers and gentlemen at the finest college in our country. It will not be easy. You will find out what you are made of. Our highly qualified faculty will do their part and you will do yours. Protecting our country is a sacred honor. This tradition of duty continues from the early days in our history when John Paul Jones proved that our Navy was a force to be reckoned with. I am honored to have you with us!" Admiral Westfield rendered a hand salute and forcefully said, "Go Navy Beat Army!"

Cheers and applause filled the gym. The class of 1942 then made their way to the main dining hall for the noon meal. This was their last unsupervised meal. All meals for the next year would include one third year Midshipmen at the table teaching the proper etiquette of eating "square" meals and punishing infractions.

The rest of the day was spent learning how to make a bed and arranging uniforms before the evening meal at 1830 hours.

Homer remarked to his roommates, "That meal was really good," and they agreed.

Then the serious organized harassment began for two weeks, with the third year Midshipmen doing everything to cause any weak member of the 1942 Plebe class to D.O.R. (drop on request) and be released before the government spent any serious money on their education. The roommates concluded that this was strategy behind the madness and humiliation.

Morning class schedules were begun with four fifty-minute classes per day and fifth and sixth classes after the noon meal. Afternoon athletics were followed by the evening meal. Then a three-hour study period. Taps was heard at midnight, with reveille at 0630. Parades were usually held twice a week. There was very little personal time.

By early October, Homer realized that he might fail calculus. Fortunately, his roommate Jim had attended one year of prep school so he would be ready for the Academy, and was able to tutor Homer and Charles, who did not have advanced math in Clute or at Roswell High School. Homer enjoyed American Naval History, German, Chemistry, Gunnery, and Tactics.

On Friday, October 30th, 1939, Homer was ordered to report to the Superintendent's office.

The Admiral's Aid de Camp, Lieutenant Commander Berkley, asked Homer to have a seat in his office, and said, "I'm having some coffee, would you like a cup?"

"Yes, Sir, thank you, Sir." Up to this point, Homer was on pins and needles, wondering what he had done wrong and if he was going to be expelled.

Commander Berkley began by saying, "Admiral Westfield and I have reviewed your complete history leading up to the lawsuit against your uncle, two lawyers, and a judge. In our opinion you have been wronged by these men, so the Admiral has granted a very unusual five-day pass so you can travel to Atlanta to testify in court. We have also granted approval for a Coca-Cola DC3 to land at our airfield and pick you up at 0700 Saturday morning. The Shore Patrol will pick you up at 0600. You will travel in your class A uniform. I don't know if you knew, that Mr. Douglas Ponder was made President of the Coca-Cola Company last week and he has arranged this. You certainly have friends in high places."

"Sir, I actually trained horses for Mr. Ponder, and he became my friend when I really needed one."

Commander Berkley continued, "Mr. Ponder has arranged priority air travel on Eastern Air Lines for your return to Washington on Wednesday morning, after your testimony on Monday or Tuesday. We will have a Shore Patrol car meet you for your return to the Academy. This way, you will only have three class days to make up."

"Sir, thank you, and please thank Admiral Westfield for me."

Commander Berkley shook hands with Homer and said, "The Navy takes care of our own."

Chapter 11
Georgia Superior Court

The Coca-Cola DC3 had just finished its required FAA annual inspection at the Teterboro New Jersey Airport near Newark. Without taking advantage of his position, Douglas Ponder had the corporate aircraft bring Homer and the crew and several others on the scheduled return trip to Atlanta's Candler Field Airport named after Asa G. Candler, the founder of Coca-Cola.

At 0700 on the dot, Homer and the Shore Patrol driver watched the DC3 make a perfect three-point landing. The plane turned at the end of the field then taxied back to where Homer was waiting, coming to a stop with the engines running while the rear door was opened, and a small ladder was extended. Homer ran out, holding his B-4 bag and his cover so it would not blow off.

When he got in the cabin, he was greeted by Larry Cohen, Sam Cornelius, Mrs. Costello, and Dr. Porter. The steward pulled the door shut and made sure everyone had a tight seatbelt before takeoff.

Homer wasn't surprised when he learned that Ned MacNeely, from the Spaulding Law Firm, had coordinated his witnesses to join the flight from Teterboro. In airline configuration, the DC3 would have 24 seats, but this executive cabin had only 14 seats arranged around tables so meetings could take place in route. It was very comfortable.

For lunch, the steward served a choice of New York deli pastrami or turkey sandwiches, chips, kosher dill pickles and Coca-Cola. Everyone had a lot to discuss during the four-hour flight. Upon arrival, there were two Cadillacs waiting. Penny and Douglas Ponder took Homer to their farm in Roswell, and Ned MacNeely had their chauffer take Larry Cohen, Sam Cornelius, Dr. Porter and Mrs. Costello to the Biltmore Hotel near his office in downtown Atlanta to begin witness prep. Homer wasn't needed because MacNeely had taken detailed notes when they first met.

The witnesses had a working dinner at the Spaulding Firm's suite at the Biltmore and turned in early. A cab was arranged to take Mrs. Costello to Christ the King Catholic Church on Peachtree Road and Dr. Porter to the First

Presbyterian Church on North Avenue. Ned MacNeely began witness preparation with Sam Cornelius at breakfast in the Biltmore coffee shop and after an hour, they were joined by Larry Cohen. When Mrs. Costello and Dr. Porter returned, they had a late breakfast. At 2 p.m. they boarded the Spaulding Cadillac for a fast trip to the Ponder's farm in Roswell.

A delicious fried chicken dinner with crackling cornbread and all the trimmings was prepared by Mary Lee Wells, the Ponders housekeeper who raised Penny. After dinner, Ned MacNeely spent an hour with Homer to review their earlier meeting and tell him what to expect in Georgia Superior Court. He explained that this is the court of general jurisdiction handling both civil and criminal law actions and the only higher court is the Georgia Supreme Court.

At 10 a.m. on Monday November 3, 1939 the Fulton County Court House was packed with observers, reporters from *The New York Times, The Newark Star Ledger, The New Jersey Herald, The Atlanta Journal* and *The Atlanta Constitution.*

The bailiff announced in a commanding voice, "Please rise, The Superior Court on and for the County of Fulton, The State of Georgia is hereby in session. His Honor Judge Walter G Bibb presiding."

Judge Bibb took his seat adjusting his black robe, picked up his gavel, gave three strikes on a wood block, then said, "This court is now hearing the case of Homer Harris and his Estate VS Benjamin Harris, Cornell Killeran, a member of the Georgia Bar, John Killeran, a New Jersey Attorney, and Andrew McCracken a New Jersey Family Court Judge."

The all-white Jury had been selected with ten men and two women. None of the Jurors had any previous knowledge of the case or knew anyone involved.

Judge Bibb looked toward Ned MacNeely and said, "Will the plaintiff please begin with his open."

MacNeely rose from the table where Homer, Larry Cohen, and an attractive young lady, associate attorney from the Spaulding Law Firm, were seated. Homer looked sharp in his uniform. Uncle Ben glared at him from the defendants table, until his attorney told him not to look at his nephew.

Ned MacNeely began with the tragic death of Homer's parents and explained the five million dollars of New York Metropolitan life insurance paid to Homer's Estate. He described the assistance provided by the Sparta First Presbyterian Church, the faculty of Sparta High School, especially Mrs. Christine Costello, and many friends and neighbors who recognized that Homer was a very fine young man with no relatives. MacNeely provided an affidavit from the principal of Sparta High School stating that Homer was an outstanding student who had suffered a tragic loss. He explained that New Jersey law stated that a person under eighteen years old could not occupy a residence without adult supervision present. He then went on to say that a respected faculty member Mrs. Christine Costello agreed to assume that responsibility. He further stated that Mrs. Costello was a widow with an impeccable teaching record. With her help Homer, was able to remain in his family home and continue with his junior year education.

MacNeely then explained the relationship that Attorney Larry Cohen and CPA Sam Cornelius had with Homer's father, and their written agreement with the Harris Estate to guard, protect, and grow the funds that belonged to Homer Harris. This included the annual audit by the highly respected CPA firm, Price Waterhouse. He submitted records from the Cornelius CPA firm showing that, during the four months of their stewardship, the investment portfolio earned $33,000 in cash and 1.5% increase in stock value before all funds and assets belonging to Homer Harris were taken over by court order signed by New Jersey Family Court Judge Andrew McCracken and transferred to his Uncle Benjamin Harris.

This was an uncle that Homer had never met and only heard mentioned by his father once, in a very negative way.

MacNeely turned to the Jury and said, "We have records that Benjamin Harris stayed at the Newton Hotel for the better part of a month, meeting with Attorney John Killeran. There was no attempt made to contact his nephew that he cared about so much, even though Newton is only ten miles away from Sparta and Lake Mohawk. The New Jersey court record will show that he was told by Attorney John Killeran not to contact his nephew until they were in court. We will provide, with birth records, that Attorneys Cornell and John Killeran were first cousins. We will prove with extensive phone records that, after detailed newspaper stories covered the loss of Homer Harris' parents and the large amount of life insurance involved was reported, the first of many phone calls was made between Cornell and John Killeran. We will prove that these attorneys accessed birth records to prove that Benjamin Harris was a blood relative brother of Robert Harris, the deceased father of Homer Harris. We have Eastern Airline records to prove that Attorney Cornell Killeran traveled to New Jersey after the relationship was verified. We have witnesses that will testify that the cousins met with Judge Andrew McCracken on two occasions at a restaurant in Newton before filing their suit for custody of Homer Harris and his Estate. Ladies and Gentlemen, we will show with court records that the last eighteen family law cases that Attorney John Killeran brought before Judge Andrew McCracken were ruled in his client's favor, with generous rewards. We will also prove, with subpoenaed bank records, that Benjamin Harris paid Attorney Cornell Killeran and his cousin John Killeran one hundred thousand dollars after he had control of the Harris Estate Funds.

We will also prove with public tax records that Judge Andrew McCracken received a pay off in the form of a $5,000 purchase price for Homer Harris' beautiful family home which, was conservatively appraised at over $100,000. Benjamin Harris signed off on the sale, and the real estate closing was handled by Attorney John Killeran.

"There is no record that we can find that the $5,000 purchase price was even paid to the Estate by Judge McCracken. These payments to the Killeran cousins and this bribe to Judge Andrew McCracken clearly show that Benjamin Harris did not protect or conserve the funds and assets belonging to his Nephew. In fact, he did just the opposite, buying in his name 1,000 acres of prime bottom land using Estate funds, adjacent to the farm owned by his wife's 400-acre farm that she inherited from her father. We would like to stipulate that Homer's Aunt Virginia had nothing to do with the actions of her husband, and should not be held liable. Homer Harris will testify that on numerous occasions his Aunt Virginia was verbally and physically abused by her husband, and kept in fear that her husband, Benjamin Harris, would cause serious physical harm to their son Sandy when he became intoxicated. We will prove that Benjamin Harris converted, for his own use, funds that belonged to his nephew Homer Harris."

Chapter 12
Looting the Estate

"In addition to the thousand acres of real property, Benjamin Harris bought a new heavy-duty Mack dump truck, a new Ford ¾ ton pickup truck for his own use, a new Caterpillar excavator, a new light duty International Cub tractor for hay cutting, and one new McCormick hay bailer. He had multiple wells drilled on his property by North Georgia Water Company with automatic cattle watering stations. He contracted with the Hobbs Fence Company to install heavy-duty fence enclosing his recently purchased thousand acres. The Hobbs Company also served as a general contractor for a new 40,000-square foot hay barn, a 10,000-square foot farm workshop and an equipment garage that could hold all of his new trucks and equipment. He acquired a prize bull, fifty cows for breeding, and three hundred and fifty young steers from multiple sources. To say that Uncle Ben went on a buying spree would be an understatement. According to bank records that we have obtained, he spent over $950,000 purchasing, improving, and equipping his property without the approval of his nephew. This is in addition to the $200,000 in legal fees Benjamin Harris paid to the Killeran cousins, and his agreed bribery payoff of the home belonging to Homer Harris at Lake Mohawk. Judge McCrackin paid only $5,000 for this beautiful 3200-square foot lake front English Tudor, easily worth $100,000 based on a recent appraisal. The taking of this young man's family home and the legal fee payments from the Estate did not have the approval of Homer Harris. These multiple acts of grand theft, embezzlement, misappropriation, conspiracy to bribe a judge by two officers of the court, and the acceptance of this bribe that took the family home from a young man who had lost his parents in a tragic accident, should be punished criminally and civilly to the maximum extent of the law. Your Honor, may we approach the bench."

Judge Bibb looked at the defense council, Blake Moore, who was representing Benjamin Harris, and said, "You may approach."

Both attorneys moved up to the Judge, and Ned MacNeely said, "I would like your permission to take the testimony of the plaintiff as early as possible, because he was given a special exception for leave from the United States Naval Academy and must return not later than Wednesday morning."

Judge Bibb asked, "Does the defense have any objection?"

"No, Your Honor, with the stipulation that Homer Harris can be recalled later today or tomorrow."

Judge Bibb said, "You may proceed, Mr. MacNeely."

Homer took the stand and was sworn in on the Bible. MacNeely began a series of questions.

"Had you ever met your uncle before your first day in New Jersey Family Court?"

"No, Sir!"

"Did your uncle ask you if you wanted to remain in your home and graduate from Sparta High?"

"No, Sir!"

"Did your uncle threaten you if the court order to move to Georgia was not obeyed?"

"Yes Sir, he said it would get messy for me if I did not go. He also told Mrs. Costello in an ugly way to get out of my house by the end of the week."

Defense council Moore said, "Objection, hearsay."

MacNeely said, "How could that be hearsay, when the plaintiff was right there in the same room with Mrs. Costello? We have Mrs. Costello on our witness list, and she can confirm this conversation."

"Objection overruled."

"Homer, please tell us what happened upon your arrival at the Harris Farm."

"Within two minutes of our arrival, my Aunt Virginia and my Cousin Sandy came out of the house to give me a warm greeting, and my Labrador retriever Buddy jumped out of the back of my uncle's truck and was immediately attacked and killed by my uncle's pit bull that was not properly tied up. I later learned that my uncle used this vicious dog in illegal dog fights where money was bet on which dog would be killed. I retrieved my dad's 45. pistol from my duffel bag and shot the pit bull. I walked over to my uncle with the pistol pointed at the ground, and told him to get me a shovel so I could bury Buddy. I had raised Buddy from a ten-week-old puppy, and next to losing my parents, this loss devastated me. Aunt Virginia and Sandy said they were very sorry, but my uncle said nothing."

"What did your uncle want you to do on the farm?"

"Nothing but chores from dawn to dark."

"Did he offer to pay you?"

"No, Sir."

"Did your uncle make any arrangements for you to enroll at Sparta High?"

"No, I had to ask him for the use of his 1929 Model A pickup truck to go into Roswell to see the principal and enroll. Aunt Virginia told my uncle that he should give me the title for the old truck since he had a new truck and he had bought her a new 1938 Ford convertible. This was the only thing he ever gave me other than a hard time about going to the Roswell Presbyterian Church with Aunt Virginia and Sandy."

"What happened after you returned from your first Sunday at Church?" "Uncle Ben liked to drink corn liquor, and he was drunk when we got home. He started raising hell with Aunt Virginia because Sunday dinner wasn't ready, and he hit her in the stomach. When she bent over, he hit her with an uppercut giving her a black eye and a nosebleed. Sandy tried to stop his father, and he was knocked to the deck, I mean floor, by a blow to his head. I was standing by the fireplace and grabbed a poker with a dull point, and shoved it against Uncle Ben's heart and pushed him up against the bulkhead, I mean the wall. He tried to take a swing at me, so I kicked him in the groin, putting him in a fetal position on top of Aunt Virginia on the floor. Sandy got up and brought me some rope, and we tied my uncle hand and foot, then dragged him out on the brick floor poach. We decided to leave him there until morning. Then we went back to help Aunt Virginia, who said, 'I'm sorry you boys had to see that.' I asked my aunt if this had ever happened before, and she said, 'Many times, I am afraid of him when he doesn't get his way.' Sandy told me, 'I'm glad you were here Homer, cus I'm not big enough to stop him from hurting my mom.'"

At this point in Homer's testimony Uncle Ben stood up and yelled "You better stop tellin' lies or I'll get you!"

Judge Bibb rapped his gavel and the bailiff restrained the defendant. Judge Bibb said "One more outburst from you, Mr. Harris, and I will have you bound and gagged for the balance of the trial. I am issuing an order of protection for your wife and son, so if you ever harm them in any way, you will spend up to ten years on a Georgia State Prison chain gang.

"You can't make my wife testify against me!"

"No, Mr. Harris, but your son can."

"Bailiff, cuff shackle and gag Mr. Harris for the balance of the trial."

Larry Cohen leaned over to Ned MacNeely and whispered, "Things couldn't be going better."

MacNeely said, "I have one more question for Homer. Did you approve any of the purchases made by your uncle?"

"No, Sir, he never shared any financial information with me, or asked my permission to buy anything."

Attorney Blake Moore said "Your Honor, I have no questions for Homer Harris."

Larry Cohen and Sam Cornelius testified regarding their administration of the Harris Estate, and the defense council asked no questions. Mrs. Costello brought a copy of Homer's Sparta High transcript for the record, and Mr. Iseman submitted a copy of Homer's senior year Roswell High transcript. Both teachers stated that Homer Harris was an outstanding student. Defense council had no questions.

The last witness for the plaintiff was Dr. Porter, Pastor of the Sparta Presbyterian Church, who testified that Homer Harris was an active member of the church and a young man with high morals.

Judge Bibb addressed Ned MacNeely and asked, "Are you ready to make your closing argument?"

MacNeely responded by saying "Your Honor, I request that all of the documents that I referred to in my open be made part of the record, and that both criminal and civil penalties against Judge McCracken, Attorneys John Killeran and Cornell Killeran be so ordered. Regarding Benjamin Harris, I would ask the court to consider his limited education, and that he was led into this fraudulent scheme by two attorneys, who are members of the Bar, and a sitting judge. The plaintiff requests that all property that was purchased with funds from the Harris Estate by Benjamin Harris be surrendered to this court for immediate liquidation and restoration to the rightful owner, Homer Harris. The incarceration of Benjamin Harris would leave no one to operate his wife's farm, so we would be satisfied with extended probation."

Judge Bibb turned to Blake Moore and said, "We are ready for your defendants closing argument."

Moore stood and walked over to the Jury and said, "The plaintiff's attorney has just stated what I had planned to ask for; probation. As attorney for Benjamin Harris, I have gotten to know this man, and he is not all bad. He has many faults, but he realizes the severe penalty if he violates the protection order just issued by this court. He is blessed with a good wife and son who will be harmed if their farm does not provide an income. He is a man with limited mental ability and education, and did not understand the numerous criminal and civil laws that the Killeran attorneys and Judge McCracken were leading him to perpetrate. It would be merciful for the court to order probation, and allow Benjamin Harris to redeem himself. The defense rests."

Judge Bibb directed the bailiff to hold Mr. Harris in confinement overnight due to his behavior in court, and return him at 10 a.m. to this courtroom for his verdict and sentencing.

On the way out of the court room, Homer handed Aunt Virginia a note that said, "My Roswell post office box is number 101 and the combination from zero is two turns right, one half turn left then right back to 1, and it will open. It is paid up for five more months, and I can send funds to you and you can let me know if you and Sandy are OK. I will send you a letter to box 101 with my address. With love, your nephew, Homer"

Chapter 13
Justice

On Tuesday morning, Judge Bibb said "The defendant and his attorney will please rise. Based on the extensive evidence presented, has the jury reached a verdict?"

The Forman stood up and said, "We deplore the actions of Mr. Benjamin Harris, but agree with the prosecution and the defense that a long period of probation may be best for his wife and son, and give him an opportunity to turn his life around. With regard to Judge McCracken, he should be extradited from New Jersey to stand trial for his criminal action. Attorneys Cornell and John Killeran should also be referred to the Georgia State Attorney General for prosecution. We believe that this court can issue a civil judgment against the judge and the attorneys to recover financial damages suffered by the plaintiff Homer Harris. The court should seize and liquidate all of the property that was purchased by Benjamin Harris using funds from the Harris Estate that belonged to Homer Harris. We recommend the Attorney General investigate any officers of the banks that are currently holding funds that belong to Homer Harris to see if they have conspired to perpetrate these criminal acts."

Judge Bibb thanked the jury for their service. He then sentenced Benjamin Harris to ten years prohibition, with a warning that any infraction will land him on the chain gang. He then issued a bench warrant for the arrest of Judge Andrew McCrackin, Cornell Killeran, and John Killeran, and referred their case to the Attorney General of the State of Georgia for prosecution. Behind the scene Georgia Governor Cole Bixby contacted New Jersey Governor Marshall Miller and requested speedy extradition of Judge McCracken and Attorney John Killeran. Judge Bibb struck his gavel three times and retired to his chambers.

Arrangements had been made by Douglas Ponder to host a luncheon for Homer, his attorneys, and witnesses at the Biltmore Hotel Coca-Cola suite. Penny was there, and had a present for Homer.

It was a nicely framed 8-by-10-inch photo of her clearing a jump on The Babe. Midshipmen were allowed one appropriate picture, not to exceed 8-by-10 inches.

Penny gave Homer a kiss on the cheek and explained that she had to head back to Emory University to prepare for a test in the morning. "I hope you get some time off and will come back to see us real soon."

Douglas Ponder explained that he had a board meeting at 3 p.m., and wished everyone a safe journey home in the morning. "I am leaving a car at your disposal if you would like to do some sightseeing. I would recommend the Cyclorama at Grant Park. It is a revolving diorama about the battle of Atlanta."

Homer shook hands with Doug Ponder and thanked him for the help that made this trip possible.

Mr. Iseman said, "I must get back to school to grade papers. It has been a pleasure meeting your wonderful friends, Homer. By the way, after all of this fine Biltmore food, you may want to have dinner at the Varsity over on North Avenue after the Cyclorama. They sell more Coca-Cola there than any other place in the world, and have the best chili dogs and onion rings you have ever tasted.

Ned MacNeely said, "I second the suggestion for the Varsity over by Georgia Tech, and the Cyclorama is amazing. I wish I could go with you, but work has piled up at my office. Thank you for all of your help with this case, especially Larry Cohen and Sam Cornelius. Working with professionals like you made this case go straight to the correct conclusion. We will stay in touch."

This left Homer, Mrs. Costello, Larry Cohen Sam Cornelius and Dr. Porter looking forward to the suggested tour and an early wakeup call from the Biltmore front desk. The Varsity lived up to its reputation.

Chapter 14
Meeting Caroline

On Wednesday morning at 7 am the Eastern Airline DC3 with *THE GREAT SILVER FLEET* painted above the windows lifted off for the 534-mile flight from Atlanta to Washington National, with a stop in Charlotte. Larry Cohen, Mrs. Costello and Dr. Porter left a few minutes later, on an Eastern direct flight for Newark. Both flights arrived on schedule, at 11 am.

Homer got to his quarters in time to be met by his roommates Jim and Charles returning from their last class. Jim started with the first question, "The scuttlebutt is that you had a Coca-Cola DC 3 land here just to pick you up? What was that all about?"

Charles added, "Everybody is saying you must be some kind of big shot."

"Well, I'm not a big shot! Remember, we're just 4th year Plebes. I had to testify as a witness in court and was given a five-day pass. Now I have to make up three days of class work and that is going to be tough."

Other Midshipmen asked Homer about his Coca-Cola trip and were told, "It was a court case that I can't discuss, but I'm not in trouble, just a witness."

This seemed to satisfy their curiosity.

The Naval Academy, realizing that Officers need social skills, announced a Plebe Hop for 4th year Midshipmen the week before Thanksgiving, 1939. Local college and senior high school girls were invited. Plebes were told that it was a command performance. Nine musicians from the Navy Band played Glen Miller songs, cookies and punch were served at one end of the old gym.

Homer saw a very pretty girl sitting in a corner with an empty chair beside her and got up the nerve to introduce himself to Caroline Dugas. She smiled and asked him if he would like to sit with her.

Homer said, "Yes, but could I get you some punch."

When he returned, Caroline told Homer that she was the daughter of Captain Dugas, who taught Naval History.

Homer said, "I'm in his class right now and it is very interesting."

She went on to say that she kept house for her dad, because they lost her mom to cancer two years ago.

Homer said, "On December 22nd, it will be one year since I lost my mom and dad in an accident that happened in the Lincoln Tunnel."

Their conversation went on for an hour before Homer said, "Would you like to dance?"

Caroline learned that Homer did not have any family to spend Thanksgiving with, and thought, 'I'll clear an invitation with Daddy.'

Faculty were encouraged to invite midshipmen that would be staying alone over holidays to their quarters for holiday dinners. As the band was softly playing "Good Night Ladies," Caroline said, "I'd like to write you."

Homer said, "Could you write your address on the empty page on your dance card, and I'll write you?"

Homer spent an enjoyable Thanksgiving dinner with Caroline and Captain Dugas. After a Turkey dinner, Homer wrote a thank you note to Captain Dugas and Caroline. Caroline wrote a letter back to Homer saying:

Dear Homer,

I was not looking forward to the Plebe Hop, but Daddy said it was an obligation. Meeting you made me glad that I was there. What I liked about you was that you were interested in me and my plans for nursing school after graduation. Other Midshipmen that I have met only want to brag about themselves. I guess I could say that I have been Navy since I was born at Bethesda Naval Hospital, so I have applied to nursing school in Annapolis and want to be a Navy Nurse. Daddy has been told that he will need to retire after this assignment, so I am hoping that we can stay here until I finish school. We should both graduate about the same time. Daddy and I would like to invite you for Christmas dinner, and hope that you haven't made other plans. Wishing you a Merry Christmas.

Your friend,
Caroline

Jim Coriello invited his roommates to visit with his family in Philadelphia for the Christmas break. Charles accepted, but Homer thanked Jim, saying that he had accepted a previous invitation.

Jim asked, "Is it with that babe that signed your picture?"

"No, the Babe is a horse I trained that belongs to Penny Ponder. Penny is riding the Babe over a jump in the picture, and she is just a friend that lives in Atlanta."

Charles said, "Listen amigo, when that fox on the horse signed it LOVE, there is more to it than you're lettin' on. If there isn't, then there is something wrong with you!"

"I hate to disappoint you, but I'm having dinner with Caroline Dugas, the same girl that invited me to Thanksgiving dinner. Staying here will give me more time to hit the books and finish the paper that I'm writing on the battle of Jutland."

Chapter 15
The Hangman's Noose Tightens

Chicago, December 22, 1938

David and Moses opened a letter postmarked Lisbon Portugal. It was written in code by reading every 4th word. It explained that a Christian friend had agreed to mail it to World Radio in Chicago and not mention any names. The news was that everything was getting worse.

'We are having trouble ordering parts and there is a big Star of David painted on the front window of our shop. Regular customers are still friendly however there are brown shirt thugs who would stand by our front door yelling insults as they entered. Other friends have applied for travel papers, but the Nazis will only allow one family member to leave so they can hold hostages. Some friends have tried forged papers and have been arrested and shot, or disappeared. This will be the first Hanukkah that we have not celebrated at services. Your mother and sister join me in sending our love.'

David took the letter to Rabbi Goldberg asking for ideas to get the family out of Germany. He suggested Irish Passports that were available for a price and said, "Does your family have any gold for bribes?"

"When Moses and I left they had gold worth about $150,000 in a hidden safe."

"Another possibility would be Palestine. The Hagenah are smuggling Jewish settlers past the British into Haifa but with war becoming more possible it is now more difficult. British policy has shifted in favor of the Arabs to gain favor and protect their interests. Shortwave broadcasts from Berlin are saying the Nazis support the Mufti and will help restore Arab land. I will contact some people who will know which way will be best, however I think time is fast running out for Jews in Germany."

David handed a $5,000 dollar donation check to his cousin to support his congregation.

Chapter 16
Plebe Year

Annapolis, December 25, 1938

After Caroline's baked Christmas ham, mashed potatoes, green beans, biscuits and pecan pie with vanilla ice cream for dessert, Captain Dugas suggested that they have coffee in his study. The conversation drifted into the Japanese aggression in China, and then Germany.

Captain Dugas solution to national defense was to double the United States fleet of battleships. Homer made the mistake of bringing up the success that Army Air Corps General Billy Mitchell had in sinking a former German Battleship with bombs.

"Why, if that ship was manned with our highly trained antiaircraft gunners, those planes would have been shot out of the sky."

Caroline could see that her dad was getting agitated, and changed the subject to the recent 14 to 13 Navy loss to Army. Captain Dugas remarked that the academic standards at West Point must be substantially lower than the Naval Academy so that professional players would be eligible.

Homer offered to help Caroline with the dishes and Captain Dugas turned on his American Bosch radio to catch the evening news. After Homer thanked Caroline and her dad for sharing their Christmas dinner, he took a fast, cold walk back to his quarters at Bancroft Hall.

Captain Dugas told Caroline "That was a wonderful dinner, just like your mother would have fixed. I wish she could have been with us. By the way, what was in the package that that he gave you for Christmas?"

"You didn't notice the gold cross around my neck?"

"That was nice, but you are too young to be getting serious. There are many Midshipmen that have more potential than this young man."

"How do you know that, Daddy?"

"I have access to all of their grades, and Homer Harris will be lucky if he graduates in the bottom ten percent of his class."

"Homer had to change from a top academic school in New Jersey to a high school in Georgia for his senior year, which did not have the prep courses that would have given him a better start here. Besides I think character is maybe more important and, Daddy, just so you won't worry, he is just a friend."

The second half of Plebe year, beginning in January 1939, went by rapidly. Homer and his roommate Charles had to study extra hard and occasionally ask for help from their other roommate Jim. Between 0630 Reveille and Taps at midnight the midshipmen had what you would call a tightly structured day.

Then came seven long weeks of Plebe Summer, beginning at dawn with rigorous physical training. The officer in charge was always a Marine Lt. Colonel, who believed in the Marine Corps way. Every Plebe had to learn how to accurately fire a 1903 bolt action Springfield rifle then clean his rifle to exacting standards. Homer and Charles fired for record expert, and Jim scored enough to be in the second tier as a sharpshooter. Jim was pleased that he was better than the bottom marksman level.

This was a compressed Marine Corps Boot Camp training program, with long marches hauling heavy packs, digging foxholes, map reading by compass, radio communication with the new walkie-talkie radios, laying telephone wire and setting up switchboards. Learning first aid and gas mask training with tear gas was as realistic as possible. Leadership positions were rotated between Plebes, and so was KP/kitchen police.

When the end of week seven finally arrived, a Rear Admiral announced at graduation that the class of 1942 were now third year upper classmen. Everyone was given three weeks leave.

Homer decided to go to New Jersey for one week, then go to Atlanta for five days. Allowing four days for travel, he would have five days to spend with Caroline in Annapolis.

On the way to the train station, Homer stopped at his post office box and found five letters. Sam Cornelius sent Homer a monthly statement, following the restoration of funds by the Georgia Supreme Court order. The original investment plan was paying interest, capital gains and dividends with a total of $4,990,552 dollars after only seven months of growth. Money was not going to be a problem.

He put the remaining letters from Hans, Mrs. Costello, Penny Ponder and Caroline in his pocket to read later, on the train. As the Erie Lackawanna Railroad started moving, Homer had to decide which letter to read first.

Dear Homer,

I am going to miss you and hope you have a safe trip to Lake Mohawk and Atlanta. I have never been to either, and hope you will take me there some day. After you return, I will have a two-week break from Nursing School and I look forward to spending time together. Right now, I'm studying for a biology test…ugh! I know you are glad to have Plebe Summer behind you. From what I have heard, it must have been rough. I'm glad our schedules worked out.

Love,
Caroline

Dear Former Business Partner,

When you get into the train station in Hoboken, give me a call, and I'll be in Dover when you arrive. You never know if the Weary Erie Railroad will get you there on schedule. I heard that your Navy boot camp at Great Lakes compared to the Army ROTC boot camp at Fort Benning was a tea party. I don't have to go through that until the end of my junior year. I'd like to hear about your summer training.

You will be pleased to see how nice your old house turned out after the repairs. Dad plans to tell you if you ever want to buy it back, it is yours. I am so glad to hear that the court case turned out the way it did. The newspapers have roasted the judge and that lawyer. They are being extradited to Georgia to stand trial. I'm glad they still have chain gangs down there. I have a surprise for you. It's called water skiing. I took an old pair of wood cross country snow skis and mounted some tennis shoes. Our Pen Yan Swift with the 22 horse will pull you up from a crouching position. It is more fun than the aquaplane board. Dad is going to give me time off from construction while you are here, and Momma is planning some great German dinners.

See you soon,
Hans

Dear Homer,

We are all looking forward to your visit. I want to hear about Annapolis. Some students have asked if you would give them a lecture about life at a service academy. With tension mounting in Europe, there is more interest in our military. There is a problem in Patterson, NJ, with a group called the German American Bund. What they are is just a bunch of Nazis in disguise. I understand that you are staying at your old house. The Schmidt's had an open house when it was finished, and I was invited. They did a beautiful repair and renovation. I have saved newspapers covering Judge McCracken and Lawyer John Killeran for you to read.

Looking forward to seeing you,
Christine Costello

Dear Homer,
I got a real laugh when you wrote about your roommate who thought I was the Babe. Please tell him that I take that as a complement. I am finished with my freshman year at Emory, and didn't flunk out. That school is hard and everyone in my class was very competitive. I'm going to be at the farm for the rest of the summer, and look forward to seeing you. I hope we can go riding together. Daddy sends his best. He wants to talk with you about a career with Coca-Cola after you finish with the Navy.

Fondly,
Penny

Homer spent his first week of his 1939 vacation visiting Hans and his family, waterskiing on Lake Mohawk, and sleeping late in his old bedroom. He invited the Schmidt's, Mrs. Costello, Ann and Charles Lindberg, Larry Cohen and Sam Cornelius to dinner at Sammy's Old Cider Mill to thank them again for their support and friendship.

He borrowed the 1929 Ford touring car that he had given to Mrs. Schmidt for a visit with Sam Cornelius so they could go over the investment portfolio in detail. On his last day, Hans asked Homer if he would like to drive the Model A to the Newark Airport to catch his Eastern Airlines Flight to Atlanta. Arrangements had been made to stay at the farm with the Ponders.

As a surprise, Penny drove to the airport in her new British racing green 1938 Jaguar Roadster to pick up Homer. She greeted him with a warm hug and asked if he would like to drive the Jag.

"It is supposed to go a 100-miles an hour, but I've never gone above seventy."

"Sure, but it will be quite a contrast to the Model A that I drove to Newark this morning."

"Don't let it get away from you, Sailor."

When they arrived at Roswell, Homer said "I could not believe a car could be this much fun to drive. The acceleration, handling and brakes are amazing. I don't think we have anything on four wheels to match the British."

Douglas Ponder got home in time for dinner with Homer and Penny. He wanted to hear all about Annapolis. Homer explained that Plebes had no privileges, however as a third class midshipman he could join the Equestrian Team, the Amateur Radio Club, and possibly the German Club.

Penny asked, "Why would you want the German Club? My Jewish classmates at Emory say that we are going to be in a war with the Nazis."

Homer explained, "If we get in a war with Germany, reading and speaking German will be a lot more valuable than French or Spanish."

Doug Ponder said, "I will be flying on the company plane to New York to meet with our Coca-Cola management team from Berlin. Homer, you would be leaving a day early, but you and Penny could fly up with me. I believe you took two years of German from Mrs. Costello in high school and had another year at the Naval Academy. How were your grades?"

"Sir, in German they were straight A's, and I'm glad to say I didn't flunk any of the really hard courses like trigonometry."

"Perhaps you would like to sit in at the meeting and translate if they stumble on some English words. You would need to consider that everything that you hear to be classified, because we have some difficult decisions to make."

"Yes Sir, I would look forward to having that experience."

"If you want to go riding with Penny and the Babe tomorrow, we could take Mr. and Mrs. Iseman to dinner at Aunt Fanny's Cabin in the evening if they are available. I was very impressed with Mr. Iseman. Is there anyone else you would like to see?"

"I'd like to see my Aunt Virginia and Sandy but I don't know how without causing a problem for her."

"I have a solution. We own the Seed and Feed Company in Roswell. Actually, we did a startup for our own convenience and it is doing well. Penny is the President, so she is getting some business experience. Our General Manager can call your uncle in the morning and tell him to come in to discuss his bill which is actually past due. When he arrives, you will get a call and can drive over to see your aunt for a short visit. We will need to be on the plane by 1 p.m."

Aunt Virginia was very pleased to see Homer. She told him that her husband was drinking heavily and is verbally abusive, but he has not hit her. She told Homer that she may need to divorce him for her sanity and so that Sandy can have a good life.

"I would sell the farm and go back to school to be a secretary. We would probably move to Atlanta so Sandy could finish at a top academic high school like Henry Grady."

"If you need money for a lawyer or anything, please let me know, and I'll send a check to the Post Office."

Penny and Homer took her car to the Coca-Cola garage in Atlanta and joined Doug Ponder and his driver for a fast ride to the airport. The flight landed at LaGuardia in time for a private dinner at the Waldorf with Dr. Rolf Dietzler, Managing Director of Coca-Cola GMBH, and his staff. The description of political and human rights conditions in Germany was grim.

The next day, the meeting began at breakfast and finished after lunch. It was decided that the parent company will stop selling concentrate syrup and remove as many employees and their families as possible from Germany. It was the right thing to do.

The Coca-Cola DC3 was ready for takeoff at 3 p.m. from LaGuardia with an amended flight plan to make a quick stop at Washington National Airport. They would drop Homer off and then continue to Atlanta Candler Field. Homer shook hands with Dr. Dietzler and Douglas Ponder, wishing the best of luck. Unexpectedly, Penny kissed him as he was heading out the door.

Chapter 17
I Can't Get Serious

Homer showed his ID to the Navy driver and made the 6 p.m. shuttle run to the Naval Academy. When he arrived at Bancroft Hall it was practically disserted. He had missed dinner. When he opened his B4 bag, he found a big corned beef deli sandwich and a note from Penny, which said:

> I want to spend more time with you. I wish we could be together more often because I think I'm falling in love with you. I need to figure out if it is friend love, or much more. Enjoy your sandwich. Hugs,
> Penny

As Homer walked to the payphone booth near the main entrance to call Caroline, he thought things were getting complicated. 'I really like Penny as a friend, and I think her dad is terrific. I have also been looking forward to five days with Caroline. They say that guys want a girl like the one that married dear old dad, as the song goes. Caroline is a lot like my mom, and I know I really care for her. Hold on fella, with three years to go here, I can't begin to think about getting serious about any relationship that exceeds friendship.'

After dropping a nickel in the payphone he heard, "Captain Dugas' quarters, Caroline speaking."

Homer was happy to hear her voice.

Arrangements were made on the phone to take Caroline sailing tomorrow. The academy had a fleet of sailboats and he would get a picnic lunch from the galley. The following day Homer and Caroline took the train into Washington and spent the day at the Smithsonian. On their third day, they visited Caroline's nursing school, and then went back to prepare dinner for Captain Dugas. After dinner they went to see *Mr. Smith Goes to Washington* with Jimmy Stewart. Over a banana split, they discussed the corruption that the movie exposed in the Federal Government.

Homer learned that Caroline had never been on a horse, and since the equestrian team members were on leave, he decided to give her a lesson on their fourth vacation day and then take an easy trail ride.

After two hours Caroline said, "I think sailing is more fun."

On their fifth day, Homer took Caroline to lunch at an Italian restaurant in Annapolis and walked around town until late afternoon. Then the Brigade of Midshipmen began arriving en masse before dark, so they said goodbye with a hug.

Before Jim and Charles arrived, Homer quietly sat on his bunk and started thinking about Penny and Caroline. In very different ways, they were both really wonderful.

'Penny has been everywhere, and has a year of college sophistication behind her. She is confident, smart, and polished. She and her dad have been in my corner since day one. I really care for her. Caroline is smart, sweet, unspoiled, understands the Navy and the demands that go with active duty. She is fun to be with. I really care for her. Right now, I hope I can keep them both as friends.'

During the last week of August, the class of 1942 was briefed on their responsibilities to the class of 1943. Homer told his roommates that he didn't enjoy harassing the Plebes, and both Charles and Jim said they agreed. Schedules were issued and the routine began. Homer's course load included second year German, Oceanography, Economics, Physics and Leadership. He was assigned to a Plebe table for meals and actually enjoyed getting to know some information about each new Midshipman.

Table conversation showed concern that some of the American population were becoming convinced that the danger to the United States was very real following German seizure of Czechoslovakia in March 1939 and the invasion of Poland on September 1st, 1939. Japanese expansion began in 1937 with the invasion of China. That triggered the naval program building toward a two-ocean Navy and the need for many more naval officers. Italy had a significant, modern navy and combined with the overwhelming number of German U Boats being launched every month, the British were hard pressed to hold the Atlantic and Mediterranean sea-lanes open. Even with the blatant aggression by Germany and Japan, there was mixed support for American Neutrality. The faculty and midshipmen at the Naval Academy could, however, read the handwriting on the wall.

Homer enjoyed 1939 Thanksgiving dinner with Caroline, and then got back to the books. During the Christmas break, he sent flowers to Caroline and Penny, and an extra-large sweatshirt that said "NAVY" across the chest to Douglas Ponder. He sent a Christmas card to Aunt Virginia and Sandy with a

$1,000 check enclosed. Homer accepted Jim Coriello's invitation for a short Christmas visit with his family in Philadelphia. Charles said he enjoyed Jim's family, but wished he had enough time to travel to Clute to be with his family. This made Homer wish that he had his family.

After New Year's Day in 1940, the second half of his third class (sophomore) year went by quickly. Caroline was deeply immersed in nursing school, so they met at the Academy chapel for Sunday protestant services and often went to lunch in town.

Caroline asked Homer how he could afford the restaurant bills and he told her, "I have made investments with some very good companies."

Chapter 18
Summer 1940

A few weeks before the end of the term, forms went out to the class of 1942 to request the type ship they would like to be assigned to for summer fleet training. Homer checked no preference, and was assigned to the USS *Perch SS176*, a Porpoise Class submarine sailing from Groton Connecticut.

After the first dive, Homer wished that he had asked for a surface ship. He was concerned when pipes started leaking after they reached a depth of only 100 ft. The air smelled like diesel fuel and the crew of five officers and 45 enlisted men left no open bunk space for Midshipmen Homer Harris, who was assigned for training. The solution was to hot bunk with a crew member and sleep when they were on duty.

Homer was rotated to assigned duties in the torpedo room, engine room, navigation, and sonar. The Captain was Lieutenant Commander Dan Dwiggins, Class of 1930, who answered endless questions. The junior officer was Ensign Nick Fain, class of 1939. During their nine-week cruise, the Perch visited Norfolk for supplies, and then on to Cuba. In Cuba the crew was given shore leave for sightseeing.

Nick Fain and Homer went to the U.S. Embassy and dropped off letters that they had written during off duty hours. Homer wrote to Caroline, Penny, Doug Ponder, Hans, Mrs. Costello, Mr. Iseman, and Aunt Virginia.

From Cuba, they ran an exercise attempting to sneak into the Panama Canal without detection. The crew of the Perch was allowed to listen to the evening BBC broadcasts that described the fall of France and intensive bombing of London, referred to as the Blitz. On the north-bound leg, the Perch ran on the surface, then practiced one crash dive before reaching the Key West Naval Station. Under the close supervision of Commander Dwiggins, Homer was allowed to dock the Perch.

The Perch received orders to remain in the Caribbean operating out of Key West, so arrangements were made for Homer to catch a hop on a Catalina flying boat that was heading to Naval Air Station, Jacksonville. From there, he could return to Annapolis by train or try to find a Navy or Army Air Corps flight heading as close as possible to the Naval Academy. The landing on the St. Johns River at NAS JAX was smooth as silk. Then the Catalina turned into a long concrete ramp, extended its' wheels and used its powerful radial engines to bring the big flying boat out of the water.

Homer went to operations and learned that a Navy R4D was warming up for a flight to Washington National Airport. He hurried to the aircraft and found that there was space available. There were ten senior officers and ten senior chiefs who had finished an I.G. inspection already on board. The R4D was the same aircraft as the Coca-Cola DC3 without sound proofing. It did, however, have reclining seats.

The conversation on the plane centered on the evacuation of several hundred thousand British, French and Belgian troops that were saved from capture off the beaches of Dunkirk by 861, ships including hundreds of civilian owned boats.

When Homer signed in at the Academy, he was told that his three-week summer leave could begin immediately. Homer called Caroline, and learned that she was getting ready to take comprehensive exams and would not have any free time for two weeks. She told Homer how hard nursing school was and, although she wanted to be together, her preparation had to come first.

Homer said, "I understand. I'll take off to Lake Mohawk, and maybe Georgia. I'm looking forward to seeing you when I get back."

"Don't be mad at me, Homer."

"Caroline, I could never be mad at you. See you in two weeks."

Homer then called Penny and spoke with Mary Lee Wells, their housekeeper.

"Why, Mr. Homer, it shore is good to hear you. You are probably callin' for Miss Penny, but she is with her daddy in Bermuda for a meetin' with the Coca-Cola folks from Europe. I probably shouldn't tell you, but they took her new boyfriend, Mr. Pick with them. I don't know nothin' much about him, but I guess he is OK. He was one of those Georgia Tech football players."

Homer thought, 'I hope it isn't serious. I could catch a hop to Bermuda because the Navy is always flying back and forth, but that may not be a good idea. I wasn't invited.'

Homer's next call was to Hans, who said, "Get yourself on up here. I just finished my summer quarter sophomore exams and need to enjoy the lake."

Hans met with Homer at the Dover train station and drove the 1929 Model A touring car up the mountain road to Lake Mohawk. Hans' mother had a Wiener Schnitzel dinner ready when they arrived. Hans' father was building new homes at a rapid pace for an average price of $4,950. Since the economy had picked up with war orders from the British, there was a housing shortage.

Both Hans and Homer were going to be starting their junior year at Rutgers and Annapolis. Homer described his cruise on the Perch and flights on the navy aircraft.

Hans said "I'll bet you are glad to have boot camp over. When I finish this year, I'm off to Fort Benning in Georgia during the summer. From what you have told me it will be really hot, like it was when you were at the farm. What will you be doing next summer?"

"I'll be on a different type of ship for a training cruise. I'm hoping for a destroyer or an aircraft carrier."

After dinner, they helped in the kitchen, which had been completely remodeled, thanked Mrs. Schmidt for a great dinner, and then moved to the radio room with Hans' dad to listen to WOR news from New York and then the 9 p.m. BBC news from London on shortwave.

Edward R. Murrow was broadcasting live with bombs dropping in the background. Fred Schmidt looked at the boys and said, "I am ashamed of Germany," then switched the dial to music from The Rainbow Room in New York.

Frida Schmidt came in the radio room and asked Homer, "Is there anyone you would like to have over for dinner while you are here? Possibly Mrs. Costello?"

"That would be great, if you could invite her."

"Well, if you boys are going water skiing in the morning, you better get some rest."

Homer and Hans said, "Yes ma'am!" and hugged Mrs. Schmidt.

Hans' dad said, "I'm glad you are here with us in your house. Please know if you ever want it back it is yours at repair cost."

"Thank you for your offer, but it is yours for you to always enjoy."

Homer and Hans walked upstairs, and Homer told Hans what was going on with Penny and Caroline.

Hans' response was, "There are lots of birds in the air, so don't worry about it. All the girls that graduated with our class, if you had been here, are now back from school and some of them look pretty good."

"There may be something wrong with me Hans, but none of them could measure up to Penny or Caroline."

"Well, let's go skiing in the morning, and you will see some of them on the lake."

Homer slept like a rock in his old bedroom. The next few days included dinner with the Schmidt's and Mrs. Costello at Sammy's Old Cider Mill, and lunches at Krogh's just off the boardwalk at Lake Mohawk. Homer was surprised when he entered the boat house, expecting to see the Penn Yan Swift that he had given to Hans when he went to Georgia, instead there was a beautiful 18-foot Chris Craft Sportsman.

Hans explained that the Judge had left it under water when he sold the house, and Hans and his dad brought it back up and removed the engine, instruments, upholstery, and drained the fuel tank. Everything was rebuilt and dual carburetors were added to the 95-horsepower engine, taking it up to 120 horses. Hans had also made a new wide pair of water skis with rubber shoes that could be adjusted.

Hans told Homer that the Penn Yan was in storage at the Marina across the lake and asked, "Would you like to sell it?"

"I might change my mind, but no, it has sentimental value to me so, I'll pay the storage."

With two weeks summer leave left, Homer decided to call Penny and see if they were back from Bermuda. Douglas Ponder answered the phone and was delighted to hear from Homer.

"Mary Lee told me you had called while we were in Bermuda and I had my secretary try to reach you at the Academy to invite you to come down, but you were not there. We have finished a cabin at a beautiful lake in North Georgia called Lake Burton, and I'm taking a weeklong vacation starting day after tomorrow. Penny and her new boyfriend are going to be there, if that doesn't cause a problem for you."

"No Sir, Penny and I have always been friends, but it may bother the boyfriend."

"Well Homer, I guess that would be his problem. Penny may be bringing one or two of her sorority sisters along."

"Would it be out of place if I asked to bring my best friend Hans Schmidt? He expected me to stay with his family for the rest of my leave. Hans will be a junior at Rutgers next year, and I know you will like him."

"Sure, bring him along. Let me know when you will arrive, and I'll send a car to the airport."

Homer asked Hans if he would like to fly down to Georgia for a week at the Ponders' Lake Burton cabin, and to bring his water skis.

"I'm buying the tickets, and a limo will pick us up at the airport."

"Do I get to meet Penny?"

"She will be there with the new boyfriend, but Mr. Ponder said Penny was bringing some sorority sisters."

Hans smiled and said, "I hope they aren't dogs with nice personalities."

Homer and Hans were met at the baggage claim by the driver holding a sign that said 'Homer Harris.' They found their bags and Hans' water skis.

The ride to Lake Burton took all of three hours on winding mountain roads. There was one area where they crossed a stream that ran across the road, and Hans said, "You are really taking me to the boondocks!"

When they pulled down the gravel road to the cabin Hans said, "Good night, I was expecting a cabin, but this place is huge."

Homer said, "They were building it last year on a lot that was leased from the Georgia Power Company for 99 years. I had no idea that it was this big, but remember, Mr. Ponder is President of Coca-Cola, and will probably use the place for business meetings."

When the driver brought the limo to a stop in front of the entrance, he said, "Well, I'm heading back to Atlanta fellas. Have a nice time."

Homer thanked him and unloaded their gear. When the driver pulled away, Homer went to the door, but nobody answered. Homer recognized Penny's Jaguar and a Cadillac that probably belonged to Doug Ponder.

"They must be here and out on the lake."

Homer and Hans walked around the house and saw two girls in bathing suits on the dock and an inboard speed boat pulling a guy on an aquaplane board behind the boat.

They walked down a steep hill to the dock and introduced themselves to a cute redhead who put out her hand and said, "My name is Emily Derieux, and this is my sorority sister Elizabeth Montgomery."

"My friends call me Lizzy. You must be Homer." Then she shook hands with Hans.

"No, I'm Hans Schmidt, and my buddy here is Homer."

Lizzy flashed a smile at Hans and said, "Well, get your bathing suit on, handsome so I can get a good look at you."

Emily said, "The house is open, just take an empty bedroom upstairs and come on down with some cold cokes and an opener."

On the way up the hill Homer said, "looks like Lizzy has her eye on you, boy, and I thought Jersey girls were forward."

When they got back to the dock the Chris Craft was being tied up, and Douglas Ponder got up on the dock and shook hands with Homer and Hans.

"I'm really glad you could make the trip."

Penny came over to Homer, gave him a sisterly kiss on the cheek, and introduced him to Pick Pickerton. Homer introduced Penny and Pick to Hans. Pick tried a crushing handshake on Hans and was met with equal force. When he tried it on Homer, he knew neither one could be intimidated.

Doug Ponder noticed the skis that Hans brought down to the dock and asked, "What have we got here?"

"Sir, they are water skis that I made."

Homer said, "Last year Hans took some old wooden cross-country snow skis and we learned to ski on them, but these are easier to get up with and handle much better with twin fins at the rear. The ski that has a toe piece at the rear can be used as a single slalom ski, but it takes a lot of practice to ski on one."

"Well which one of you would like to give us a demonstration?"

"I think Hans should, Mr. Ponder, because he came up with the idea."

Hans put on the skis and sat on the end of the dock. Homer tied a 75-foot rope with a wood handle attached to the ring at the stern of the 18-foot Chris Craft, which was exactly like the one that Hans and his dad restored. When the boat pulled away, leaving 15 feet of slack in the line.

Hans yelled, "Hit it," and Mr. Ponder gave it full throttle. Hans hit the water standing up and immediately jumped a wake.

Penny said, "Wow, that looks like a lot more fun than the aquaplane. You ought to try that, Pick."

"It looks easy Penny, you will have to try it too."

When they made a pass by the dock, Hans kicked off a ski and continued cutting far to one side and then the other. Penny jumped in the crystal-clear water and swam out to retrieve the ski, and then handed it to Pick on the dock. Finally, Hans fell off, and Homer helped him back in the boat.

Mr. Ponder said, "Do we need to go back to get the other ski?"

Homer said, "No Sir, I can get up on one."

Homer got up on the first try and put on a good show. Finally, after twenty minutes, Homer sprayed water on the dock from his wake. On the next circle, he tossed the rope up in the air and went over 100 feet to the dock before dropping into the water by the ladder. The three girls gave Homer a round of applause.

Penny said, "It's your turn now, Pick."

Hans said, "Do you want to start with two skis in the water? It's easier."

"No, I'll do the dock start like you did."

Penny drove the boat and Hans handled the rope. When they had 15 feet of slack in the rope, Hans yelled "Hit it!"

Penny gave full throttle, and Pick launched through the air and came down flat on his belly. Mr. Ponder, Lizzy and Emily laughed, and Homer could not help but smile.

They circled Pick in the water and Hans, gave him instruction for getting up. This time he fell backwards. On his next try, he fell forward.

Hans told him not to pull the rope into his chest. "Keep your arms straight and knees bent until the water feels hard then stand up."

On Pick's next try, he got halfway up and fell sideways.

"You are trying to stand up to soon. When you get up, keep your knees partially bent and your arms straight."

On Pick's fifth try, he started falling backward and pulled the rope up to his chest again.

Hans said, "Just stay in a crouch with your arms straight, and let the boat pull you up."

Penny said, "This is your last try for today."

This time, Pick fell backwards again, so they picked him up.

After the boat was tied up, Mr. Ponder said, "Okay kids, lets' get dressed and we will drive over to LaPrades Camp for dinner."

On the way up the hill, Homer said, "It's harder than it looks, Pick. In the morning, Hans and I will take you out without an audience and you will be successful. The lake will be like glass, and without the boat, waves that we had today it will be easier. Hans' family have the exact same Chris Craft up at Lake Mohawk, so I'm sure Mr. Ponder won't mind, but we will ask."

Dinner was served family-style, with fried chicken, corn on the cob, green beans and crackling cornbread. It was delicious.

Over coffee and apple pie, Mr. Ponder said, "Since everybody doesn't know everybody, perhaps we could go around the table and you can give us a short resume. Penny will you go first?"

"I'm Penny, and everyone except Hans knows me. I will be going into my junior year at Emory University in Atlanta and I'm a Phi Mu sister. My major is international business. My hobbies are horseback riding, boating, and Georgia Tech football, which is how I met Pick. Since Pick is sitting next to me, I'll let him go next."

"I'm Pick Pickering and I've been dating Penny for three wonderful months. I graduated from Tech last June, with a degree in industrial management, and played football. I am now serving as a commissioned officer in the U.S. Army, as a Second Lieutenant and am the assistant G-4 doing POL, that's petroleum oil and lubricants, inventory checks for Third Army. I live in the BOQ at Fort MacPherson. I am enjoying one week of my 30 day leave with you fine folks."

Lizzy said, "Well, I'm next. I'm Penny's sorority sister and live at the Phi Mu house at Emory. I'm from Rome, Georgia and plan to be a teacher when I graduate next year. My major is French, and my minor is Art. Emily, you are next."

"I'm Emily Derieux and I'm from Cumberland, Maryland, at least for now. My dad is the Plant Manager at the Celanese Amcelle Plant, and we have been transferred around the country at least six times. My major at Emory is Chemistry. I'm a Phi Mu, and live at the sorority house."

Mr. Ponder said "Okay Homer, you are up to bat."

"I'm Homer Harris and my home, for now, is the United States Naval Academy. I was originally from Lake Mohawk in New Jersey, however I spent my senior year at Roswell High School, where I met Penny. I will be starting my second Midshipman year which, in civilian terms, is my junior year in college. Two weeks ago, I finished a seven-week training cruise on a submarine. I am fluent in German and have a variety of naval and civilian courses behind me and in front of me. Hans, you are up."

"I'm Hans Schmidt, from Lake Mohawk, New Jersey and I am going into my junior year at Rutgers University. I am in Army ROTC, and majoring in business. Homer and I have been friends forever. I would like to thank Mr. Ponder and Penny for having me for this visit. I have never been to Georgia and, although I live on a beautiful lake with nine miles of shoreline, Lake Burton, with sixty-two miles of shoreline is really spectacular. I will be back in Georgia next summer for boot camp at Fort Benning, and I'm looking forward to getting the straight scoop from Lieutenant Pickering about Benning."

Doug Ponder smiled and said, "It is my pleasure to welcome you outstanding young adults to our extended family. With the talent and character at this table, I know our country will do well."

Hans and Homer were able to get Pick up on skis after three tries the next morning. For the next two days, Hans and Lizzy stayed glued to each other. Homer helped Doug Ponder with projects on the cabin, and played gin rummy with Emily. Penny and Pick took long boat rides. Homer decided to leave in the morning with the Coca-Cola mail courier on his return trip to Atlanta, because a Navy R4D flight was leaving Naval Air Station Atlanta for Washington at 1700.

When Homer returned to Annapolis, he found two letters in his mail box. The first was from Caroline.

Dear Homer,

I have missed you so much. I hope you will call me the minute you get back from New Jersey. I felt so bad about staying in the books for those tests and not seeing you. I barely passed chemistry and I could have flunked out if I didn't cram for all the subjects.

Love, Caroline

The second letter was from Aunt Virginia.

Dear Homer,

I am writing you for advice and help. Your uncle took his frustration out on Sandy and gave him a thrashing for no good reason. I have decided to divorce him. I don't have any money for a lawyer, or even know who to go to. Could the lawyer that handled your case help me? I will keep checking the post office box and hope to hear from you soon.

With love, Aunt Virginia

After a good night sleep, Homer called Caroline and asked her out for dinner at their favorite Italian restaurant. Then sat down and wrote to Aunt Virginia.

Dear Aunt Virginia,

I was sorry to hear about Sandy, but know that you will both have a better life on your own. The law firm that handled my case was the Spaulding Law firm in Atlanta and the lead attorney was Ned MacNeely. His phone number is Willow 9899. I will contact him and guarantee your legal bill. They can also help you sell the farm for a good price, and then my CPA Sam Cornelius can help you invest the money and create an income for you and Sandy. Going back to secretarial school sounds like a good idea. You are a fine person and deserve a happy life.

Your caring nephew,
Homer

Dinner conversation with Caroline filled in details on all of the time that they were apart. Caroline discussed nursing school, and Homer told her about his cruise on the USS *Perch* and then his visit to Lake Mohawk and Lake Burton.

"Caroline, I have nine days before class starts. Do you think your dad would allow you to go with me to the Schmidt's home at Lake Mohawk for two or three days? Mrs. Schmidt is like a second mother, and she would love to meet you."

"I'll ask Daddy tonight. Would we be going up on the train? Would I have a separate bedroom? Could she call Daddy to extend the invitation? Please call me in the morning, to find out if I can go."

Caroline gave Homer a hug and a real kiss at her front door.

At 0900, Homer heard, "Captain Dugas quarters, Caroline speaking."

"Caroline, this is me."

"Yes, Daddy said yes if Mrs. Schmidt calls him."

"I'll make train reservations to leave tomorrow morning. We won't need to get dressed up, just casual clothes, a bathing suit, and a dress for church on Sunday. I will set it up right now with Mrs. Schmidt." "Homer, I'm so excited. I hope your friend Hans will be there. I'm looking forward to meeting him."

When Homer called Mrs. Schmidt, she said, "I would love to have Caroline come tomorrow with you, but you will have a surprise. Hans brought a girl that I think you have met named Lizzy back from Georgia. I can put both girls in the guest room with twin beds."

Homer thanked Mrs. Schmidt, and gave her Captain Dugas phone number. Homer thought about having Caroline and Lizzy together. 'No doubt Lizzy will give Penny a complete report on Caroline, but so what? I'm not hiding anything.'

Hans and Lizzy came down to the Dover train station in the Model A touring car, arriving just as the Erie Lackawanna came to a stop.

Caroline thought Lake Mohawk was beautiful, and Mrs. Schmidt went out of her way to make her feel welcome. Lizzy kept a running conversation with Caroline about nursing school and life at Annapolis. Lizzie talked about Emory, life in Georgia, what she thought about Penny's new boyfriend, and how she thought Hans was a keeper. The girls hit it off.

For Saturday dinner, Caroline and Lizzy helped Mrs. Schmidt dip thin veal patties in a bowl with parmesan cheese, eggs, parsley, salt, pepper, nutmeg and milk. Then they fried the Wiener Schnitzel until brown in a butter-filled pan.

Lizzy said, "We never had anything this good in Georgia."

The girls helped clean up the kitchen and then joined Homer, Hans, and Mr. Schmidt in the radio room. When they switched from WOR News to shortwave radio Berlin, Lizzy and Caroline couldn't understand a word so they went to the dining table and played a new card game called canasta.

After Church on Sunday, Homer invited Caroline, Mrs. Costello, the Schmidt's, Lizzy, and Hans for lunch at Krogh's just off the boardwalk at Lake

Mohawk. During the conversation around the table, Fred Schmidt talked about the new houses that he was building for civilians that were being hired at Picatinny Arsenal, creating a demand that was overwhelming. Hans mentioned that the Army received an appropriation of six billion dollars in June 1940, which was more than the total for the last sixteen years to support a growing 1.2 million man Army.

Mrs. Costello said, "After signing a non-aggression pact, Hitler attacked the Russians and may defeat them. I am so glad to be in America."

Caroline added "My daddy is a Navy Captain, and he has been saying that without the British Navy and the Royal Air Force Hitler would be in London."

Lizzy added, "Well, maybe I should have majored in German instead of French."

Homer said, "What I'm hearing is connecting the dots. It won't be long before we could be at war with Germany. Our Navy is modernizing the older ships, and we are building new ships so we can have a two ocean Navy. Japan has been building battleships and aircraft carriers for the last three years at a much faster pace than us. The German U Boats are making it very difficult to get supplies to England through their wolf packs. What really concerns me is that a large percentage of American pacifists do not want to properly prepare in case we are drawn into the conflict. We are enjoying prosperity and what may be a false sense of security."

Frida Schmidt said, "On that happy note, why don't we head back to our house for apple strudel with vanilla ice cream?"

When the check arrived, Fred Schmidt grabbed it before Homer could get to it.

The weather on Sunday afternoon was beautiful. Homer and Caroline had gone to the Sparta Presbyterian Church and The Schmidt's, Lizzy and Mrs. Costello went to Don Bosco Catholic services. Mrs. Costello thought something might come of this, since Hans and Lizzy were both Catholic.

The afternoon was spent teaching Caroline and Lizzy to water ski. Hans had finished a second pair of skis on Saturday and put a cote of spar varnish on them, so they were dry enough to use Sunday afternoon. Both girls thought skis were much more fun than the aquaplane board.

Dinner on the Schmidt's back deck facing the lake included grilled hamburgers or cheeseburgers, chips, and a salad.

Caroline thanked the Schmidt's for a wonderful visit, and said, "I wish tomorrow wasn't our last day."

Hans grinned and said, "We'll keep you and just send Homer back to school."

Caroline thought he was serious, and replied, "I can't do that, we want to stay together. Don't we, Homer?"

Homer just gave her a hug.

The train ride to Annapolis was on schedule, arriving in time for dinner at their favorite Italian restaurant. Caroline put her head on Homer's shoulder on the cab ride to Captain Dugas' quarters. When they arrived, Homer shook hands with Captain Dugas, and thanked him for letting Caroline make the trip.

Caroline hugged her dad and said, "Daddy, I had a really great time, and you would like the Schmidt's. They have a beautiful home on the lake that used to belong to Homer's parents. I learned a new sport called waterskiing. Homer's best friend Hans' girlfriend Lizzy was visiting, and also learned to ski. She is going to be a junior at Emory University in Atlanta. Mrs. Schmidt taught me a new recipe for Wiener Schnitzel that was delicious. I'll have to make it for you."

"Well Homer, you brought my little girl back safely with a suntan. You both are going to have classes starting day after tomorrow, so I suggest you get ready for a very important year."

"Yes, Sir. Have a good evening."

Chapter 19
The Pace Accelerates

Homer began his second year class schedule (his junior year), with Navigation, Seamanship, Oceanography, Leadership, Ethics, Law, Political Science, and Psychology. There was a feeling of urgency among the faculty and midshipmen. World conditions were continuing to deteriorate, and debate was being held in Congress over the need for a peacetime draft.

Homer shared his cruise experience on the USS *Perch* with his roommates. Jim was assigned to a Great-War-era four stack destroyer that mapped Greenland and Iceland. Charles was assigned to an oiler that made two trips between San Diego and Pearl Harbor, and refueled a submarine returning from Wake Island. All three roommates agreed that this was going to be a tough academic year, with very little personal time.

Homer made a trip to the post office at least once a week, and found several letters in October.

Dear Homer,

The divorce is now final as of October 1, 1940. Sandy and I have bought a small house in Ansley Park near the Governor's Mansion, so he can be in the Henry Grady High School district. The farm was sold for $520,000.00 to the Georgia Cattle Company. The Spaulding Law Firm was very helpful, however they will not send me a bill. They say the bill has been taken care of, I guess by you. Mr. MacNeely has been a wonderful lawyer. He has recommended some investments to give me an income and I would like to know what you think about putting $50,000 dollars in Coca-Cola, $50,000 dollars In Georgia Power, $50,000 dollars In DuPont, $50,000 dollars In General Motors, and $50,000 In the Citizens and Southern Bank stock. The dividends will give me $7500 per year and the remaining cash will add about $1000 in interest from the bank. That is more than enough for us to live on. I have enrolled in Massey Secretarial School and am learning typing, shorthand and filing. When I graduate, they are placing graduates with Delta Air Lines, Southern Railroad,

Coca-Cola, and a number of smaller companies. So far, no trouble from your uncle. He was hired by the Cattle Company who turned my house into an office and bunk house. I hope you will come to see us. Our phone number is Maple 9890. I will always be your loving Aunt Virginia, using my maiden name, Mills.

Please know you are in our prayers,
Aunt Virginia and Sandy

Dear Homer,
Here is an interim report on your investments through September 1940. The total is now $5,189,600.00 - up from $4,449,552.00 during the same period last year. All of your stocks are performing very well so I would not recommend changing any allocations. If you are in Atlanta, please try to get together.

Best wishes,
Sam Cornelius

Thanksgiving and Christmas dinners, 1940, were spent with Caroline. He sent flowers to Penny, Mrs. Costello, and Caroline. Homer decided to stay at the Academy, because the extra study time would help pull his grades in Oceanography and Navigation up to a passing level.

Homer told himself, 'I can't afford to flunk.'

The course load was considerably more difficult than his first two years. Aside from the 1940 Army-Navy game 14 to 0 win over Army, there was very little recreation. Caroline and Homer continued to meet every Sunday at church, and usually had lunch together in Annapolis. After classes resumed in 1941, a new program was added to all Midshipmen's schedule that included an evening briefing by a faculty member after dinner that covered world events. Questions could be submitted in writing, and several would be selected for discussion during the next briefing.

Homer was shocked when the briefing on January 24, 1941, described his former neighbor Charles Lindbergh's testimony before Congress recommending a neutrality treaty with Hitler.

The briefing officer Commander Tom Perkins said, "I can't believe Lindbergh would be so naïve to think that any pledge that Hitler has ever made would be honored. Just look at the Russians fighting for their lives at Stalingrad. The non-aggression pact that Hitler and Stalin signed wasn't worth the paper it was written on."

During the February 10th briefing, the Midshipmen were told that Congress passed the Lend-Lease act because the British had run out of money and we couldn't let the Nazis take England. Churchill bravely thanked the United States, saying, "Give us the tools and we will finish the job."

The March 30th, briefing officer, Commander Tom Perkins, explained that all German, Italian and Danish ships found in United States waters would be placed under protective custody. Questions were now allowed from Midshipmen, who were called on.

Jim Coriello asked, "Sir isn't this likely to cause a declaration of war by the Germans and Italians?"

Commander Perkins said, "I don't think they want to bring us into the war, at least until they finish off Russia and are willing to lose a dozen or so ships to keep us out. They are hoping that the America First Committee and Mr. Lindberg will keep telling the American people that this isn't our war."

During the April 11th briefing, Commander Perkins explained, "If England fell, then Iceland or possibly Greenland would be a staging base for a direct attack on America, so the United States acquired full defense rights on April 9th, 1941. On April 10th, the USS *Niblack* dropped depth charges on a German U-Boat to drive it away from survivors from a sunken Dutch freighter. This first shot against Germany did not draw a response and the grateful sailors were rescued."

On May 21st the United States Freighter SS Robin Moore was sunk by a U-Boat off the coast of Brazil. The next day training cruise assignments were issued to the class of 1942. Homer was assigned to the USS *Benson*, a modern five main gun destroyer with a top speed of 37.5 knots. After a shakedown cruise, the Benson sailed from the Boston Navy Yard on June 28th, 1941 in route to Iceland with Homer assigned to work side by side with LTJG Herb Nicholson in navigation. The Benson carried the first full company of U.S. Marines to begin relieving British troops that had been guarding the island.

Homer recalled that his roommate, Jim Coriello, described mapping Iceland and Greenland during his training cruise last summer.

On their return from Reykjavik, Homer rotated through Radar, Sonar, Gunnery practice, shooting at icebergs, and finally the 50,000-shaft horsepower engine room. After returning to Boston, the Benson was ordered to conduct patrol exercises off Portland, Maine. At the end of nine weeks, Homer transferred at sea to a PBY Catalina mail plane and returned to Boston, then took a train to Annapolis to begin his three week leave.

Chapter 20
Passage to Portugal

Chicago, August 10, 1941

David and Moses Goldberg met with their cousin Rabbi Solomon Goldberg at his home in Tinley Park. David explained to his cousin that their every fourth word code system had worked until June of 1941, and then they got a letter that was not in code, saying,

Welt Radio in Dusseldorf had been sold to new owners, who would not be ordering any more radio sets or tubes from Amerika.
Signed, Your Father,
Abraham Goldberg

Moses turned to his cousin and said "This sounds bad! We've got to do something."

The look on the Rabbi's face told David and Moses they were not going to like what he was about to say. "We may have waited too long. The Hagenah reports a major final round up of German Jews. This doesn't mean that our family is not in hiding. Many Christians are risking their own lives to shelter old Jewish friends in hidden attics or cellars. We are not at war with Germany, at least not yet, so they should still recognize U.S. Passports. I have connections and will get naturalized U.S. citizen passports for your mother, father and sister. Either you, David, or Moses will need to travel to Dusseldorf with as much gold as possible carefully hidden to use for bribes and, of course, the passports. If I might suggest that Moses looks less Jewish than you, David. He will need a very short haircut and a training session with a person from Hagenah before he departs. We can use some influence to get him a seat on the Pan Am Clipper from Rio de Janeiro to Lisbon with a stop in the Azores for fuel. Be ready to go in four weeks."

On September 14, 1941, Moses left Chicago on a Delta flight to Atlanta, then Eastern to Miami and connected with the Pan Am Clipper to Rio. Moses had concealed 100,000 dollars in American Gold Eagle Coins and 20,000 in one-carat diamonds. His passport was in a pocket in his briefcase and the other three Passports were carefully sewed in behind the lining of his small suitcase. After a two-day hotel stay Moses went to the Clipper terminal two hours before scheduled departure and learned that he had been bumped from the flight. The U.S. State Department and Military passengers had bumped all of the non-high priority passengers. The scramble for seats on the next flight began, and another week went by before he would have a chance for a seat. A Pan Am agent apologized, and told Moses that it looked good for the October 3rd flight.

When this flight didn't work out, Moses thought about bribing someone at Pan Am, but decided he might be turned in and go to jail in Brazil. He decided to wait one more week and then find a ship.

Moses sent a wire message to David, saying, 'I have found a neutral Portuguese freighter heading to Lisbon and booked passage after being again turned away at Pan Am.'

The SS Saint Augustin left Rio on October 15th with an expected arrival November 3, 1941. It was a fairly new refrigerator ship, with a cargo of Argentine beef and coffee beans. There were five passenger cabins with two occupants, and Moses was the only passenger traveling alone in the sixth cabin. Passenger meals were served in the captain's dining room and the food was very good. Two Brazilian coffee brokers from Fortaleza were traveling on business and they were friendly. Both spoke English. A retired banker from Lisbon was traveling with his wife and he spoke English, but his wife did not. Fortunately, Moses knew how to play bridge making an English-speaking foursome. The other passengers were from Paraguay and Argentina, and spoke Spanish.

The ship had a small library. The cabins had a speaker system that would announce meals and could broadcast shortwave radio broadcasts from around the world. While walking down the corridor, Moses passed one of the Argentine cabins with the door ajar, and could hear radio Berlin. He thought, 'I better stay away from these people.'

Halfway to Portugal the ship started rolling. An announcement was made that dining service was being suspended until they could divert far enough away from an Atlantic hurricane. The new arrival day November 7th was announced.

That was wishful thinking. This already slow freighter was bucking headwinds and didn't arrive in Lisbon until November 10. Following this miserable 25-day trip, Moses was walking like a sailor on dry land. After going through a very brief Portuguese customs visit, Moses went to the U.S. Embassy for a recommended hotel and information on train schedules.

The young American behind the desk suggested three hotels and then tried to talk Moses out of going to Germany. He said, "Your name suggests you are Jewish, and we are hearing horrible things happening to Jews in Germany. Even though you have a legitimate business reason to go to Dusseldorf, we could not help you if you just disappear. With that serious warning, here are the train schedules, Sir."

Moses thanked him, caught a cab to a four-star hotel, then fell asleep with his clothes on. The next morning, Moses found an iron and ironing board in a closet and pressed his suit. The last thing he could do was send this suit with secret pockets to a drycleaner.

After breakfast on an outdoor patio Moses took a cab to the train station and purchased a second-class ticket leaving at noon November 12 for Dusseldorf, with a change in Madrid and another in Toulouse Vichy France, then on to Dijon in German occupied France.

Germans in black leather coats and sinister looks boarded the train in Dijon demanding papers. They took Moses passport and removed him from the train to an office in the terminal. After he heard the train depart a Nazi SS officer and two enlisted men entered the room. The officer glared at Moses for several minutes and then said in English

"I see you are an American Jew. Why are you going to Dusseldorf?" For this likely question, an answer had been prepared in Chicago.

"My company is owed a large sum of money for radio sets, tubes, and other parts that we have sold and delivered to Welt Radio in Dusseldorf, and I am going to try to collect. In this file you will see the invoices that have not been paid." "

How do we know, American Jew, that you are not a spy?"

"I am just a businessman from a country that is not at war with Germany, Sir."

The officer handed the invoice file back to Moses and said, "You will be met in Dusseldorf. Take him back to the ticket counter and put him on the next train."

Moses decided to only speak English, so it was difficult to arrange a new ticket on a good schedule. The new ticket would take Moses into Germany at Saarbrucken leaving at 10 p.m. November 13th, with a change in Frankfurt, then a twelve-hour layover before catching an express to Dusseldorf arriving at 8 a.m. on November 14th. Two hours out of Dijon, a railroad bridge was blown up by the French resistance and the engine and five of the ten cars plunged into a small river. Fortunately, Moses had the last seat in the back of the tenth car and was not injured.

The French conductor told the passengers who were in the fifth through tenth car to stay quietly in their seats while German soldiers swarmed all over the undamaged cars. When the sun came up, everyone that Moses could see was asking for food and water. They received no response from the conductor.

Finally, at 2 p.m. on November 14th, the conductor and a German officer told the passengers to gather their baggage and start walking down the tracks back to Dijon. They would be met by a special train that would come for them. Two German soldiers were detailed to see that all passengers stayed together. After five hours, several elderly passengers fell to the ground alongside the track. The soldiers were asked to stop and wait for the train that would rescue them, and they agreed.

One soldier and two Frenchmen went down a hill and found a small stream, and filled one canteen and the sleeves of a raincoat that were tied off at the cuff. After several trips, everyone had a drink of water and then tried to stay warm during the night. Finally, at daylight they could hear a steam engine pushing a flatcar and a boxcar down the track in reverse. The passengers were loaded and arrived at noon on November 15th back in Dijon. After some bread and wine supplied by local townspeople, the passengers were interrogated one at a time and then returned under guard to the passenger depot. It took the French Railway System five days to locate another train and an abandoned track that could be used at very low speed to go to Saarbrucken.

Moses was now on German soil on November 20th, and was afraid that the next interrogation would come to a tragic end for him. However, he was pleasantly surprised when an old, overweight, regular army officer said in English, "Please sit down. You have had a terrible time trying to get to Dusseldorf. The report that I have is that this is a business trip to collect money that is owed your company in Amerika. Could I see your passport and collection invoices?"

Moses said, "Yes, Sir!" and handed the folder and passport to the officer. When the officer handed everything back to Moses he included a paper allowing him to go to the Saar Hotel to check in for five days until a seat was available for Frankfurt and then Dusseldorf. Moses thanked the officer for his assistance. After checking in he went straight to the bathtub and came close to falling asleep in the warm water. The five restful days passed quickly. Moses never left the hotel. He enjoyed a hearty European breakfast and excellent early dinner before the dining room became crowded. Every evening he would find a discarded newspaper and take it back to his room. He thought since I only speak English the hotel staff may wonder why I have them in my room so I'll say just to look at the pictures. The overnight train left for Frankfurt at 6 p.m. on November 25th and arrived the next morning. The Frankfurt Dusseldorf express was delayed without any explanation. Moses spent November 26th in the station asking for information every two hours until he overheard a conversation between two railway employees saying that the tracks had been bombed again by the British. Moses went across the street and checked into a second class hotel for the night. In the morning he learned that train service would resume on the evening of November 28th, so one more night in a flea bag hotel with a bath down the hall was the best he could do. At 6 p.m. on November 28th, Moses had his papers checked and boarded a first-class, high-speed train with a deluxe dining car and a bar in the club car. He couldn't wait to see Dusseldorf, his hometown. What would he find? Would his family be alive? About fifty percent of the passengers were in Army, Navy or Luftwaffe uniforms. Moses tried to be as inconspicuous as possible. Everything was on schedule until the express passed Bonn and then pulled to a stop in a tunnel. The conductor passed through the car and made an announcement that an air raid had caused a rockslide and we would remain safe in the tunnel until it is cleared. Moses heard several officers announce that they would go to the rockslide and see how long it would take to clear the track. He thought to himself you never hear radio Berlin say anything about stuff like this. When the officers returned, they told the other passengers that half of a hillside was down on the tracks and they heard it was going to take one or two days to get the equipment in to clear the track. The conductor assured the passengers that we have heat and food for all and will do our best to make everyone comfortable. November 29th through December 3rd were spent on the train. At 11 p.m. December 3rd the train started moving slowly at first as it cleared the rockslide area then picked up speed arriving in Dusseldorf at 7 a.m. on December 4th.

When he got off the train two Gestapo agents came up on either side and said "Come with me." Moses was interrogated in an office at the train station and held until December 6. His papers and the debt collection story held. Moses was told to check in when he was leaving Dusseldorf.

He thought to himself, 'It could have been much worse. I need to find a cab and see if my family is at home, but first I need to convert some currency.'

The kiosk in the train station charged more than the bank but they were happy to accept five American gold eagles. Moses then went out to the main entrance to find a cab.

He took a chance and said in German, "1849 Rotterdamer Strasse on the East Bank of the Rhine."

The driver put the diesel Mercedes in gear and pulled away. When they arrived, Moses paid the driver and walked up to the front door of his family home.

When he rang the doorbell, a heavy German woman that he had never seen before came to the door and said, "No solicitations," and started to close the door.

Moses said, "I am looking for Abraham Goldberg."

The woman said, "Those filthy Jews don't live here anymore. Are you one of them?"

Moses thought quickly and said, "No I am here to collect a large amount of money owed to my company."

The woman said, "Well you will never see them again. Heil Hitler." Then she slammed the door.

Moses went back to the sidewalk and then turned north, walking sadly for two blocks until he came to the home that belonged to some very close Christian friends, Wolfgang Muller and his wife Monika. When he lifted the big brass knocker, he hoped that they were still there.

Monika came to the door with a surprised look and said, "Moses, is this really you? Come inside, it is cold out there. What are you doing in Germany?"

"Mrs. Muller, my brother and I have been unable to contact our parents or my sister, so we decided that I should come over to try to bring them to America."

"Oh Moses, come in and take your coat off and I will fix you some hot coffee. Let me tell you what I know. About seven months ago, the Nazis rounded up every Jewish person that they could find in Germany. Dr. Goebbels the Minister of Propaganda released stories that the Jews were being well treated in new cities that were built in Poland but there are horrible rumors about these places."

"Thank you for the coffee. When I went to our home, a nasty woman said my family did not live there anymore. Did they just take the property and give it to Nazis?"

"I am afraid that happened many times all over the country. My husband and I think it was horrible, but if we said anything, we would be shipped off too. Wolfgang will be home soon. I'm sure he will be glad to see you and he will know more than I do."

When Wolfgang Muller saw Moses, he appeared shocked.

"Moses, how in the world did you get here?" After taking off his coat, he shook hands and placed his right hand on Moses shoulder. "I am glad to see you, but these are dangerous times. I am deeply saddened about your family. There was nothing we could do. It all happened at night and they were gone. You know your father and I both served together in the Medical Corps during the Great War. We have been friends ever since. Monika and Ruth were best of friends and you and our youngest son Heinz were best friends. Heinz had a choice to wait and be conscripted into the Army or volunteer for the Luftwaffe. He is now in pilot training at Stuttgart. Our oldest son, Karl, joined a scientific expedition formed by Himmler to do research in Tibet of all places. He was their radio operator. They left Germany about three months after you and your brother moved to Amerika. We would receive a letter at least every two or three weeks, and then they stopped. The Army sent a rescue party but they could not find a trace of the twenty men. It has now been over three years and they have been declared dead. Mother and I still have, hope but as time passes, we know Karl is gone."

Moses said, "I am so sorry about Karl, we didn't know."

"Have you a place to stay?" asked Mrs. Muller.

"Not yet, I just arrived this morning and was hoping to be with my family."

"Well, you stay with us here. I have been preparing Italian spaghetti for dinner and we have plenty. Wolfgang, you could get Moses to look at your shortwave radio and adjust the antennae."

"I would like to hear about Amerika from you, Moses. We know you are helping the English, but thank goodness we are not at war with each other. I think Germany is getting stretched pretty thin in too many places."

"I don't know about that Mr. Muller, but many Americans do not want us in a war. Even Charles Lindbergh is leading a group called the America First Committee, and he has resigned his commission in the Army Air Corps."

After dinner they sat around the radio and listened to the BBC even though that was verboten.

Moses went on to say, "You know, my brother David and I established World Radio in Chicago, and the business is now three times the size of Welt Radio here. Being in the business, we have a very powerful shortwave receiver and hear Berlin and London loud and clear. To us, the BBC is more truthful than what we hear from Berlin. For example, the train that I was on from Dijon was sent into a river when the French blew up a bridge, but you never hear anything but good news on German radio. I think that is what Americans call propaganda."

Monika Muller said "We agree, but are afraid to say anything. I know you must be tired. Please make yourself at home in Karl's room, and we will see you for breakfast. Wolfgang leaves the house at 7:30 so he can open the pharmacy at 8:00, so breakfast at 6:30."

"Before I go upstairs, Mr. Muller, could I ask if you know anyone who might know where my family has been taken without causing any trouble for you?"

"I may be able to find out something, but it will take a few days Moses. I suggest staying in the house so you will not be picked up for random questioning. Even if we find them how do you plan to get them out of the country?"

"Sir, I have with me valid United States Passports for my sister, mother, and father stating that they are fully naturalized citizens. Using my U.S. passport, I was able to get in so we should be able to get out. The word at home is that Germany doesn't want us in a war until they have finished off the Russians. I was stopped and interrogated multiple times, and they always let me go. I also have gold for bribes if necessary."

"Nothing would make me happier, Moses, than to save your family, our dear friends, but don't get your hopes set too high."

"Thank you, Mr. Muller, and good night Mrs. Mueller."

In the morning of December 7th, 1941, Moses had a light breakfast with the Muller's and spent the day reading magazines and newspapers. He adjusted Mr. Mullers' radio antennae, cleaned and tightened contacts and checked all of the tubes. One tube was weak, but fortunately there was a storage box with replacements. When this was completed, the signal strength was increased by twenty percent. That evening, they enjoyed broadcasts that came from Vienna and London.

Just before turning the set off after the 9 p.m. BBC news, the news reader came back on with a flash report saying American radio broadcasts have reported an aerial attack on Pearl Harbor Hawaii by Japanese aircraft. Radio Berlin was playing popular music.

Moses said, "Let me see if I can find one of the 50,000 watt, clear channel stations in America. Sometimes you can get a signal skip off the ionosphere and hear a station thousands of miles away, just like it was local."

WOR on 710 KHz in New York was the first to come in clear, and they said that many ships had been sunk and thousands killed. WSB on 750 KHz in Atlanta had the same report.

Moses said, "Let's try further west," and began to pull in KFI 740 KHZ in Los Angeles, and they were rebroadcasting a clear channel station KGMB on 590kHZ that was only 10,000 watts of power from Oahu.

The Hawaiian announcer was emotional. He described battleships blowing up, flames everywhere, aircraft being shot down, thousands killed and hospitals overflowing with injured.

Wolfgang Muller said, "This is bad, we have a mutual defense pact with Japan and Italy. I pray that this doesn't cause us to go to war with America. I am going to turn in but if you want to try to get more reports, Moses, please do so."

All of the streetlights were off and the homes had black out shades. Mrs. Muller checked her shades, hugged Moses, and went up to bed.

In the morning, Wolfgang contacted a cousin in the Dusseldorf Police Department about the Goldberg family. When asked about his interest Wolfgang told his cousin that some friends from Amerika were concerned because they had not been able to contact their relatives, which was the truth.

His cousin told him that there are long lists and it might take a few days. "Weren't these the Jews that had the good radio repair shop? If it is them, they are probably working in a radio factory. There are several factories around here making aircraft and tank radios."

On the evening of December 8th Wolfgang returned home with the information from his cousin and that gave Moses some hope.

On December 11th, the morning newspaper headlines shouted *WAR DECLARED ON AMERIKA.* Radio Berlin reported that both Germany's Fuhrer, Adolph Hitler, and Benito Mussolini announced an Axis Pact of Steel with Japan.

Moses said to himself, 'Now I've had it, I'll never get out of Germany.'

That evening, Wolfgang Muller sat down with Monika at his side and said, "Moses, if the Gestapo find that we have been hiding you we are all dead, so we need a plan. You will never get out of Germany now, and your Passport will be a ticket to a firing squad as a spy. I have discussed this with my wife, and she is in agreement that we allow you to assume our son Karl's identity. You will need to turn yourself in to the authorities with a good solid story. We have lots of information about the expedition to Tibet and who was in the group. You are an expert with radios and Karl was the assigned radio operator. You were installing an antennae on a mountain top, and heard gunfire down at your camp but when you could get down the mountain everyone was dead and the camp was looted. It has taken all this time to walk home from Tibet.

"You had no money and had many problems making the long trip, but you are here and want to be of service to the Fatherland. Ask if it would be possible to enlist in the Krieg's Marine as a radio operator. The Navy will be far away from areas where you might encounter Heinz, but if that occurs you just happen to have the same name as his brother but you never met the other Karl Muller. You will have Karl's birth certificate and, since you are the same size, wear his clothes. We will need to teach you every important thing that happened in his life. We are risking our lives to do this."

Moses said, "I can't ask you to do this."

"No, you are no longer Moses, you are Karl Muller, you are our family, and we are telling not asking. This will keep us alive and all you will have to do is be a German again."

After two days of memorizing facts, Karl Muller went to Navy recruiting and told them his story. He was given a series of tests on radio technology and he passed with flying colors. Following a brief background check, a senior Captain administered the oath and told Karl that he should report in two days for transport to radio school in Kiel.

Chapter 21
The Home Stretch Year

Annapolis, August 10, 1941

The nine-week summer training cruise on the USS *Benson* was a first-class learning experience for Homer.

Delivering the first U.S. Marines to Greenland was a mission not just an exercise. His roommates, Charles and Jim, were back in their quarters at Bancroft Hall, getting unpacked from their nine-week summer training, when Homer arrived. They compared notes on their assignments.

Jim was assigned to the aircraft carrier USS *Yorktown CV5*. The Yorktown had been transferred from the Pacific to strengthen the Atlantic Neutrality Patrol, so Jim flew on a PBY Catalina to Bermuda to join the Yorktown. They made two patrols from Bermuda to Newfoundland. There were U-Boats all over the area, but they had orders not to fire on the U.S. Navy. Charles was assigned to the battleship USS *Texas BB35* serving as a flagship for the Neutrality Patrol in the Atlantic. Although the Texas was commissioned in 1914, The Big T was continually updated and received radar just before Midshipmen training began in June 1941. The Benson sailed alongside the Texas through rough seas approaching Greenland.

None of the roommates had time to plan anything special for their leave. This was their best summer. After a good night rest, Jim left for Philadelphia and Charles for Clute, Texas.

Homer called Caroline in the morning and met her for lunch. Fortunately, she was on summer vacation from nursing school. She wanted to hear about his cruise on the Benson, and asked Homer what he would like to do for at least two weeks.

"Caroline, what would you think if we made a trip to Georgia? I could call Penny and see if they were going to be at Lake Burton. I'm pretty sure they would invite us. My Aunt Virginia wrote to me that she has finally divorced my rotten uncle. It would be nice to see her. She has a house in Atlanta, but I don't think that would be a good place for us to stay, because she said it was small. I could also see my cousin Sandy. I would like to take Mr. and Mrs. Iseman out to dinner, if it wasn't for his help I wouldn't be at the Naval Academy. Plan B would be to go back to Lake Mohawk if Hans is back from ROTC boot camp at Fort Benning. Then Plan C would be to stay here, unless you have some other ideas."

"There are a lot of places that I would like to go, but all I care about is being with you. You know I love you. Daddy should know that he can trust you and me after three years, so I'll take his temperature when he gets home. Call me in the morning"

"If we weren't in a restaurant I would put on a PDA, (Public Display of Affection) because Caroline, I love you too."

Caroline had baked chicken, acorn squash, and green peas for dinner with her dad. When they were finished, Caroline said, "Daddy, Homer just got back from his summer cruise on the destroyer USS *Benson* and we would like to go to Atlanta to visit friends."

"I don't know if that is a good idea. I've said all along he may not have the grades to even graduate next year. If he does make it, he'll be in the bottom ten percent, and the bottom ten turn out to have lousy careers in the Navy. There are so many young men here that are more promising than Homer Harris, so you ought to open your eyes. If your mother was alive, she would be able to talk some sense into you."

"So I guess the answer is 'yes, Daddy, we can go to Atlanta.'"

"Don't smart off with me, Caroline. I only have the best interest in your welfare."

"Daddy, it won't be long before I am a BS Registered Nurse, and I know how things work. I know what the academy regulations are. I have tried to be a good girl all my life, and you don't seem to appreciate that I have my head screwed on right. The last thing I would ever do is embarrass you with a scandal. I don't know if Penny Ponder, who is a friend of mine, and her dad who is, by the way, President of the Coca-Cola Company, are even going to be in Atlanta. Homer did not want to call them to set up something if I could not go. Homer also has an Aunt Virginia and his cousin Sandy in Atlanta that he would like to visit. He is going to call me in the morning, and I need to let him know. You have to trust my judgement someday, Daddy!"

"I do trust you, I just don't think you should make a long trip with a young man that you are not married to. This isn't your honeymoon. "Then why did you let me go to Lake Mohawk last summer?"

"First of all I spoke with a very responsible mother who would have you as her house guest and you were only away for three days. The situation is completely different."

"If I can't go to Georgia what about going back to Lake Mohawk? Homer only gets three weeks leave and needs a vacation and so do I."

"I would rather you spend your time off meeting some other promising young men to see what you may be missing."

"I don't want to meet any of your promising young men! So Daddy, this is what it is all about. You just don't like Homer, and I know he has more character, morals, kindness and good judgment than any of the promising young men that you think are hot stuff! I will tell Homer to go see his aunt and whoever else he wants to see for three weeks, and I will just stay here cook your meals, clean your quarters, and study for next semester. Does that make you happy?"

Caroline went to her bedroom and closed her door for the night. In the morning, she told Homer about her disagreement with her dad, and that he should have a good three week leave and tell Hans and Penny that she sends best wishes.

"Caroline, if you are here, I will stay here."

"You should really go see your Aunt Virginia to make sure she is all right. If you want to stay for your whole leave, I will understand. Daddy can't stop us from meeting at church. As you can tell, I am really upset with him!"

Homer caught a flight to Atlanta, rented a car at Candler Field, and checked in at the Biltmore Hotel. He called Aunt Virginia that afternoon, and she asked him to please come over for dinner.

Homer said "Why don't you let me take you and Sandy out for dinner?" and she agreed.

After dinner, they went back to her house in Ansley Park. Sandy was going to summer school and had homework, so Homer had two cups of coffee with Aunt Virginia and learned that she would graduate from Massey Secretarial School in three months. Her finances were in order and there had been no contact with his uncle.

Homer gave Aunt Virginia a big hug and said goodbye to Sandy. "Please keep in touch and let me know if you need anything."

The next morning, Homer called Mr. and Mrs. Iseman at home, because school was out for the summer and arranged to drive out to Roswell and take them to dinner at Aunt Fanny's Cabin in Smyrna. He also called the Ponder's farm and spoke with Mary Lee, their housekeeper. He learned that Penny and a bunch of her sorority sisters were on a train going to Hollywood to tour the studios.

"Mr. Ponder, he is in town and I know he would like to see you Mr. Homer. I will tell him tonight when he gets home or if he stays in town, he always calls me to let me know about dinner. Where are you staying?"

"At the Biltmore"

"That is where Mr. Ponder stays when he is working late."

Before Homer left the Biltmore to pick up the Iseman's for dinner, the phone rang, and it was Douglas Ponder.

"Homer, I'm glad to hear you are in town. I'll stay in town tomorrow night and we could go to Mammy's Shanty up on Peachtree for dinner. I 'm looking forward to hearing about your junior year and getting caught up on everything. I wish Penny was here, but she is on a sorority girl trip to California."

Dinner with the Isemans gave Homer a chance to hear that Roswell High School was continuing to turn out good graduates. The main topic was the Isemans' deep concern for what was happening to the Jewish population in Europe. Homer shared some unclassified information from the Naval Academy briefings and his own belief that we would have to help the British or they would be invaded.

Mr. Iseman told Homer, "Several Jewish organizations are trying to smuggle as many into Palestine as possible. Our sources tell us that the Arabs are lining up with the Nazis and are being promised that they will get back the land that Jewish settlers legally purchased from them. It is not a pretty picture."

Homer said, "What Hitler wants strategically is the Suez Canal and the oil. We are assisting the British effort to hold them back and are sending tanks and all sorts of equipment to them through President Roosevelt's Lend Lease Plan."

Homer thanked the Isemans for all that they had done for him before saying goodnight.

Homer put a 'do not disturb tag' on his door at the Biltmore and slept in late. At 11 a.m., he ordered a sliced turkey sandwich and a coke from room service, then got cleaned up and dressed in casual clothes. Then he took the elevator to the top floor, where the WSB Radio studios were located. They had a bank of Associated Press teletype machines with a large magnifying glass in front of the printed pages so they could be read by visitors behind a glass window. Every few minutes a, producer would come over and tear off the pages to make up a news broadcast.

Homer was glued to the page report coming out that President Roosevelt was returning to Washington from a secret meeting in Newfoundland with Winston Churchill, where they created the Atlantic Charter. He thought to himself, 'I'm really glad that we are backing the British with everything we can send them. I know that the British troops that I met this summer in Greenland were thankful for our help.'

When Homer returned to his room, there was a message under his door saying *MEET YOU AT THE CC Suite at 5 p.m./DOUG.*

Homer had sent his uniform out to be dry cleaned and pressed, so he looked sharp when he knocked on the Coca-Cola suite door. The attendant invited him in, and explained that Mr. Ponder would be about twenty minutes late. It turned out to be thirty minutes, and when Doug Ponder came in he apologized then gave Homer a handshake and a hug.

"I have missed seeing you. It is a shame Penny is in California and won't be back for another week. Homer, you have about a year of catching up to do with me. So lets' start off with dinner at a new restaurant just down the street called Mammy's Shanty."

Doug Ponder was most interested about the deployment of Marines to Greenland that had made the news. When Homer explained that he was there on the USS *Benson*, Ponder said, "I am so proud of you!"

They talked about world affairs, U-Boats, and then Ponder brought up Penny's boyfriend Pick.

"You met him at Lake Burton Last summer. I don't think he has any ambition. You know he was promoted to first Lieutenant and he was given orders to leave his staff job and take over a basic training company at Fort Jackson South Carolina and he pulled strings to allow him to continue measuring oil storage tanks. I hate to say this, but I think a big reason for courting Penny is that he thinks I will give him a big job with Coca-Cola. It seems that Penny is beginning to see that he is a good-looking, shallow person. I'd call him an empty uniform, but it is not officially over yet."

Homer thought to himself, 'this sounds like Captain Dugas being protective, but with justification.'

"I was not jealous of Pick, but simply not impressed." Homer said "It will be interesting to see what happens. I only wish the best for Penny."

Homer told Mr. Ponder that he had seen his Aunt Virginia and everything was going well for her. She will be finishing secretarial school in about three months and has her finances in order thanks to Ned MacNeely.

"For the first time, she seemed happy."

"You know we hire secretaries at Coca-Cola, so please tell her to apply. I think as you do, that she is a good woman who deserves a good life and I can keep an eye out for her. Don't mention that I even brought this up, however."

Doug Ponder said, "What happens next?"

"Sir, I'm going to leave tomorrow to get ready for my last year at the Academy. I have a tough schedule, and then who knows what will be happening in the world."

Doug Ponder smiled at Homer and said, "You know, I never had a son, so I'm un-officially adopting you, so stay in touch.

"Thanks for dinner, Sir. I will stay in touch and again appreciate all that you have done for me."

They shook hands and said good night at the Biltmore.

Homer returned to Annapolis in the late afternoon on Saturday and called Caroline, who remarked "You have only been gone four days. Did you get to see everyone you wanted to see?"

"I had dinner last night with Mr. Ponder and the Isemans the night before. When I arrived, I saw Aunt Virginia and Sandy and took them to dinner."

"What about Penny?"

"She was on a sorority trip to Hollywood, touring the studios."

"Well, I am glad you are back. I have had an unpleasant time with Daddy. We will talk about it when we are together."

"Am I allowed to see you?"

"Yes reluctantly. What about church tomorrow?"

"I'll be there."

After Church, Homer and Caroline took a walk toward town, and then caught a cab to their favorite Italian restaurant. Caroline began the conversation.

"Homer, I will be blunt. I don't want to hurt your feelings, but Daddy wants me to see other promising young men. He wants me to be interested in only the top five percent of the class."

"Well Caroline, I am what I am. This is a hard school and most of the Midshipmen have better grades than me, but I am doing my best. I am good in some areas, but weak in math. I would be gone, except my roommate Jim has been able to tutor me when I was close to failing calculus. If you need to have dates with other guys to keep peace at home, I won't like it, but I will understand."

"Daddy has started bringing his best students to our quarters to discuss some strategy for a paper they are writing or some other excuse, but it is really to introduce them to me. I can see right through him."

"My fear, Caroline, is that you may find a good guy that has more potential than I have, and you will make a choice. Whatever happens, you have the right to make your own decision."

"Homer, you know how I feel about you. That isn't going to change. I am going to be extremely busy with school and keep some control over my own life. You have time left on your summer leave, why don't you see if Hans is back from boot camp and go see him? Being away for a few days could avoid a dust up with Daddy or some of his 'Promising Young Men.' Daddy thinks he is doing the right thing for me, but I know my heart."

"I know my heart too."

When Homer returned to Bancroft Hall, he called to see if Hans was back from boot camp.

Mrs. Schmidt answered the phone and said, "Homer, I am so glad to hear your voice. Hans is on a train right now and will be coming into the Dover train station at 3 p.m. in the afternoon tomorrow. Why don't you come up and surprise him? He is bringing Lizzy, the girl that he met last summer. I think you know her."

"Thank you, I'd love to come up for a few days, but I don't want to be a fifth wheel or be in the way."

"Don't be silly, you know friends you would like to see, and we really want to see you."

"Okay, I will try to get in before 3 p.m., but I will call if there is a change."

"Thanks again for having me." Homer called Caroline and told her he was leaving on an early train in the morning for Lake Mohawk.

Hans arrived first, and borrowed a cap from a porter. Then walked up to Homer from behind and said "Can I carry those bags Sir?"

What a surprised look on Homer's face! Homer was expecting Lizzy, but there was another girl that he recognized from last summer. Lizzy hugged Homer and said, "You remember my sorority sister, Emily Derieux."

"Of course, she beat me consistently at gin rummy when we were at Lake Burton."

Emily gave Homer a light kiss on the cheek and said, "We decided not to go to California with ten of our sorority sisters. This sounded like more fun."

After dinner Hans, Homer and Hans' dad Fred went to the radio room with a brandy.

Fred Schmidt said "Before we hear about your summer military experiences, I would like to make a toast. Here is to the United States Army and Navy! May they always keep us safe."

Homer said, "Hans, what happened at Fort Benning?"

"Well I'll be honest, at times I thought they really wanted to kill us. This was designed to make people without guts drop out. We had very little sleep. They took us about thirty miles from camp at night in open cattle trucks and dumped us off with a 50-pound pack on our back, a O3 Springfield rifle, a steel pot on our head and one canteen of water. This was called a road march to contact the enemy, and they flew over us with piper cub observation planes and dropped bags of white flower that burst and stuck to our perspiration-soaked bodies. Then they had aggressors fire at us, so we had to go through deep brush. Our company started with 144 cadets and finally arrived at camp with 126. 18 dropped out and were sent home for good. We fired every type of weapon except artillery or tanks and I qualified on the rifle range as an expert.

We had wire and radio signal training, first aid, chemical gas training, and land navigation compass training. Leadership positions were rotated. I'm probably in the best physical shape that I have ever been in. What about your cruise Homer?"

"My nine weeks were spent on the USS *Benson*, a new fast destroyer that made the news when I was on her because we took the first load of Marines to Greenland to relieve the British so they could use their troops fighting the Germans. I was rotated through Navigation, Sonar, Gunnery where we shot at icebergs with our 5-inch guns, and finally down in the engine room. I was allowed to relieve the Coxswain and steer the ship for several hundred miles. The thing I liked was that this was a real mission. There were U-Boats all around the area but they didn't fire at us and we didn't drop depth charges on them."

Fred said, "I'm really proud of both of you boys!"

He turned on the radio and pulled in the BBC loud and clear. The lead story was about President Roosevelt banning the export of aviation fuel except to Britain and Canada. The news reader reported the large number of German aircraft shot down over the last 24 hours by Spitfire and Hurricane fighter squadrons, and British losses were reported to be light.

Mrs. Schmidt and the girls finished in the kitchen and were upstairs admiring the first quilt that she had ever made. "I've made many wedding dresses, but this has been a challenge."

During the next week they enjoyed boating, skiing, cook outs, and made several trips to the movies in Newton. Hans let Homer know that he was getting serious with Lizzy.

Emily shared with Lizzie, "I don't know why I can't get Homer interested in me. He is nice to me but that seems to be it."

Homer had lunch with his attorney, Larry Cohen, and dinner with Mr. and Mrs. Sam Cornelius. Sam gave Homer a complete briefing on his investments and made some suggestions to buy more shares of Boeing and DuPont. The U.S. economy was continuing to grow.

Homer invited Mr. and Mrs. Schmidt, Mrs. Costello, Hans, Lizzy, and Emily to Sammy's Old Cider Mill in Mendham for a lobster or steak dinner. They had to take two cars, so Homer and Emily went with Mrs. Costello in her Woody Ford Station Wagon. They all sat on the front bench seat, and Emily tried to cuddle up with Homer.

During the return trip Mrs. Costello told Emily that Homer had given her the car for a Christmas present. Homer thought, 'I wish she hadn't said that.' Emily couldn't wait to tell Lizzy who would tell Penny.

After a relaxing eight days, Homer thanked Mr. and Mrs. Schmidt for a great visit. Homer told Hans to stay in touch as they rode down the mountain to the Dover train station in the 1929 Ford touring car. Hans and Lizzy were in the front seat and Emily with Homer in the back.

Emily held Homer's hand and said, "I really like you and hope you will write to me, at the same Phi Mu sorority house address as Penny."

Homer thought, 'I don't want to lead her on,' and said, "It is going to be a busy year, but I'll try to keep you all posted."

On the train ride back to Annapolis, Homer thought, 'this is going to be a tough year, I hope I make it.'

He digested the news in the New York Times, the Newark Star Ledger and picked up a Washington Post when he changed trains for Annapolis. All of the stories pointed toward going to war to save Great Britain.

When Homer got back to Bancroft Hall he just went to bed and thought, I'll call Caroline in the morning. Charles Forrest was his first roommate to return for their first class (senior) year. He spent his leave on the family ranch in Clute Texas, moving cattle around and observing the oil rig that was drilling on their property. Homer told Charles about his trip to Atlanta and Lake Mohawk, but left out the details about Caroline. They decided to go in town for lunch and when they returned Jim Coriello was unpacking his stuff.

Jim stayed with his family in Philadelphia and looked up a few old girlfriends. He was glad to hear that Charles and Homer had a good time during their three-week leave.

Homer said, "I'm going down the hall to see if the phone is available to call Caroline."

"Captain Dugas quarters, Caroline speaking."

"It's me. I'm so glad to hear your voice."

"Oh Homer, I have missed you, I mean, really missed you! When can I see you?"

"What about Church and lunch after?"

"I'll be there. I love you."

September 1941

The fall class schedules were posted, and the class of 1942 entered their first year (senior year).

Homer, Jim and Charles said to each other, 'this is the home stretch.'

The faculty briefings after dinner covered the tenuous situation in England and the supply difficulties with U-Boats sinking ships faster than they could be built.

A new briefing officer, Commander David Owens, with extensive experience in China and the Philippines, answered many questions about Naval and Army defenses in the Pacific. He felt that the 25,000 U.S. Army troops providing training and logistics for the 100,000 man Philippine Army would be able to stop any Japanese invasion on the beach. The Naval strength in Subic Bay and Cleveite with the Army Air Corps land-based aircraft would smash any invasion fleet. Commander Owens assured the Midshipmen that their massive fleet in Pearl Harbor could handle anything coming from Japan.

His recurring statement that stuck was, "Peace in the Philippines and our allies Pacific territories will only continue through strength."

Homer noticed an academic shift in emphasis away from politics, the humanities, economics, and law to Naval and Military subjects. Homer and his roommates could feel the pace quicken.

From time to time the dinner briefings showed films that would be of interest. The September 29th, official Navy film showed the first Liberty ship, the SS Patrick Henry, being launched just two days ago at the Bethlehem Shipyard in Baltimore.

Commander Owens noted that these ships cost only two million dollars and had a nautical range of twenty thousand miles. "Plans are in the works gentlemen to build a thousand of these big, slow, ugly, ships. New shipyards are being opened in Jacksonville, Florida, and several in California to turn out these ships like we build automobiles on a production line. Without these ships, there is no way we can support our allies or our own forces if necessary. Are there any questions?"

One of the Plebes put up his hand and asked, "Sir, how fast do they go, what kind of power do they have and are they armed?"

Commander Owens said, "Those are good questions. This ship can sustain eleven knots, for you recent civilians, that is thirteen miles per hour. The current design has a four-inch deck gun mounted in the stern, anti-aircraft guns fore and aft and the propulsion comes from one 25 hundred horse steam engine. Now, lets' move on to an exciting new twin engine Army fighter from Lockheed."

The projector showed the first P-38 Lockheed Lightning making a fast, low pass over an airstrip. "The performance of this plane is classified, but it will scare the hell out of the Germans or the Japanese."

Somebody in the back yelled GO ARMY! Hands shot up, and Charles asked, "Can this plane be adapted for carrier duty?"

Commander Owens laughed and said, "Leave it to a first classman to ask me a question I can't answer. I really don't know, but my Naval Aviation buddies tell me that we have some hot new carrier planes that are coming soon. Thank you for your attention gentlemen, now back to the books."

When the roommates were back in their quarters, Charles said, "You know, I've heard that a graduate from the Naval Academy could be commissioned in the Army Air Corps. If that's true, I'd like to fly that P-38! What do you think?"

Homer replied, "I think the Navy would remind you of all the money they have spent so you could be a sailor."

Homer was only able to see Caroline during the last Sunday, September 30th. After Church they had dinner, and Homer explained that every spare minute was study time and Caroline understood.

She said, "I am going through surgical rotation. That includes overnight duty in the emergency room. There has been no time for Daddy's *Promising Young Men,* in case you were wondering."

The October briefings increased the tension in the air. Commander Owens gave details to the Midshipmen about the October 17th torpedo attack near Iceland on the destroyer USS *Kearney* that killed eleven sailors.

"The German U-Boat Captain said he was shooting at a British ship and the U.S. Destroyer got in the way."

Then on October 31st the Destroyer USS *Ruben James* was torpedoed also near Iceland with the loss of one hundred Sailors. Due to heroic damage control effort, both destroyers made port.

The day before on October 30th, the President signed a billion dollar Lend-Lease bill to send supplies to the Soviet Union. That meant that those Liberty ships will be heading to the ice-free Russian port of Murmansk.

Homer only made one trip to the Post Office in October, on his way to Church with Caroline on the last Sunday in October. Caroline packed sandwiches and potato chips and two bottles of Coca-Cola in a small basket and, since it was chilly, they found an empty Sunday school classroom to have an indoor picnic.

Caroline said, "Did you hear that President Roosevelt has changed Thanksgiving Day from the third Thursday in November to the fourth Thursday, November 27th. Daddy said the Thanksgiving leave will be Wednesday, Thursday, and Friday because of the Army Navy game."

"I did hear about the date change but the word about leave hasn't come out yet."

"Daddy said he would like to have at least three Midshipmen for Thanksgiving dinner on Wednesday before the game, so I'll tell him that I knew he wanted three and I have taken care of it. I hope you and Jim and Charles are available."

Homer broke into a grin and said, "Caroline, you are devious!"

Sunday evening, Homer told his roommates, "Penny Ponder will be available real soon. The First Lieutenant doggie that she has been dating looks like he will get his Dear John letter before long, and her sorority sister Emily Derieux is drawn like a moth to Naval Academy uniforms. She is a very pretty redhead, and she is smart. Maybe we could invite them up for the Army Navy game on November 27th. I'll see if they could stay with Caroline."

Captain Dugas signed an invitation letter for both girls, and sent it to the Phi Mu sorority house mother.

Homer called Penny who said, "Daddy agreed we could go, and he would pay for the tickets. He will have a limo bring us from Washington National to Annapolis then pick us up when we need to come home. I explained to Emily that you would be escorting Caroline and your two roommates would figure out who would be the lucky winner for her. She is on cloud nine! I don't know if you knew that I called it off with Pick. He just wasn't right for me, and probably because I was always comparing him to you. Timing is everything."

Penny and Emily arrived at the Academy on Wednesday November 26 in time for early Thanksgiving dinner with Captain Dugas, Caroline, Homer, Charles and Jim. They would all take the special train to Soldier Field in Philadelphia for the game the next day. Jim Coriello's family invited the roommates and their dates for dinner at their home after the game, and Homer arranged for a limo to bring them back to Annapolis.

Emily asked Penny, "How can he afford this?"

Penny said, "Don't worry about it, he is well off."

Emily said, "I thought he might be because last summer his teacher said he bought her a Ford Station Wagon for a Christmas present. I forgot to mention that to you."

"Emily, Homer does kind things and never wants anybody to know. He is the most genuine young man I have ever known."

Homer wondered which roommate would connect with Penny, and horses did the trick. Charles laid on his Texas cowboy charm and told Penny she could bring her own forward seat saddle when she came down to Clute to visit the family ranch.

He said, "I'll have the best quarter horse you've ever ridden ready."

When Emily mentioned that she was a chemistry major at Emory, University Jim's eyes lit up. "Chemistry is my best subject. After prep school, I got a summer internship with DuPont in Wilmington Delaware before coming to the Naval Academy. If I decided to leave the Navy I would try hard to join DuPont."

Emily added, "I have had three years of paid summer jobs working for Celanese. I have been in quality control at the Cumberland Maryland plant and at the Narrows Virginia Plant. Both plants make cellulose acetate fiber."

For the rest of the visit Emily and Jim connected with chemistry, in more ways than one. When the limo arrived on Saturday November 29th to take Penny and Emily back to Washington National, the roommates came to Captain Dugas quarters to say goodbye. Caroline hugged Penny and Emily, Emily laid a big kiss on Jim, and Charles hugged Penny.

When Penny got to Homer, she gave him a light kiss on the cheek and whispered in his ear "I'll always love you."

Homer noticed tears in Penny's eyes when she quickly jumped in the limo.

As the limo pulled away, Homer said, "Well, Navy won 14 to 6 and the fun is over, we better go hit the books."

He hugged Caroline, and Charles and Jim thanked her for hosting Penny and Emily. Homer met Caroline at Church on Sunday and took a cab to their favorite Italian restaurant.

Caroline said, "Lets' try to do this again next Sunday."

Commander Owens called a special briefing after the noon meal on Saturday December 6, 1941 "Gentlemen, President Roosevelt has made a personal appeal for Peace to Japanese Emperor Hirohito. Something is up, but we don't know exactly what. Normal Japanese radio traffic has gone silent. I do not think the President would make this unprecedented contact with Japan if he thought that Admiral Nomura, the Japanese Ambassador, was playing straight with us. The new Civil Air Patrol that Mayor LaGuardia formed this month under the Army Air Corps has spotted, this morning, two U-Boats between Sandy Hook and New York Harbor. The light planes dropped dye markers and called the Coast Guard. There was a Navy PBY U-Boat sighting just off Norfolk yesterday and submarine activity that we believe to be Japanese close to Wake Island. This briefing should be considered confidential and not discussed with anyone outside of the Naval Academy. Enjoy the rest of your weekend."

Homer and Caroline met at church for the December 7, 1941 service at 10 a.m. and then went into Annapolis for lunch. Homer brought letters from Hans, Penny, Aunt Virginia, and Doug Ponder for her to read.

Hans was in love with Lizzy and they are getting engaged. Penny thanked both Homer and Caroline for a really nice visit. Aunt Virginia has had an interview followed by a good offer with Coca-Cola for a secretarial job at the Atlanta bottling plant on Spring Street, which was not far from their Ansley Park home. Sandy is doing very well at Henry Grady and really liked the teachers. The letter from Doug Ponder told Homer about Aunt Virginia joining Coca-Cola.

He wrote, 'Penny had a great time at the Army Navy game. She really enjoyed meeting your roommates and being with you. You have my best wishes for the second half of your senior year. Best regards, Doug.'

Caroline said, "You have some very nice friends and roommates. I think Jim and Emily really have something going, but I don't know about Charles and Penny."

When they returned to the Academy, people were yelling, "TURN THE RADIO ON."

Homer went in Captain Dugas Quarters with Caroline, and the old battleship Captain was huddled over the radio in the living room. Reports were coming in over WOR in New York City that Pearl Harbor was under attack by Japan early Sunday morning Hawaiian time. The Captain said, "It sounds serious. I was afraid something like this would happen. This was a sneak attack covered up by that lying Jap Ambassador. The report says we have lost all of our battleships at Pearl. Homer, I think you should get back to Bancroft Hall. There will be instructions coming for all the Midshipmen."

Charles and Jim were in their quarters when Homer arrived. Jim said, "I guess you have heard about Pearl. Vice Admiral Westfield has scheduled a briefing for all Midshipmen in the dining hall at 1500."

When the Admiral approached the microphone, you could hear a pin drop. "Gentlemen, our Naval and Army Air forces in Hawaii have been dealt a devastating blow by Japanese carrier aircraft. We were not at war with Japan, and they struck without warning. We have lost our battleships and a number of other warships. Early reports several thousand dead. Fortunately, our Carriers were at sea and are at full fighting strength. We are down but not out! You and the Midshipmen before you will have responsibilities that you might not have imagined yesterday. You will meet these challenges, and the United States Navy, will win so help me God. Commander Owens will have a briefing with more details here at 2000."

The Admiral turned to the American Flag on the podium and executed a crisp hand salute. The follow up briefings added detailed information as it came in.

December 8, 1941

President Roosevelt finished a speech to Congress declaring war on Japan and was then joined by Admiral Ernest King, General George Marshall, and Mrs. Roosevelt in the oval office at the White House.

Admiral King said, "Mr. President, that was your finest speech."

General Marshal agreed and said, "Mr. President, we have many immediate needs in the Army, and I am sure the Navy as well, but Admiral King and I have agreed that one of our top priorities is an immediate shortage of junior officers for both services. We would like your approval to accelerate the graduation for the class of 1942 and possibly 1943. We have already taken steps due to the increasing tension to concentrate on Military and Naval subjects. By eliminating the other courses, we can have about 500 Cadets from the 1942 class ready to graduate as Second Lieutenants, I would hope by the end of February or maybe just a little later."

Admiral King said, "Mr. President, the Navy will have 563 Midshipmen ready for their commission as Ensigns on about the same time schedule."

President Roosevelt said, "That is good because these fine young men will be the backbone of both services. What can we expect from the ROTC programs?"

General Marshall said, "We are working on that time schedule and number. The universities may be reluctant to graduate our boys if they omit courses for substitute military subjects that will be necessary to get them ready."

"Give me a list and I will tell these university presidents that we can lose this war and then they won't have their damn universities. If they won't cooperate, we will commission them without their degrees."

Both General Marshal and Admiral King said, "That should do it, Sir."

Chapter 22
Assigned to the *Leopard*

December 11, 1941

Karl Mueller passed the radio technology tests with the best score that had been earned to date at the school. The Kommandant had him brought to his office for congratulations and a promotion from Soldat (seaman recruit) to Matrosenobergefreiter (seaman apprentice). He was told that he was going to the advance class in Bremerhaven and would not have to sit through the basic class.

"You are a promising young man, and you will have a good career in the Krieg's Marine. Pick up your orders from my Feldwebel (petty officer first class) in the outer office. He will give you transportation passes. You are to go directly to the Advance Radio School without any delay. When you graduate you will be promoted again."

"Thank you, Sir."

The advanced radio course was easy for Karl. The twelve-week school covered all phases of broadcasting including radio direction finding, signal jamming, use of the enigma code machine, repair of transmitters and receivers. The use of radio direction finding (radar) and basic sonar. Upon graduation, students were promoted to Funkmann (radioman second class) and were assigned to sea duty, radio listening stations for intelligence, repair facilities or instructors at the basic school in Kiel. It was known that the best students were assigned sea duty. Karl's orders directed him to the Bremen shipyard to join a new raider the *Leopard*. This was a disguised commerce raider and U-Boat supply ship with six hidden 4-inch 100MM naval guns. Unless you looked closely the *Leopard* appeared to be an ordinary cargo ship. Her hull was designed like a fast destroyer and she had multiple diesel engines developing eight thousand shaft horsepower. The *Leopard* had a range of thirty thousand nautical miles at a speed of 15 knots and a top speed of 22 knots. She carried one hundred torpedoes to replenish U-Boats at sea and the ability to transfer diesel fuel and food.

On March 1, 1941 the *Leopard* sailed at night with Karl assigned as second radioman. The *Leopard* would fly whatever flag was convenient on her way around the cape of good hope picking off unsuspecting British cargo ships heading to Australia.

Chapter 23
Graduation

Annapolis, February 28, 1942

Admiral Ernest King Commander in Chief of the U.S. Fleet approached the microphone at the Graduation and Commissioning of 563 Ensigns.

"Thank you, Admiral Westfield. You and your faculty have done a fine job for our country preparing the class of 1942 to defend our country.

The President made the decision to accelerate your graduation because the United States has been thrust into a war that we cannot afford to lose. We are building our strength at a rapid rate and will soon be able to go on the offensive. We have however powerful enemies across the Atlantic and Pacific Oceans, and they have been preparing for war with us for several years. Let me assure you, however, Germany, Japan, Italy, and several other countries have made a momentous mistake to take on the United States of America. President Roosevelt made the statement to General Marshal and myself, that the Naval Academy and West Point class of 1942 will be the backbone of their services. Gentlemen, you will have assignments all over the globe, they will be difficult, and you will meet each challenge. With your service and millions that have come before you, we will prevail. God bless you and God bless the United States of America."

The commissioning continued and hats went in the air. Following the ceremony, orders were issued to each new Ensign with priority travel documents.

Jim Coriello received orders to join the aircraft carrier *Hornet*. Charles Forrest was assigned to a mine sweeper operating from Pearl Harbor. Homer was given an envelope directing him to the Superintendent's office at 1600. When he arrived there were nine other new Ensigns waiting in the outer office. Homer knew that his grades were not the best, but he had been commissioned. When he looked at the others who were waiting it dawned on him that they were the bottom of the graduating class of 1942.

When they were ushered into Admiral Westfield's large office, they automatically stood in line at attention, until the Admiral said, "Stand at ease gentlemen. I know you are wondering why you did not receive orders right after commissioning. You are all commissioned officers in the United States Navy and will retain your commissions, however due to an extreme need in our logistical fleet, the Merchant Marine, you are being detailed to serve as First Mate Navigators on very high priority Liberty ships. Without these ships and their valuable cargos, we cannot support our own Navy or Army. Should the captain of your assigned ship be unable to perform his duties, you will assume command. You will be paid at the Merchant Marine rate, which is equal to a Navy Lieutenant O-3. I wish to emphasize how important this assignment is, and when it is over you will transfer back into the Navy at an appropriate rank. Commander Owens is here with your orders and travel priority documents. God bless you and Godspeed on your assignments."

When Homer got back to their quarters, Jim and Charles were packing up.

Jim asked Homer, "What was going on with Admiral Westfield?"

Homer sat on his bunk and held his head in his hands for several minutes before answering. "I'm ashamed to tell you. Ten of us who must be the bottom of the class have been detailed to the Merchant Marine as First Mate Navigators. Crap! I'm not even in the Navy! If they didn't think I could be of use on a ship, they could have at least put me on a PT boat. The Admiral said that when this assignment was over, we would be returned to the Navy. Who knows how long that would be?"

Jim and Charles did their best to raise Homer's spirits, but they could tell that he was deeply depressed.

Charles stepped out in the hall and said to Jim, "We can't leave him like this."

Jim replied, "We can stay a few minutes, but we have to go. He will be all right. I will get in touch with Caroline and she will take over."

Charles said, "I don't know if that won't make things worse. You know Captain Dugas will lay a big 'I told you so' on Caroline."

Jim replied, "This will just be a temporary setback for Homer. He has overcome tragedy before, and he will get a hold of himself. Caroline will understand the situation and stand by him. All we can do is wish him the best, but we have to go."

When his roommates said goodbye, Homer sat on his bunk and thought, 'How can I tell Caroline…what a failure I am…when Daddy gets finished rubbing it in on Caroline, I won't have the girl that I hope to marry…I have let her down…I've let myself down…God knows I tried to make better grades. I probably should have gone to Rutgers with Hans.'

After an hour, someone knocked on the door and said, "Homer, you have a phone call"

When Homer got to the phone, he heard Caroline say, "I know, I still and will always love you. When do you have to leave?"

"The orders have me on a train for Jacksonville Florida at 0600."

"I'm borrowing daddy's car and I will be over to Bancroft in one hour to pick you up. We will have dinner in town, and then I want to spend every minute with you before you leave me at the train station. No arguments."

Homer and Caroline stayed at their favorite Italian restaurant until the owner, Rocco Dragonetti, who they had grown to like over the years, came to their table and said, "My friends, I hate to say but I must close for the night. It is now eleven and the door has been locked since ten. Everyone is gone now but us. I hope to see you again soon."

Caroline drove to the Annapolis train station and parked her dad's 1940 Buick two door right next to the station. There was light snow on the ground, so every half hour Caroline would start the car and run the heater.

"What can you tell me about your orders?"

"I'm on the 0600 train to Washington and then the Southern Railroad to Atlanta and then the Florida East Cost to Jacksonville. I am to report on March 3rd to a Liberty ship called the SS *Earl Horne*. I will be the First Mate Navigator and second in command."

"That doesn't sound so bad compared to some of the junior officer assignments that they will hand out to your classmates. Homer, I know it will work out all right."

"I will give it my best, but if they ever transfer me back in the Navy, I will be so far behind others from this class the idea of a good career is shot before it starts. I am so sorry that I have let you down Caroline. Your daddy was right, you should be meeting his promising young men."

"Homer, don't talk like that. I would marry you right now if we had time."

Caroline started the Buick ten times to run the heater before the train pulled in.

Homer kissed Caroline for the last time and said, "I'll always love you. Stay here, it is cold outside. I'll write whenever I can."

Homer threw his duffel bag over his shoulder and boarded the train while Caroline sat in the car with tears in her eyes.

Terminal Station, Atlanta, March 2, 1942, 0600

The Southern Railroad Dixie Flier arrived with nine very old extra cars added to the rear of the regular ten car train packed with Army and Navy personnel. Homer thought the Union Army probably used them for the last time bringing troops home in 1865.

Homer was familiar with Terminal Station. He remembered the scene from *Gone with the Wind*, with several thousand dead and dying Confederate soldiers laying along the tracks right here without medical attention. The large waiting room had been changed since his last time there. In the center was a series of tables, about 25-foot round, with 5-gallon size glass jars, each bearing the name of one of the 48 states, and the March of Dimes logo. The Southern and North-Eastern states contained more donated money than the Western States.

Another area was partitioned off with a banner over the entrance in red, white, and blue saying "**USO Service Personnel Only**." Homer was wearing his only Ensign uniform, so he went in and had coffee and donuts before boarding the Atlantic Coast Line Orange Blossom Special for Jacksonville at 1030 hours. This was a modern train with air conditioning, set up with three seats on the right side and two on the left.

When Homer got on board, it was completely full except for one open seat at the front of the car facing to the rear. Two Army Lieutenants were facing forward and a third was in the rear facing seat next to his. When the train started south behind a diesel engine, the four young officers facing each other introduced themselves. The three Army Second Lieutenants wore khaki uniforms with collar brass indicating that they were Armor Branch.

The guy next to Homer stuck out his hand. "I'm Charlie Cox, from Augusta, Georgia."

Then, sitting across from Homer; "I'm Buddy Vaughan from Dallas, Texas."

"I'm Todd Dwyer from Rochester, New York."

"I'm Homer Harris from Lake Mohawk, New Jersey. Where are you guys headed?"

Todd responded for his buddies. "Since I'm senior to these two by a few days, we're all heading to Jacksonville to pick up a boat ride. What about you?"

Homer replied, "I'm heading to Jacksonville to join a ship as well."

Buddy said, "We gathered you were in the Navy, cause your sailor suit was a good clue."

Homer asked, "Just curious, it looks like you are all the same rank so Todd, why are you Senior?"

"I graduated a few days ahead of these guys, because Norwich in Vermont is the oldest of six military schools in the U.S. and we have that privilege, so my date of rank is earlier than theirs. That gives me the right to pull rank and order them around."

Buddy let out a "Ha-ha," and said in a Texas drawl, "You know how these Yankees are, and this one is just full of himself! And for the record, Texas A&M has twice as many generals as Norwich or Charlie's school, North Georgia College, combined."

Todd volunteered, "We just completed the Armor school at Fort Knox and are the advance party for our platoons that are coming behind us by a couple of days. Say, where did you go to school for Navy ROTC?"

"I didn't, I graduated from the Naval Academy at Annapolis but I'm being detailed as a Lieutenant in the Merchant Marines for a temporary period. Do you guys know the name of the ship that you are reporting to?"

Buddy said, "It is a Liberty ship called the SS *Earle Horne*."

Homer said, "This is some coincidence, that is a brand-new Liberty ship, and I will be the First Mate Navigator."

Todd added, "Well, I hope it is up to the job, because we will be putting twenty M-4 Sherman tanks on board. Do you know where we are going, Homer? It must be someplace warm because we weren't issued any winter equipment."

"I don't know. Sometimes you don't get to open your orders until you have put out to sea." Todd said, "We have one more platoon leader who is supposed to be with us. He is a party boy from the University of Georgia, so I would guess Gabe Silver probably eased into the club car and is getting tanked up right now."

Buddy said, "I don't know how he ever got a commission, or got through the Armor School."

Charles said, "You're not from Georgia, so you wouldn't know his pappy is the Lieutenant Governor."

At 1930 the Dixie Flier arrived at the Jacksonville Terminal and then continued on to Miami. The Lieutenants had vouchers for the Seminole Hotel downtown, so Homer had a choice and decided, rather than report this late, he would try for a room at the Seminole.

The Army had two rooms reserved for the Lieutenants, but they did not see Lieutenant Silver get off the train, so Todd said, "You can bunk in my room and since there were no other rooms available"

Homer said, "Thanks, but I'll move if he shows up."

It turned out that Second Lieutenant Silver brought his blood alcohol level up to 2.0 and fell asleep in the club car. When the conductor woke him and asked for his ticket, he was forced to buy a coach seat to Miami or be put off the train.

After breakfast, Homer and the Lieutenants took a cab to the Talleyrand Docks on the St. Johns River, and found the Liberty ship SS *Earl Horne*. The

Lieutenants went to the Harbormaster's office to find out when their tanks were scheduled to arrive.

Homer went up the ships boarding ladder and carried his duffel bag to the main deck, then asked a crew member where Captain Strenger might be found.

"He's on the bridge."

When Homer got to the bridge, there was a very thin, weathered-looking, grey-haired man, who wore weathered khaki pants and a short sleeve shirt with four stripes on his shoulder boards.

Homer guessed he was sixty-five years or older, and said, "Sir, are you Captain Strenger?"

"Who the hell do you think I am, Sonny?"

"Sir, I'm Ensign Homer Harris and I have orders to report as your First Mate and Navigator."

"Let me see your orders."

The Captain pulled a very thick pair of glasses from his shirt pocket and proceeded to study the orders. He took his glasses off and looked directly at Homer with blue bloodshot eyes. "What kind of experience could you possibly have at your age?

"Sir, I have navigated on a submarine and on a fast destroyer and have passed every navigation course at Annapolis."

The captain said sarcastically "I'm so impressed. You did bring your sextant, I hope."

"Yes Sir."

"You need to go to the Army Navy store in town to get some khakis. That's what we wear, so you can put away your navy uniform. Boson' Mate Bates here will show you to your cabin. We are supposed to receive a trainload of tanks some time tonight, so you get back as soon as possible to help with the loading. One more thing, I don't know how many soldiers will be arriving to make up the tank crews, or where we are going to bunk them or feed them."

"I can help on that, Sir. On the train from Atlanta I sat with the three Army Platoon Leaders who were the assigned advance party for the *Earl Horne*. They will have twenty Sherman tanks that weigh 33 tons each and have a crew of five, which will total one hundred troops. They are bringing their own K rations. The last time I saw the Lieutenants, they were going to the Harbormaster's office to check on their tanks and the ammunition shipment that goes with them. The troops are coming in on a train from Fort Knox sometime tomorrow."

The Lieutenants had a message waiting at the Harbor Masters Office that said: 'Captain Brumley, the Company Commander, suffered from appendicitis and that he and the First Sergeant would join the company by air at their destination. Master Sergeant House, the platoon sergeant for the fourth platoon, will be in charge of the troops during the movement. Second Lieutenant Todd Dwyer will act as senior officer during the ocean deployment. When you are fully loaded you will report to this command and sail as ordered by the Navy.'

Homer returned to the *Horne* with four Khaki pants and shirts.

Chapter 24
Preparations for Sea

Since his orders made him a Lieutenant, he also purchased a pair of collar insignia double railroad track Lieutenant bars and a pair of brown combat style boots that would go with a brown web belt. With this outfit, Homer tried to look like he was on the same team as Captain Strenger. When Homer got to his cabin he changed and returned to the bridge where Captain Strenger was just starting a meeting. He introduced Homer Harris.

"Mr. Harris has been loaned to the Merchant Marine by the Navy. He will serve as First Mate and Navigator. Mr. Harris, I'd like you to meet our Chief Engineer Rosco Brown, who has been with me for over twenty years. To my right is our Coxswain Evan Jones and our Boson' David Bates, and the most popular man on the ship, our cook, Leroy P. Brown. Yes, they are related, along with another relative, Abraham Lincoln Brown, who is our Engine Room Chief. We will be taking on six hundred and sixty tons of Army tanks, twelve thousand rounds of main gun ammunition and fourteen thousand pounds of small caliber ammunition, and one thousand gallons of military MO gas for the tanks. The Army is including enough K Rations to feed one hundred tank crewmen for what I am told will be a long trip. I am open to suggestions as to where we are going to berth these one hundred passengers. We don't have enough sanitary facilities on the ship for an extra hundred people to use the head and relieve themselves. I would like for the First Mate and Chief Engineer to stay behind and start working on these problems. The rest of you can return to your duties."

After everyone else had left, the three Lieutenants were brought up to the bridge and introduced by Homer to the Captain. They had received the same cargo information that Captain Strenger had just discussed from the Harbor Masters office.

Lieutenant Dwyer said, "Sir, I have received orders that I will serve as senior officer. Two of our officers are here and will assist in any way possible. We have one more officer that has been delayed."

Captain Strenger explained that a Liberty ship is a cargo ship, and not designed to carry one hundred extra people.

The Captain said "I can solve the space problem for your officers by putting four bunks in my cabin, and I will move to my sea cabin that is right off the bridge. My furniture can be taken below to make room. I have asked Mr. Harris our First Mate and Chief Engineer Brown to figure out accommodations and sanitary facilities for your troops. Our small galley will be able to provide hot coffee, soup, and hot water for washing, but that is about all we can do. I expect your tanks will arrive later tonight and we will begin loading immediately. Our boson has a loading plan to stage ten tanks as deck cargo on the port side and ten on the starboard. All of the other cargo will be distributed according to weight in our fore and aft hold space. Are there any questions? If not, I suggest that you get my cabin set up and then inspect the ship, and give me suggestions in the morning for berthing and sanitation."

That evening the Lieutenants helped pack up the captain's cabin and set up four bunks then joined the crew in the wardroom for a pot roast dinner. Homer joined them at a table for four where the discussion began about the problem with Lieutenant Silver.

Buddy Vaughan said, "If he doesn't get here by the time our troops arrive, and he misses a movement at a time of war, he will spend the rest of his life in Leavenworth."

Charlie Cox said, "I'll be dammed if his daddy will be able to get him out of a court-martial for something that serious."

Todd added, "In my opinion we will be better off with Sergeant House taking fourth platoon.

Homer said, "I've never met this guy, but he sounds like a real loser."

Todd added, "Worse than that, he is an alcoholic loser with no leadership skills and an inflated ego. It wouldn't surprise me if his troops didn't throw him overboard some dark night."

In the morning, Homer and Rosco Brown the Chief Engineer met with Captain Strenger with suggestions for the Army troops.

Chief Brown led off. "Cap'n, there ain't no empty space inside except down in the hold on top of the ammunition where we can put these soldiers, so that won't work. Mr. Harris and I think the best thing to do is build a latrine right on the stern and rig up a system where we can dump 55-gallon drums of waste at night using our aft crane to pick up the drums and wash them out overboard. We can surround this thing with plywood and paint it to look like part of the ship. Then over the aft cargo hatches we can rig a canvas tarp cover with sides that can be secured in case we run into weather."

Homer added, "I learned from the Lieutenants that the troops have air mattresses and army blankets that can be arranged under the tarp cover. Each tank has issued a small Coleman stove to warm up K rations for the crew. This will be anything but a luxury cruise for the tankers, but they will make it work. I suggest that we rig safety lines around this area also in case of bad weather. We don't have nearly enough life boats or quick launch solid rafts so I will get inflatable life rafts from the Navy, Coast Guard, Army Air Force or anywhere else they can be located and enough life jackets. The Lieutenants were sure the Army didn't issue life jackets."

Chief Brown said, "I'll have my guys start work building this out if we have your okay, Captain."

Captain Strenger nodded and said, "Get moving. We are almost finished loading the tanks and the troops can arrive anytime."

Homer continued with the Lieutenants, who were included but stayed silent in the Captains meeting and said, "I will go to Naval Station Mayport and Naval Air Station Jacksonville. Todd, I would like for you to go to the Coast Guard, Charles and Buddy can see if the Army Air Corps can give us Life rafts and jackets. Send a message to the Harbormaster's office with your scrounging results and I'll check in every hour. I will prepare a letter of request on Merchant Marine stationary for you to present. This will explain that this is a classified SECRET mission and will be charged on their books to the U.S. Merchant Marine Maritime Administration."

Buddy asked, "Do you have authority to do this?"

"No, but they will probably lose the paperwork and if not, it will take a year to go through channels. Sometimes you have to use the system against itself. We aren't going on a joy ride, and there is no way we could get what we need through channels."

By late afternoon they collected all that they needed with a little to spare delivered by Navy, Coast Guard, and Army Air Corps trucks. The paint wasn't dry on the latrine when busloads of troops began arriving from the Jacksonville train station. Sergeant House and the other Platoon Sergeants had pulled off a clean movement and were congratulated by their Platoon Leaders.

The troops were called into formation on the dock by Sergeant House, who reported to Lieutenant Dwyer. "All present and accounted for, Sir."

Lieutenant Dwyer introduced Lieutenant Harris, the First Mate, who explained that this was a cargo ship and not designed for more personnel aboard beyond the crew.

"We have made modifications to accommodate you on the aft deck under shelter, and will provide all the support that we have available. We have members of our crew available to assist your boarding. This is a high priority

CLASSIFIED war time mission, and no outside communication will be allowed once you are aboard. I will see you on the ship."

After the tankers got settled on the aft deck Leroy Brown brought ten gallons of Chicken Noodle Soup out from the galley to supplement whatever K rations were selected by each soldier.

During dinner, the Lieutenants and Homer asked for their attention. Homer began by asking how many men smoked, and about seventy percent raised their hands. He then proceeded to explain the smoking lamp and light discipline.

"You can get this ship sent to the bottom by making just one mistake showing a light at night. The only safe area that is screened off is the latrine at night and that is if there are no aircraft anywhere in the area. I have been in close proximity to Nazi U-Boats in the North Atlantic, and they like to follow garbage trails to locate their next victim, so you can't throw anything overboard. If you see anyone about to make a mistake, you stop them. Our crew will now distribute inflatable life jackets for lack of a better name called Mae Wests. They have one compressed CO_2 bottle to use in an emergency. We have placed inflatable life rafts under your tanks. I would suggest that you open one up tomorrow and get familiar with the instructions. There is enough to go around but if you don't know how to use this life saving equipment then it is your loss. I have received a report that the paint is now dry if anyone needs the temporary head or what you call the latrine at the stern of the ship. Thank you for your attention."

Lieutenant Dwyer announced, "After you have cleaned your mess kits and policed up your area, all tank crewmen will mount up and check all of your control systems. Drivers will start their engines in neutral with the parking brake firmly set and continue running them for fifteen minutes. You will open your radio net and perform a communication check then shut down. If there are any problems report them immediately to your platoon sergeant."

Homer went to the bridge to let the Captain know that the tanks were about to start up.

When they did Captain Strenger said, "Those things make a hell of a lot of noise. What kind of engines do they have?"

"Sir, I was told they have a 425 horse Ford V8."

During the engine run up, Second Lieutenant Gabe Silver arrived in a taxi. Lieutenant Vaughan spotted him and sent his platoon Sergeant Bobby Lowery down to the dock and told him to stay there until the run up was complete. Homer went down to the dock and returned a salute from Silver. He told Silver to follow him to his quarters. No one offered to help with his gear.

When Silver got to the Captains former cabin, he said, "Well this isn't too bad. At least we have a private bath."

Lieutenants Dwyer, Vaughan, and Cox were standing in the room when Sterling arrived. Lieutenant Dwyer said, "Captain Brumley had a medical emergency and is not coming with us. I have been designated Senior Officer in Charge and my first order to you, Silver, is sit down and write your complete explanation for not being with your platoon when we left the train in Jacksonville on 2 March 1942 at 1930 and note that it is now 4 March at 2000 when you arrived at the SS *Earl Horne*. This information will be placed in the ships log."

Homer heard one long blast of the ship's whistle and hurried to the bridge.

The Captain said, "We are getting underway, take in all lines. Hard port rudder. Give me three short blast signals and reverse slow."

The *Earl Horne* began slowly backing into the mid channel without tug assistance.

When sufficient distance was achieved, the Captain said, "Maintain hard right rudder and give me slow forward."

With this skilled maneuver, the 441-foot long Liberty Ship moved to dead center in the channel and headed to the Atlantic Ocean. The two oil-fired boilers provided 2,500 shaft horsepower from the triple expansion steam engine, moving the SS *Earl Horne* at 11 knots, or 13 miles per hour.

Chapter 25
The First Leg

March 4, 1942, 2300 Hours

After the St. Johns River jetties were passed, the SS *Earl Horne* was joined heading south by a Navy Destroyer on the port side and a Coast Guard Cutter on the starboard closest to shore. At 2315, a flashing light signal was sent from the destroyer: 'You have lights showing in multiple places.'

Homer copied.

Homer picked up the microphone, sending loudspeaker announcements. "Platoon Leaders and Platoon sergeants to the bridge on the double"

When they arrived, Homer told them to inspect the ship and correct any lights showing. Charles got to the Platoon leaders' cabin, and found a porthole open and bright lights on. He turned off the light and closed the porthole, then went looking for Lieutenant Silver.

Several other areas were corrected in the troop section aft. Coleman lanterns were being used with inadequate screening. The destroyer was using a cone over the signal search light to restrict the light pattern and sent a second message; 'Lights out complete now.'

Captain Strenger called Homer by his first name and said, "Lets step into my cabin, it's time to open our orders. Watch me open the safe and learn the combination. You and I are the only ones authorized access to the safe."

The Captain removed a large envelope marked TOP SECRET in red ink.

'SS *Earl Horne* is to proceed at best speed to the Panama Canal and use high priority to transit same. During transit you will be contacted for a naval intelligence briefing prior to exiting. Your final TOP SECRET destination is Sidney Australia. You are authorized to draw any supplies you consider necessary from Navy or Army supplies. Do not announce your final destination until you have exited the canal and are at sea in the Pacific.'

Homer said, "Captain, I would suggest using the Army chain of command calling the Platoon Leaders to the bridge so we can brief them on the Panama Canal part of our orders. They will brief their Platoon Sergeants, who will brief

132

the Tank Commanders and their crews. I would also like to set up a watch system using the tankers. Each tank has five crewmen so I would suggest one man at the bow, one on the port and starboard side amid ship, and one at the stern each serving a two-hour watch. Each tank has binoculars and they have short range walkie-talkie radios, so we can keep one on the bridge for instant communication. I can brief the observers on things to look out for. The Army officers can work out a 24-hour schedule, if this meets with your approval, Sir.

"Homer, I'm glad they had this kind of training at Annapolis." The Captain stood beside Homer when he briefed the four Lieutenants. "At daylight, we should be passing Daytona. If there is any question about the need for lookouts, remind your troops that just off Daytona a week ago the Texaco Star oil tanker was torpedoed and sunk. We have 1292 nautical miles from Jacksonville to the Panama Canal and, even with an escort, these are dangerous waters."

05 March 1942: at Sea
Ships log: Passed Daytona at 0600.
        Passed Miami at 2000
        All is well.
06 March 1942: at Sea
Ships log: Passed Key West at 1600.
        In route to Cancun
        All is well.
07 March 1942: at Sea
        All is well.
08 March 1942: at Sea
        Passed Cancun at 2200
        In route to Colon Panama
        All is well.

March 9, 1942, at Sea
At 0700 Coxswain Evan Jones attempted to wake Captain
Bronson Strenger in his day cabin off the bridge. Coxswain
Jones contacted the First Mate Homer Harris who determined
Captain Strenger had passed away in his sleep.
Lieutenant Todd Dwyer was called to the bridge.
Both Lieutenants Harris and Dwyer have had extensive first-aid training and concluded that the Captain was dead. Chief Engineer Rosco Brown was called to the bridge and agreed.
The Captain was deceased.

Chief engineer Brown said, "I knew this day was comin'. The captain had a bad heart but didn't want anybody to know. He trusted me with his will. Would you want me to go and get it?"

On the outside of the envelope, it said: {Last Will and Testament of Bronson Strenger} *TO BE OPENED IMMEDIATELY UPON MY DEATH.*

Homer said, "Under these circumstances, as a senior officer, will you, Chief Brown, please open and read the contents?" The Will was signed and notarized. Chief Brown read:

I, Bronson Strenger, being of sound mind, do hereby leave all my possessions that I may have aboard any ship that I am on to the members of my crew. Any funds that I have in the Seaman's Bank of New York should be distributed to the Merchant Marine Welfare Fund.

Since I do not have any living relatives, I wish to be buried at sea.

Homer sent a flashing light message to the Navy Destroyer and the Coast Guard Cutter:

'*Captain Bronson Strenger has died of natural causes verified by U.S. Army Officer Lieutenant Todd Dwyer and Merchant Marine Chief Engineer Roscoe Brown. First Mate Homer Harris, Annapolis Graduate, has assumed Command. Captain's Will requested burial at sea and will be conducted under way. No option to preserve deceased due to lack of refrigeration.*'

The will and a copy of the message to the Navy and Coast Guard were made part of the ships log. At twelve noon The Captains body was committed to the deep. Homer led the crew and Army personnel in the Lord's Prayer. A message came from the destroyer:

'*Regret your loss carry on.*'

The balance of March 9th was a somber day for everyone aboard the *Earl Horne.*

Ships Log 10 March 1942: at Sea
    In route to Colon Panama
    All is well.

11 March 1942: Nearing Panama Canal 1030 hours.
    Navy and Coast Guard signaled you are in security zone
    Hold position for Pilot. Radio traffic approved. Good luck.

Chapter 26
The Canal

When the pilot boat arrived, it was threading its way to the *Earl Horne* through twenty-five ships waiting their turn for passage through the canal. When the pilot reached the bridge, he told Homer that his ship had number one priority and took over directing the Horne past anti-submarine nets to the first lock at Colon. Homer felt relieved being in a safe area for a few hours.

After attaching lines fore and aft to an electric mule railroad engine, The Captain was instructed to disembark and was met by a Navy Ensign who Homer recognized from the class of 1941.

The Ensign said, "My orders are to bring the Captain to the intelligence briefing at Fort Sherman, and suggest the Captain assign some personnel to secure fresh milk and vegetables."

Homer said, "I am the Captain, Homer Harris class of 1942."

The Ensign looked surprised and stared at the Lieutenants twin railroad track bars on Homer's collar, and said, "I'll be dammed. How did you pull this off?"

"I assumed command when the Merchant Marine Captain had a heart attack and died. The Navy and Coast Guard were advised of the command change."

Homer returned to the ship and saw Lieutenant Vaughan near the gangway. "Buddy, can you organize a party to get some fresh food? I'm going to a briefing and should be back in a couple of hours. I'll catch up with the *Horne*."

Homer got in the Ensign's jeep for the uphill trip to Fort Sherman.

The briefing was conducted by U.S. Navy Commander Kevin Owens. New charts were distributed by a Senior Chief. The Commander began by welcoming the three Captains to Fort Sherman.

"In approximately six hours, unless you need to fuel at the Fort Amador tank farm, you will exit Balboa into the Pacific and head to your destinations. Gentlemen, this is Indian country. We will provide a Navy escort for each ship until dark or until the next night if you depart after 2400. We are flying Pacific air cover for two hundred nautical miles in all directions. You should maintain radio silence unless you have enemy contact. There are Japanese I-Boat long range submarines operating all over the Pacific Sea Frontier. Recent intelligence places a number of German U-Boats trying to block off Australia. Eight cargo ships have been sunk in New Zealand and Australian waters in the last month. If that wasn't enough to be concerned about, we have a report that a Q Ship Raider named the *Leopard* has been operating in the area. It will look like a cargo vessel and may be flying any number of flags. We have British reports that the *Leopard* mounts camouflaged four-inch guns and also serves as a supply ship replenishing torpedoes for a wolf pack. Reports indicate that the raider can make twenty knots and will either sink its' victim on sight or fire a shot over the bow if the Germans think they can transfer fuel or food before sinking their target. This is firm information from British survivors. Are there any questions?"

Homer was returned to the *Horne* as it was clearing the second of three Gatun Locks. During the third lock a canal pilot boarded to guide the Horne through Gatun Lake and the narrow Culebra Cut under her own power. The canal pilot departed when they reached the Pedro Miguel Locks and the mules took control of the ship on the downward steps to the Pacific. The last two Locks placed the SS *Earl Horne* at Pacific sea level. Homer maneuvered to the fuel tank farm under the 16-inch guns of Fort Amador.

Fueling was not completed until 0200 on 12 March. This would give the Horne eighteen hours of Navy escort before the remaining 8,598-mile, unescorted trip. While the Chief Engineer and the Engine Room Chief were handling refueling, Homer called a meeting of the Platoon Leaders and Platoon Sergeants in the wardroom.

He gave them a run down on the intelligence briefing at Fort Sherman, and explained, "The escort will leave after eighteen hours and we will be sailing for twenty six days on our own. Our biggest risk is submarine attack. According to Naval intelligence, there are both Japanese and German subs that we could encounter. There is also a disguised German raider operating in New Zealand and Australian waters. Your lookouts may give us some time to either evade or fight. When I was at the Naval Academy, I did a report on using high velocity gun fire to intercept torpedoes before they could reach the ship."

Homer uncovered a chart that showed a 75-millimeter armor piercing tank round with a velocity of 2030 feet per second, which could travel one mile through the air before losing accuracy and the same round fired into water could go 34 feet. He then showed a drawing of a Sherman tank with the main gun depressed firing into the water and intersecting a torpedo.

"When we are at sea on our own, we will practice with two tanks on the port and two on the starboard side. We can use a 30-caliber machine gun to lay a track similar to a torpedo and give your gunners practice putting a shot on the nose of the torpedo."

Lieutenant Silver interrupted and said, "Aren't we supposed to have authorization to touch the cargo. That ammunition is meant for our destination which by the way is what?"

Homer replied, "If you haven't figured out where we are going, I'll let you know right after we clear Balboa, and that ammunition won't be any good at the bottom of the Pacific Ocean. On all of the tarps covering your tanks I want you to stencil in black paint TRUCK-M1 and face that toward the sea. The German raider that is also operating where we are going has a history of stopping cargo ships to take off fuel and food before they are sunk. If this happens to us, we will pop the tarps off and fill the raider full of holes before he knows we are well armed and powerful."

Silver then said, "Why don't we wait here until we get a real captain."

Lieutenant Charlie Cox said, "Sit down Silver and shut up. If we had a cargo captain, he wouldn't know anything about naval warfare. I'd rather fight than sit there and be a dead duck."

Homer said, "I will take full responsibility for using some of our cargo ammunition."

Roscoe Brown came in the wardroom and announced, "We have finished refueling and my cousin told me he has lighted the boilers and will have full steam in twenty minutes."

A tug was waiting with a line on the bow to pull the *Horne* away from the fuel dock. A Great War era, four stack destroyer was waiting just off Balboa in the Gulf of Panama to escort the *Horne* for the next eighteen hours.

Chapter 27
Pacific Danger

Homer picked up the microphone on the bridge and said, "This is the Captain, I know you have all been speculating on our destination and now that we are at sea I can tell you that we have an eight thousand mile voyage to Sidney, Australia. Your tanks are going to General MacArthur."

Homer heard a cheer go up. "We will be passing through very dangerous waters, so you lookouts need to be at maximum alert 24/7. Light discipline is critical. You are authorized to arm each tank with a full basic load of main gun armor piercing, high explosive, and white phosphorus ammunition. Some of your 30-caliber bow machine guns are not obstructed, so they should be armed along with your fifties. In the morning we will practice removing the tarps and simulate firing. Gentlemen, the *Earl Horne* is a fighting ship that just looks like a cargo ship."

Morale was high, except with Lieutenant Silver, who was going around trying to get support for returning to the Panama Canal.

Ships Log: March 12, 1942

At Sea: Tarp removal and dry fire practice conducted from 0800 to 1100. Tank Basic ammunition loads have been checked and are complete. Lieutenant Dwyer had the bottom escape hatches removed and began crew practice entering the tanks from underneath with tarps still in place. Drivers and bow gunners were stationed behind the tanks and at a short whistle signal would quickly pull the tarps off of their tank.

Ships Log: March 13, 1942

At 0200 the Navy destroyer sent a flashing light signal, "Wish we could go all the way with you. God Bless the USA." Homer sent a message back, "God Bless the U.S. Navy. Fair winds and following seas."

Homer turned to the Coxswain Evan Jones at the helm and Lieutenant Buddy Vaughan beside him on the bridge and said, "Well we are on our own for about 24 days. Buddy, if you will stay on the bridge with Evan while I take a walk around the ship, and then you can send someone up to relieve you. I will catch a couple of hours rest in the day cabin off the bridge with the door open, if you need me."

In the morning, Todd Dwyer had a cup of coffee on the bridge with Homer and the assistant coxswain able seaman, Blake Trailer, from Louisville Kentucky.

Todd said, "Wouldn't it be a good idea to teach Buddy or Charlie or me some navigation skills, in case something happens to you, Homer? We all understand land compass navigation, but there aren't any grid square maps to refer to on the ocean."

"Not a bad idea. We can hold class on the bridge when you can work it into your schedule. By the time we get to Sidney, you will be the only master navigators in the Army."

Homer made a decision to head due south for 20 hours, so that the *Horne* would be about three hundred nautical miles below the regular sailing lanes and increase their chance of not running into the enemy. At 2200 hours, Homer used celestial navigation and showed Todd, Charles, and Buddy how to take a star shot and fix their position before turning on a direct course to Australia.

Ships Log: March 14, 1942
On course, No enemy sightings.
Anti-torpedo training going well.
Monitored radio messages report Japanese landings in the Solomon Islands increasing the threat to Australia.

Ships Log: March 15, 1942
On course, No enemy sightings.
Weather beginning to deteriorate.

Ships Log: March 16, 1942
On course, No enemy sightings
Entering squall line seas 6 to 8 ft.
Monitored radio messages report American and Philippine forces
Retreat to Corregidor.

Ships Log: March 17, 1942
On course, No enemy sightings

Fifty percent Army personnel experiencing sea sickness affecting lookout schedules. Radio messages report General Douglas MacArthur has arrived in Australia from the Philippines by order of President Roosevelt.

Ships Log: March 18, 1942
   On course, No enemy sightings
   Weather improving seas 4 to 6 ft.

Ships Log: March 19, 1942
   When Lieutenant Dwyer told Silver to get off the bridge, Silver drew his 1911 A-1 45 semi-automatic weapon, pointed it at Captain Harris and ordered him to return to the Panama Canal
   As Chief Engineer Brown attempted to take the pistol from Silver, he fired a shot, striking Coxswain Jones in the leg. Lieutenant Dwyer un-holstered his side arm and struck Silver in the head with the butt of his pistol, rendering him unconscious.
   Lieutenants Dwyer and Vaughan placed a tourniquet on Coxswain Jones and using the ship's medical kit administered morphine applied sulfa powder, and sewed up the flesh wound. Since Liberty ships do not have a brig for prisoners, Captain Harris ordered the
   eight-by-twelve-foot paint locker emptied and had Silver locked behind the chain link fencing.
   The following charges against Lieutenant Gabe Silver entered in the ship's log are as follows:
   Mutiny on the high seas at time of war
   Attempted murder
   Cowardness in the face of the enemy
   Wrongful discharge of his firearm
   Wounding of a member of the ships Merchant Marine crew while in the course of his duties.
   Witnessed and signed by: Captain Homer Harris, Lieutenant Todd Dwyer, Chief Engineer Roscoe Brown)

   Lieutenant Dwyer requested Homer to make an announcement for Sergeant House to report to the bridge.
   When he arrived Homer said, "I guess you know what just happened."
   "Yes Sir, its' all over the ship."
   Lieutenant Dwyer said, "Well Sergeant House, fourth platoon is yours and it is for the best. You can see in the Ships Log the serious charges against Silver."

"Sir, I'm glad to have him out of my hair. I've never seen a worse officer in my sixteen years of active duty and, no offence, I've seen some rotten apples."

Homer said, "I'm going to ask Charlie Cox to be the temporary Master at Arms to see that Sterling doesn't cause a disturbance or do anything that would endanger the ship. Now gentlemen, let's get back to normal."

Ships Log: March 20, 1942

On course, No enemy contact

Anti-torpedo training continued.

As a precaution, Captain ordered 20 improvised depth charges be made using one high explosive tank round taped to a satchel charge with a delayed fuse. The purpose is to drive a submarine from the area.

One successful test was made.

Ships Log: March 21, 1942

On course no enemy contact

Practiced tank battle station drills.

Ships Log: March 22, 1942

At 0615 starboard side look out reported a periscope wake three o'clock.

Homer and Todd were having a cup of coffee on the bridge. Bow and Stern lookouts verified the sighting.

Homer grabbed the microphone. "Battle stations, tank! This is not a drill."

Todd yelled, "On the way to my tank."

Tank #15 and 21 were at amid ship on the starboard side. Tarps were off, and armor piercing 75-millimeter rounds were loaded and ready to fire when tanks 15 and 21 started tracking one inbound torpedo. At 150-foot distance from the *Horne's* hull both tanks fired, and almost immediately a mountain of water shot up and the *Horne* was rocked to the port side by ten degrees.

Homer thought, 'Why doesn't he fire another torpedo?'

Luck was with the *Horne*; the sub was Japanese, and they had fired their last torpedo.

Homer ordered assistant Coxswain Blake Trailer "Hard right rudder." "Sir, that will head us into the sub!"

Homer said calmly, "That is the idea. If he stays down we will start dropping our fake depth charges to scare him away but if he comes up to use his deck gun on us, we will be broadside and fill him full of holes."

Trailer said, "Look Sir, he's coming up!"

Homer grabbed the loudspeaker's microphone and said, "Remember your training and take out his radio antennae first so he can't call for help. Good shooting, he is meat on the table!"

Ten tanks on the starboard side fired twenty armor piercing rounds each before Homer announced, "Cease fire."

The Japanese I-Boat looked like it was made out of Swiss cheese but since all of the holes were above the waterline it wasn't about to sink.

Homer announced, "Platoon leaders to the bridge."

When they arrived, Homer said "We have an opportunity to board this sub and get all of their naval codes, charts, and radio frequencies. This is a volunteer job."

The three Lieutenants and Sergeant House all said they want to go.

"So you are going to make me decide. Buddy, you take six men armed with Thompsons, Forty-fives, grenades, and a satchel charge to toss into the forward deck gun magazine on your way off the sub. If there is enough of their deck gun ammo, the explosion should crack the sub open so she will sink. Make this quick, I don't want to hang around here too long."

When they returned, the boarding party had two large packages wrapped in oil cloth. They had just secured their motorized lifeboat when the sub belched a ball of flame from the bow deck and cracked itself in half.

At 0725 the sub disappeared beneath the waves. The tankers and the crew of the *Horne* burst into a genuine whooping and hollering celebration.

After a couple of minutes, Homer picked up the mike and said, "To all Army and ships' crew personnel, WELL DONE! You have made history! Now lets' get back to work as there are probably more of them out there."

Ships Log: March 22, 1942 continued:

At 0615 sub spotted by lookouts. One torpedo was fired at the USS *Earl Horne* and tank 15 and 21 engaged with armor piercing rounds and destroyed torpedo before it could strike hull.

Japanese sub surfaced and was sunk by ten tanks from the First and Second platoon company A 40th Armor.

After dark they examined the contents of material captured from the sub and Buddy said "We got all the paperwork and maps. I just hope it is good stuff because I can't read a lick of Japanese."

Homer said, "It must be or it wouldn't be on board. Now, while you repack this stuff, I'm going down to talk with the third and fourth platoon who didn't fire a shot. We didn't know if another sub was off the port side."

For the next 7 days, the sea was calm and there were no enemy sightings. Training continued and morale stayed high. Personal time was spent playing cards and writing letters that could be mailed in Australia. Homer made an announcement that no naval action could be mentioned in any letters, and that the Platoon leaders would need to review the contents before the letters were sealed. The troops enjoyed sunbathing and saltwater showers.

In the evening of March 28th, radio reception was very good so the BBC report of a determined British raid on the French port of Saint Nazaire came in loud and clear over the *Horne's* loudspeaker. The British destroyer HMS *Cambletown* was packed full of explosives and completely destroyed the port when it was remotely steered into the docks and detonated. The BBC also reported that the island of Corregidor in Manila Bay was holding out against massive Japanese attacks.

Another story covered push back on the new conscription law in the United Kingdom, including women up to the age of 45. The troops commented that the Brits must be desperate if they are drafting older women. Homer and the Platoon leaders decided that putting the war news on the loudspeaker would help the troops to realize how serious things were.

Ships Log: March 31, 1942

> On course. At 1400 Stern lookout reports possible smoke from vessel.
> Weather clear, Sea calm.

Homer checked his charts and determined that the Horne was about 2100 nautical miles from Australia, then called a meeting with the Platoon Leaders and Platoon Sergeants.

"Gentlemen, this may not be anything to worry about, but you remember the warning about a German raider that was disguised to look like a cargo ship. The Navy had reports that it was operating off Australia and supplying a U-Boat wolf pack. They said it was capable of 20 knots, so if we see a ship gaining on us, we may assume that it could be the raider. We have about eight hours before dark, then we will change course due south for four hours that will put us fifty miles from our prior course. If it is the raider, and he has radar, he will pick us up and we will have to fight.

Ships Log: April 1, 1942

At 0700 corrected course after attempt to evade unidentified ship that has been gaining on us for seventeen hours. Estimate distance astern to be 6 nautical miles.

Announced Tank Battle Stations.

Homer could see that this was no ordinary cargo ship as it closed the distance to the *Horne*. It was flying the Union Jack, trying to appear British. The ship continued advancing on the port side of the Horne, complying with the rules of the nautical road for a vessel passing another.

When they were abreast of the *Horne* at 0900, a large caliber shell was fired in the ocean in front of the *Horne* and a loudspeaker ordered them to stop in English with a German accent. The Union Jack was lowered, and the Swastika flag was raised. Homer signaled the engine room, 'SLOW ASTERN.'

The voice from the raider asked, "What is your cargo?"

Homer answered on his loudspeaker "We have trucks, diesel fuel, and food."

He hoped the Navy Commander's briefing at Fort Sherman was accurate and the raider would move in close to pump off their fuel before sinking the *Horne*.

When the raider was three hundred feet from the *Horne*, Homer hit the deep steam whistle and the tarps came off. Tank 31 took out the radio antennae and radar with one high explosive round. Tank 41, closest to the bow of the *Horne*, put a high explosive round through a front window on the raider's bridge. Tank 45, at the stern of the *Horne*, concentrated on the rudder breaking it loose at the top and since the raider was also in reverse, the rudder was pulled into the propeller blades, causing a complete jam.

When guns on the raider began to be uncovered, the tanks quickly destroyed them with main gunfire. Ten fifty caliber machine guns raked the raider and anyone who was seen moving met their maker. Armor piercing ammunition was used in the area below the funnel where the engine room was probably located. After ten minutes, the raider was a smoking wreck on the port side. The tanks had expended five hundred rounds of main gun ammunition.

The feared German raider, the *Leopard*, was sitting dead in the water.

Homer announced on the loudspeaker, "First and Second Platoons, prepare to board the raider."

Homer maneuvered the *Horne* alongside the raider. Master Sergeant House and Lieutenant Cox told their unhappy loaders and gunners to remain with their tanks, in case something happened on the starboard side. This gave them a boarding party of thirty men using the tank commanders, drivers and bow gunners armed with Thompson sub machine guns, 1911 A-1 pistols and grenades.

Lieutenant Cox and the Third Platoon started their sweep at the bridge, and Sergeant House led the Fourth Platoon to the stern. All of the tank commanders had walkie-talkies.

Homer had to come on the net and say, "Cut out the chit chat! Unless you have a problem or need help!"

Sergeant House came around the undamaged port side of the raider and kicked in a door leading to the infirmary.

Three nurses were chained to bunks wearing very little clothing. They were hysterical. Two nurses had British accents, and one sounded Australian.

The older British nurse said, "Thank God you are here! The keys are in the desk. Please get these chains off!"

Staff Sergeant Billy Powell, 43 Tank Commander, found the keys and quickly unchained the nurses. Sergeant House used his walkie-talkie to contact the bridge, and requested three army shirts to be brought to the port side aft of the raider.

"We have three nurses who will need medical attention and help getting on the *Horne*."

The Australian nurse picked up Sergeant Powell's Thompson and opened fire on a row of lockers across the cabin. Pools of blood ran out the bottom of two lockers.

The Australian nurse said, "The so-called doctor and his assistant abused us in the worst way for profit. They just got what was coming to them!"

Two troopers from the First Platoon arrived and gently helped the nurses back to the *Horne*. Lieutenant Cox came around the port side passing the bridge that looked like a raw hamburger factory inside and came to a locked door.

Cox used his Thompson to pick the lock, and kicked the door open. There were two Germans in Navy uniforms standing, wide eyed, with their arms pointing straight up.

Toward the rear of the radio room, the smaller of the two said, in perfect English, "I am American. I am Jewish. I will help you."

The large German said "Juden," and reached for his luger pistol.

Before he could get it out of his holster, Lieutenant Cox stitched him up with a short burst from his Thompson.

The smaller radio operator said, "My Name is Moses Goldberg from Chicago. I got trapped in Germany after Pearl Harbor. I went back to Dusseldorf to try to get my family out, but the war started."

Lieutenant Cox called to Staff Sergeant Hank Holbrook and said, "Hank, take this guy under guard to the Captain on the bridge. We'll let the Captain figure out if he is legit."

On the way out the door Moses said, "There are prisoners locked up in the forward hold and nurses in the aft infirmary."

The boarding party freed 14 British seamen from the hold near the bow. When Moses got to the bridge, he started by telling Homer there were four U-Boats operating in the area.

Homer said, "I'm sure there are. Keep him under guard. I'll deal with him when we are out of here."

There were several fire fights, and finally Homer said, "Let's wrap this thing up. I want a head count when we have everyone on board."

Moses said, "Sir, there is a spare enigma machine, codes, radio call signs and cyphers in the closet under a tarp in the radio room closet."

Homer called Lieutenant Vaughan on the walkie-talkie and said, "Buddy, take four men to the raider radio room on the port side behind the bridge and get anything that looks valuable from the closet. Grab as many German hats and Jackets as you can carry. There are Nazi flags in the closet and a phonograph that has a German national anthem record on it. Lieutenant Cox, stand by the torpedo storage and when the last man is back on the *Horne*, set the satchel charge on top of the torpedoes at max delay. I think that is five minutes. If it is less, tell me now."

"It is five minutes, Captain."

Homer called Engine Room Chief Abraham Brown and said, "We are about to blow up the raider, so I need all the steam you can give me to get us the hell out of here."

"Sir, you just give me the signal and we're gone."

According to Lieutenant Cox's estimate, there were forty torpedoes in the hold where he tossed the satchel charge bag. The *Earl Horne* was 2,000 feet away when the torpedoes went off, creating a small tsunami that lifted the stern and propeller almost out of the water.

Ships Log: April 1, 1942 continued

At 0830 the German raider, the *Leopard*, fired a shot across the bow and ordered the SS *Earl Horne* to stop. The Third and fourth Platoons of Company A 40th Armor engaged and defeated the *Leopard*, an armed German raider. Lieutenant Charlie Cox and Master Sergeant Frank House lead two boarding parties and rescued fourteen British Seamen and three nurses. An enigma machine, codes, cyphers and other intelligence information was captured. Charges were planted that blew up forty torpedoes and sunk the raider at 0930. All Army personnel returned to the ship without injuries. Tank guns were cleaned, and ammunition was restored to full basic load. Army personnel and rescued nurses rendered first aid to the rescued seamen.

Homer turned his attention to Moses Goldberg. Moses explained that being Jewish with an American passport would guarantee a trip to the firing squad in Nazi Germany after Hitler declared war following Pearl Harbor.

"My brother, David Goldberg, at World Radio in Chicago can verify who I am. I went home to Dusseldorf to get my mother, father, and sister out, but they were gone. Christian friends took me in and gave me an ID that belonged to one of their sons who had been declared dead. I used that ID to enlist in the Navy rather than be drafted into the German Army. I hoped to get to a neutral country where I could jump ship and find an American Embassy, but you rescued me first."

Homer said, "That is some story, Mr. Goldberg. I hope it is true. Now, I am going to ask you some questions so that the FBI can verify your credentials. First, when you were growing up did you have a dog? If so, what was your dog's name? What was your mother's name before she was married? What is your social security number? What kind of car did you have in Chicago? And last, so I don't waste my time or the FBI's, what are the names of the two baseball teams in Chicago?"

"Sir, they are the White Sox and the Cubs."

"Moses, I am going to proceed believing that you are for real and have you and our radio operator, Josh Gordon, set up a clandestine radio station using your frequencies and call signs and the enigma machine. After the FBI clears you, I will have you take an oath and Join the U.S. Navy. I am also a commissioned naval officer. We will contact the U-Boats one at a time; meet them and sink them."

Moses said, "We will first need to contact Berlin and tell them that the *Leopard* was badly damaged in an air attack and an SOS was responded to by an American Liberty ship, which our brave crew and Captain Heinkle captured. We have transferred our guns and torpedoes so now we are the *Leopard2*, ready to continue supporting the wolf pack. Berlin has special recognition codes for the U-Boats and they will be told what we look like otherwise they would sink us."

"If this works, Moses, we will sink four more subs."

"More subs, Sir?"

"Yes, we have already sunk one. Moses, you will be under armed guard until we hear from the FBI, but get busy. It may take a few days."

The encoded message was received at Pearl Harbor and retransmitted to the FBI in Chicago. 24 hours later, the FBI replied confirming Moses Goldberg's story. By this time the *Leopard2*'s radio station was ready to transmit to the four U-Boats.

Homer called a Platoon Leader and Platoon Sergeant meeting to go over a plan of deception when the German subs came in for refueling. "Gentlemen, I have weighed the choice of making a straight run for Sidney Harbor as the *Earl Horne* and hope that we don't encounter any U-Boats. This is Moses Goldberg, who some of you have met. He was trapped in Germany with his U.S. Passport and chose to join and hide in the Krieg's Marine to avoid a firing squad. Our finding him serving as a radio operator on the *Leopard* has given us a bold but I think safer alternative. A story was fed to Berlin that we were captured by the air attacked damaged raider and we are now the *Leopard2*. We will bring the wolf pack in one at a time and sink them, like shooting fish in a barrel. We have partial German navy uniforms and flags that we will display as they approach. We will be playing the German National Anthem, '*Deutschland*' over our loudspeakers. Moses will communicate in German and some of us in uniform will do the smiling and waving routine. When they are broadside, we will fill them full of holes just like the Jap sub."

Ships Log: April 3, 1942

0400 On Course. Calm seas.

Following establishment of *Leopard2* identity with Berlin radio, contacted U-Boat 246 by radio and confirmed refueling location.

Homer entered the radio room and asked Moses, "How far do you estimate that sub is from us."

"By the strength of the signal, Captain, I would guess no more than twenty miles."

"Moses, how do you feel about sending these subs to the bottom?" "After knowing what the Nazis are doing to my people and probably my family, I will enjoy seeing every shot tear them up."

"Well Moses, get on your Nazi uniform, and get ready to make some announcements over the loudspeaker."

Homer went back to the bridge and announced, "BATTLE STATIONS, TANKS, remember to take out the radio antennae first or we will have three more U-Boats looking for us. Raise the Swastika flag and get ready to play

148

"*Deutschland*" over our loudspeaker. To all of you imitation Germans, put on a good show. This will be over in a few minutes."

Before leaving the radio room, Moses sent a message to the sub, asking how many torpedoes they required fore and aft.

The answer came back, "Stern fully loaded, need ten forward."

Homer brought the *Horne* to a dead stop, and U-246 approached slowly on the starboard side.

He picked up his walkie-talkie and said, "Buddy, concentrate second platoon fire on the stern. They have a full load of torpedoes back there."

"WILCO--24 and 25 put your AP (armor piercing) in the stern and hit those torpedoes!"

Tank 15 and 21 took out the radio antennae with HE (high explosive) and the fifty caliber machine guns cut down four waving Nazis on the conning tower of the sub. It only took two rounds into the stern to hit a torpedo and a heavy muffled explosion cracked U-246 in half. The stern section went down quickly, and water began filling the forward section, causing a loud whistling sound coming out of twenty tank round holes. U-246 was gone in less than four minutes.

Homer turned to Moses on the bridge and said, "That was almost too easy."

Ships Log: April 3, 1942 continued

At 0730 hours the *Earl Horne* posing as the raider *Leopard2* contacted U-246 for refueling and sunk same in less than four minutes. Resumed course to destination. No further enemy contact.

Homer calculated that the *Horne* had 1750 nautical miles to reach Sidney.

At 1200, Homer picked up the microphone and said "I wish we could do more for you sharp shooters, but the best I can do is issue one cold Becks Beer from the crate that we took off the raider."

A loud cheer went up when Leroy Brown and his mess assistant began handing out the Becks.

Sergeant House said, "The Nazis still make the best beer that I have ever tasted!"

The *Horne's* radio operator, Josh Gordon, put the recording of *the Star-Spangled Banner* on the loud speaker as they pulled down the swastika and ran up Old Glory.

Ships Log: April 4, 1942

On course. Calm seas. No enemy contact.

Ships Log: April 5, 1942

On course. At 2300, made radio contact with U-234 and established refueling location.

Ships Log: April 6, 1942

At 1400 hours close radio contact was made with U-234 and the *Leopard2* was advised that all torpedoes had been expended. 200 rounds of main gun ammunition expended. Lieutenant Dwyer led a boarding party to plant satchel charges in the deck gun ammunition hold on U-234. At 1500 hours the explosion cracked the sub open and it sank quickly. No Army personnel were injured.

Ships Log: April 7, 1942

On Course. No enemy contact. Light rain and calm seas.

Ships Log: April 8, 1942

At 0530, radio contact was made with U-288 and U-199 operating together. Both subs had engaged the Royal Australian Navy Cruiser Outback and an Escort Corvette and sunk both. They had expended all of their forward torpedoes. They would arrive at the *Leopard2* at 1100 hours.

Moses brought the message to the bridge. Homer called for the Platoon Leaders and Sergeants to report to the bridge ASAP.

When they arrived, Homer said, "We have a difficult situation coming up. Moses has told me that when two subs arrive at the same time with the old *Leopard*, they come abreast on opposite sides for refueling. This means we will need all four platoons to be fully manned. The only extra people we have to wear the Nazi uniforms are in our engine room, but they are black. There are no black Nazis so pick out eight of the British sailors and dress them up. You know the drill. Have the flags ready and put "*Deutschland*" on the loudspeaker."

At 1115 both subs approached from astern; U-199 went to the starboard side of the *Horne* and U-288 went to the port side. Homer didn't waste any time hitting the ship's deep whistle. The tarps were pulled off by the driver and bow gunner of each tank and the fireworks began. The gunners on tank 25 and tank 45 concentrated on the stern of both ships and the radio antennas were destroyed with high explosive rounds from tanks 21 and 41.

On U-199, three German sailors jumped off the conning tower and tried to man their deck gun and another sailor tried to get to their anti-aircraft guns behind the conning tower. They were shredded by fifty caliber machine gun rounds.

After 150 main gun rounds had been fired by the first and second Platoon, they hit a torpedo in the stern of U-199 and it cracked open and quickly sank. On the port side of the *Horne*, the third and fourth Platoon were having a more difficult time with U-288. It appeared to be a newer sub and had a thicker hull. Penetration was achieved by putting two or three rounds on the same spot and finally opening a hole.

Sergeant Billy Powell, tank 43 Commander, told his loader to put WP (white phosphorus) in for the next two shots, and he managed to put both rounds through an existing hole. Smoke started pouring out of a dozen holes and a raging fire started to cook off the main gun ammunition and the torpedoes at the stern. Five minutes after the first WP rounds started the fire, the stern torpedoes and the deck gun ammunition exploded at the same time. U-288 did not need a boarding party.

Homer went on the loudspeaker and said, "Well done, tankers! You guys have really made history this time. Adolph Hitler can't build them as fast as we can sink 'em."

A cheer went up from everyone on board, especially the nurses and the rescued British seamen. Homer calculated that they were only two hundred and fifty nautical miles from Sidney and before he could send a radio message requesting an escort, Moses received a radio message from a German Milch Cow. This was a submarine oil tanker. The message requested a meeting fifty miles east of the *Horne's* position.

Homer asked Moses to tell him all that he knew about this oil tanker sub.

"I saw one in Bremerhaven and it was huge, probably four hundred feet long with a beam of fifty to sixty feet. It can carry as much petroleum as a standard size conventional oiler. It may have only two torpedo tubes in the bow."

Homer weighed the options: to continue to Sidney or to backtrack and capture or sink the Milch Cow. If he continued to Sidney, the Germans would realize that the raider and four U-boats were gone and probably give the oil to the Japanese. The Milch Cow is headed their way, so he decided to risk steaming two hours east to try to capture this prize.

The *Horne* displayed the swastikas and dressed the fake German crew. When the Milch Cow was abreast of the *Horne*, Moses made an announcement on the loudspeaker that the Fuhrer had ordered a picture for all German newspapers, with one hundred percent of the crew on the bow of the giant sub. They were told to line up and pass a note pad down the line putting each sailor's name in order.

After they lined up, Moses sent a message to the Milch Cow and it was answered by the radio operator left behind.

Moses put on his most aggressive Nazi voice over the loudspeaker and chewed out the captain for violating an order from the Fuhrer. "Captain, do you want this insubordination reported to Berlin or is this just an oversight?"

Quickly, the radio operator and the sailor that was sent for him were on the bow deck.

Moses announced, "Move further forward and closer together."

Homer gave a tap on the whistle and the First Platoon tarps came off and Lt Dwyer fired a burst of fifty caliber rounds between the crew and the conning tower into the water. The swastika came down and the Stars and Stripes went up. Moses told the crew that they were prisoners, and if they did not throw any firearms that they had with them into the ocean, they would be executed. The captain and three other officers threw their lugers in the water.

Moses announced, "You will climb a cargo net and follow instructions when you reach the bow of this vessel."

Homer sent Chief Engineer Brown and Boson Evan Jones down a cargo net from the stern of the *Horne* and secured a line between ships. Eight of the British seamen were sent down to the Milch Cow carrying a walkie-talkie for Chief Brown. When the Germans reached the *Horne*, 32 members of the crew were huddled into a tight group with four U.S. Army tankers holding submachine guns on them.

Moses told them over the loudspeaker, in German and then in English, "If you move or do not obey a command, you will be shot!"

Chief Brown was good at figuring out mechanical things. With the help of Moses translating German words that were spelled for him over the radio, the Milch Cow began to move forward on the surface.

Homer rang the engine room and ordered, "All ahead slow."

He then contacted Chief Brown and told him to maintain a 200-yard separation directly behind the *Horne*. Slowly, both ships began to increase speed until at 11 knots.

Chief Brown called on the radio, saying, "I am unable to keep pace with you."

Homer had the *Horne* slowed from 13 to 10 knots.

Ships Log: April 8, 1942 Continued

At 1115 Hours U-199 and U-288 came along both sides of the *Horne* to be resupplied and both were sunk by main gun fire from twenty tanks of Company A 40th Armor. At 1300 hours radio contact was made between the *Horne* and a German Milch Cow submarine oil tanker U-698. A decision was made to capture or sink the German vessel. At 1600 hours the German submarine and 32 crew were captured by Army, Merchant Marine and rescued British seamen. The *Horne* and the captured German vessel are in route to Sidney with expected ETA in 27 hours.

Ships Log: April 9, 1942

At 1000 hours radio contact from the USS *Horne* was made with the Royal Australian Navy requesting an escort for two American ships approximately one hundred miles east of Sidney Harbor. Estimated arrival Sidney 1900 hours. Two Harbor pilots requested.

Following the Australian Navy contact, Homer called a platoon leaders and platoon sergeants meeting on the bridge.

"Gentlemen, we are not completely out of the woods yet, but we are getting close. In about nine hours we should be tying up in Sidney. We will pick up two pilots and Chief Brown will take our oil tanker submarine to their oil docks. Our pilot will take us to an area for unloading your beautiful tanks. First, we will get military help to transfer the German prisoners. We need to make it clear that the Germans can have no outside contact or our intelligence information that you have captured will be worthless. The next group to cover secrecy with will be the British sailors and the nurses. I will do this while you are briefing your troops. When we arrive, it will get pretty busy so I would like to say a few words of appreciation to your troops for the magnificent job that they have done. Any questions?"

Sergeant House asked, "Sir, any idea where we are going once we are off the ship?"

"No, but I am sure we will be contacted by our Navy and Army brass because they will know we are arriving. Lieutenant Dwyer, I would like to borrow two of your troopers with their Thompson's to stay with Moses and me as guards until I get the intelligence material delivered to Naval Headquarters. Once this is done, I will return them to you."

"No problem. I will send you two E-6 Sergeants."

Two Australian corvette escorts picked up the *Horne* and the Milch Cow exchanging flashing light signals. Ten miles outside Sidney Harbor, a pilot boat arrived and put one pilot on the submarine and the other pilot on the *Horne*. Both American ships were carefully guided around minefields on a very dark night.

Ships Log: April 10, 1942

The SS *Earl Horne* was directed to a military dock in Sidney Harbor at 0300 hours and secured, then the engine room was told to shut down.

Homer lowered the gangway and disembarked with Lieutenant Dwyer when they contacted an obviously low level representative from the Harbor Master's Office. An American Navy representative was requested on a high priority. In addition, Australian or American Army personnel were required to take over thirty-two dangerous German prisoners.

The representative said, "You better come with me, mates. This is above my pay grade."

Homer started making phone calls to the Australian Army Headquarters handling port security.

A Major from the First Light Horse Cavalry said, "We will send two armed men and a Constable from Harbor Police to take over your prisoners."

Homer said "This is Captain Harris. Let me speak with your commanding officer."

"I am the commanding officer, old chap. How can I be of service?" Homer said to himself, 'be diplomatic, then said, "Major, these are very dangerous Nazi prisoners who must be held in complete confinement or one of the most important intelligence captures of this war will be compromised. You will need at least ten well-armed troops and a very secure place to keep these Nazis."

"No problem with a secure place. They will be 500-miles in the outback in a maximum-security camp, run by our troops, who hate Nazis."

"When can you pick them up? We have them under guard on the USS *Earl Horne* tied up to dock D 12."

"I will round up two paddy wagons so they will be securely locked in, and we should be there in one hour."

"Thank you, major. Could I have your name for our ship's log?" "Certainly, I am Major Horace Copthorne of the First Australian Light Horse. This sounds interesting, I'll be coming down with our troops and look forward to meeting you, Captain Harris."

At 0800, the prisoners were gone and ten of the tanks were lifted by the large dock crane on to the dock. Then an olive drab four door American Buick with small flags on both front fenders pulled up alongside of the boarding ladder. An American Army Colonel was helped out of the back door by the Sergeant driver.

Homer stepped outside the bridge and saluted. The Colonel returned the salute and told the Sergeant to go on the ship and have the Captain come down to the car.

When Homer reached the Colonel, he saluted again and said, "Homer Harris reporting as ordered, Sir!"

The Colonel said, "General MacArthur requested the captain."

"Sir, I am the Captain," Homer replied.

The driver opened the other door and General MacArthur joined the Colonel and Homer.

Homer saluted the General and said, "It is an honor, Sir. I am Homer Harris, an Annapolis graduate detailed to the Merchant Marine." MacArthur shook hands with Homer and said, "I came down personally to thank you for getting these tanks through to me. I know how dangerous it was for you. By the way, are they still teaching gunnery at the Naval Academy?"

"Yes, Sir. That was my best subject."

"Colonel Willoughby, I'd like you to transfer Lieutenant Harris to that critical coastal artillery slot."

"At what rank, General? He would be the equivalent of an O-3 Army captain so I would recommend Major's oak leaves so he will have more authority with the Aussies."

"That seems appropriate and he merits a Bronze Star."

Colonel Willoughby pinned on the oak leaves and the Bronze Star. General MacArthur said, "Report to my headquarters, Major Harris, as soon as possible."

"Yes Sir!" Homer returned to the bridge and told Lieutenants Vaughn, Cox and Dwyer what had just happened.

Homer said, "I didn't have an opening to tell him what we have done but you can rest assured I will write up everyone that disserves recognition. The way MacArthur is handing out rank you will probably be colonels. Next, I'm going to find a truck and take Moses and the sergeants that you have loaned me guarding the classified information to Naval Headquarters."

Homer gathered the ship's log and had the troops help load a lorry that was reluctantly surrendered by a British Petroleum driver. When they arrived at the Headquarters front gate, they were stopped by two U.S. Marines armed with Springfield bolt action rifles. Sergeants Billy Powell and Hank Holbrook pulled out their Army ID's and Homer showed his Merchant Marine papers.

The senior Marine Sergeant said, "What about this guy?"

Homer said, "He has been cleared by the FBI, but it is a long story. We need to bring this truck into the compound, and I need to see the commanding officer."

"Well, you ain't doing neither!"

"Sergeant, do you have a phone out here?"

"No, it is inside the gate"

"I suggest you guard me while I contact the Admiral's Aid, or the Chief of Staff." "

Why don't you tell me what this is about?"

"Sergeant you don't have a security clearance high enough for me to tell you what time it is. If you don't take me to the phone now you will find out what a naval officer who is ticked off can do to a sergeant's career!"

Homer spoke with Commander Raymer who was Admiral Bryan Hickox aide and explained that he has very sensitive highly classified material on a borrowed truck that needs to come in off the street.

The Commander told the Sergeant, "Bring the truck inside and unload whatever is being guarded. Then let the truck back out. I am sending someone down to escort this officer with you to my office."

Homer told Sergeants Holbrook and Powell, "Stay with this stuff and do not let anyone touch anything. I'll take Moses with me."

Chapter 28

Australia, UK, and the USA

When Homer entered Commander John Raymer's office, he saluted, and realized how scruffy he looked.

"Sir, we just arrived from Jacksonville Florida at 0400 with twenty Sherman tanks for General MacArthur, and I have what will be one of the most highly classified secrets of the war out in your courtyard under U.S. Army guard."

"Well Mr. Harris, what do you have?"

"Sir, with all due respect, I am sure the Admiral will read you in on this, but it will be his place to do that not mine."

"Let me see your identification."

Homer gave the commander his Merchant Marine ID and volunteered, "Sir, I am also a commissioned Naval Officer detailed to the Merchant Marine."

"Who is this guy?"

"Sir, this is Moses Goldberg. He is an American citizen. I have verified this with the FBI, and I will vouch for him. He does not have an ID."

Commander Raymer instructed Homer and Moses to have a seat then he entered Admiral Bryan Hickox office.

The Admiral told Commander Raymer, "Bring them in and stay in the office."

Homer came in the office, stood at attention and saluted the Admiral. "Sir, I am Homer Harris, an Annapolis graduate detailed to the Merchant Marine and I would appreciate it if you would review the Ships Log of the SS *Earl Horne*. It will explain why we are here."

Admiral Hickox took the log from Homer, but said, "I don't have all day to read this so why don't you give me the Readers Digest version and please take a seat."

"Yes Sir, thank you Sir. I was the First Mate on the SS *Earl Horne*, a Liberty ship loaded with twenty Sherman Tanks, ammunition, and one hundred tank crewmen sailing from Jacksonville, Florida. South of Cancun, the Captain passed away from natural causes, and I assumed command. After Passing through the Panama Canal, we encountered a Japanese sub that fired a torpedo at us. I instructed the Army tankers to use a technique that I developed for a term paper at the Academy and used tank main gun fire to blow up the torpedo before it could strike our hull. Army Lieutenant Dwyer led a raiding party and captured the Japanese naval codes, cyphers, maps with their mine fields and a lot more. That material is in your courtyard under Army guard. The next enemy encounter was with the German raider the *Leopard*. They overhauled us and fired a shot across our bow. We defeated the raider with tank fire and captured a German Enigma coding machine, their codes, cyphers and a lot more. This gentleman next to me is Moses Goldberg. He is an American citizen that I verified with the FBI. He was trapped in Germany with a U.S. Passport when the war started and joined the Krieg's Marine with a fake ID to avoid a firing squad and was the second radio operator on the *Leopard*. We established a fake radio station and brought four U-Boats in and sunk all four."

At this point, Admiral Hickox was astounded. "You mean, son, you sunk five enemy submarines and the raider and captured a windfall of intelligence with a Liberty ship? My GOD! You are the greatest American Naval Hero since John Paul Jones!"

Commander Raymer said, "Sir, just before we came in, I got a message that a huge submarine oil tanker was off loading enough oil to supply our Navy and the Australians for a month. Captain Harris, did you have anything to do with this?"

"Yes Sir, we captured that Milch Cow and turned over thirty two Nazis crewmen to the First Australian Light Horse who said they were going to a very secure POW camp in the outback. We also rescued fourteen British seamen and three nurses from the raider. The Milch Cow had a new four rotor Enigma machine and extensive charts. Fortunately, we had no casualties."

Commander Raymer said, "You weren't kidding when you said this was top secret. We will need to ensure that the prisoners are sequestered and everyone else knows that they must maintain complete secrecy."

Admiral Hickox said "John, get clean uniforms for these gentlemen, and then we will go over to see General MacArthur. That will give me time to digest the ships log"

When they returned, Homer explained that the General had met him this morning and transferred him into the Army as a Major for costal artillery.

"Well, we will get that reversed. This report will astound the General. We need you to develop the torpedo intercept tactic and that is a Navy job. There won't be a problem because the General is reasonable. He will probably award a Silver Star to both of you."

"Admiral Hickox, I took the liberty of unofficially swearing Moses into the U.S. Navy. He graduated from the advanced course at the Krieg's Marine radio school. I would appreciate your making him legitimate?"

The Admiral said, "Raise your right hand, Lieutenant Goldberg." He turned to Commander Raymer and said, "John will you take care of the paperwork."

Homer said "One more thing, Sir. We have an Army Lieutenant Platoon leader that went off his rocker and we have him locked up in our paint locker. He is charged with mutiny, attempted murder, discharging his firearm, and wounding our Merchant Marine Boson while he was on duty at the helm. Details are in the Log."

Admiral Hickox said, "Leave him locked up, we'll let the Army handle this."

While Homer and Moses drew khaki uniforms and got cleaned up at Navy Headquarters, Admiral Hickox called General MacArthur. "Douglas, I need to bring some incredible information to you that can't be discussed on the phone. I will also be bringing the Liberty Ship's Captain that you met this morning and another amazing gentleman."

"Come right over, Bryan. I can't wait to hear what this is about."

When they entered General MacArthur's office, Colonel Willoughby and the General rose and shook hands with Admiral Hickox. Then the General asked them all to have a seat.

Admiral Hickox said "We appreciate you making time on your schedule for us General. I don't think you will be disappointed. I believe you and Colonel Willoughby met the Captain of the Liberty ship that delivered the Sherman tanks to you this morning."

"Of course, we have poached a fine officer from the Navy to become my Coastal Defense Artillery officer."

"General, I believe you will want to put him back in the Navy when you hear what is in the Log of this Liberty ship. Captain Harris developed a battle plan with three Army lieutenant platoon leaders and one master sergeant platoon Leader that destroyed a Japanese torpedo before it could strike the Liberty ship's hull. Then the Sherman tanks sunk the sub that fired it. Later in the voyage, they were engaged by the German raider, the *Leopard*, and sunk it. Two Army boarding parties rescued fourteen British seamen and three nurses who were being held captive. Then they rescued Moses Goldberg, an American citizen who was trying to help his family escape the Nazis when the war with Germany was declared. He joined the Krieg's Marine with a fake ID

159

to escape a firing squad and was made one of two radio operators on the *Leopard*. He was instrumental in bringing four U-Boats to the Liberty ship with an elaborate deception that Captain Harris and Mr. Goldberg developed. They sunk all four U-Boats with tank fire. The final act of brilliance was luring a German submarine oil tanker to the Liberty ship and capturing the vessel and crew. We have just pumped off enough oil to run our Navy and the Australian Navy for about a month. The most amazing achievement is your Army troops have captured all of the Japanese Naval codes, cyphers, charts and more. They have done the same with the Germans and we now have two Enigma code machines and all of their charts, cyphers and maps worldwide. This intelligence will save many lives."

Homer thought, from the look on General MacArthur's face, that this was the first good news that he has heard since the war started.

General MacArthur got up from his desk and came over to Homer and put his hands on both of his shoulders and said, "I am so proud that we have young men like you coming out of Annapolis. Captain Harris, I am going to submit you for the Medal of Honor and, with my blessing, return you to the Navy. I see that Mr. Goldberg is now a Navy Lieutenant. Colonel Willoughby, will you call a photographer in and help me award the Silver Star to both of these fine officers. Captain Harris, you will be here for a few days while we copy all of the intelligence information then we will send you and Lieutenant Goldberg by air to Bletchley Park the code center in London. Colonel Willoughby will work with you to prepare decorations for all of the Army personnel that deserve recognition. I plan to send a personal letter that will be delivered by you in person to General George Marshal, Admiral Earnest King and President Roosevelt. Colonel Willoughby, you will implement the tightest secrecy protocol possible. I am looking forward to reading every word in the log of the *Earl Horne*."

Admiral Hickox said, "Thank you, General. We will have a log copy brought to you this evening."

General MacArthur replied, "I hope, before you leave, you gentlemen could join my wife Jean and I for dinner."

Admiral Hickox responded with a smile and said, "It has been a long time since I saw you and Jean together in Manilla. It would be a pleasure for me and these fine officers. Sir, I do have a question that I would like to clear with you regarding an appropriate rank for Captain Harris when we transfer him back to the Navy. Would you concur that O-5 Commander would be appropriate?"

"That seems appropriate."

"We do have a problem Admiral, with all of the personnel that accomplished this astonishing series of victories at sea. We can't allow them to be placed in an area where they could be captured because the top-secret intelligence information must be protected."

When General MacArthur was ready to dismiss people, he had a way of pleasantly changing subjects. "Gentlemen, I don't think we have anything scheduled for tomorrow night, but I will clear this with Jean and call you in the morning."

On the ride back to Naval Headquarters, Admiral Hickox said, "I forgot to bring up using the General's long-range liberator transport for your trip to England. I have one that is assigned to me that is not decked out like the one assigned to General MacArthur. We will make triplicates of everything and for safety sake, I want to use two aircraft to make sure the intelligence gets through. Commander Harris, you will be on one of the liberators and Lieutenant Goldberg will be on the other. It will probably take three days to get everything photographed, copied, and measured. The SS Silverfish will be ready to leave for Pearl soon and we will send back up copies of everything on her in case neither of you make it. There are some very good uniform shops in Sidney so you will be able to outfit yourselves before leaving. You can contact Commander Raymer in the morning to draw a partial pay and have photos taken for your IDs."

When the driver pulled up to the Headquarters, Admiral Hickox went on to say, "My driver will take you to the Army and Navy BOQ. I would expect you are tired. Have a meal and a good rest."

"Thank you, Sir."

In the morning, Homer looked at his watch and said, "Moses, up and at em! It is 0800. We have a lot to do."

They both rolled out of their narrow Army cots and found the head for a hot shower. Then after breakfast they hitched a ride to Naval Headquarters to draw their partial pay and have their IDs made. Commander Raymer asked Homer, "Would you like a driver or take a jeep from the motor pool and find your way around?"

"A jeep sounds good."

"Here is the address of two tailor shops that have Navy uniforms. I would remind you that you are driving on the wrong side of the road so be careful. Here is my phone number if you need something."

"Thank you, Sir!"

"Homer, you don't call me Sir, we are both Commanders. After what you did, you should be an 0-6 and I should be saying 'Sir' to you. If you and Lieutenant Goldberg are free for dinner, I have found a terrific Italian restaurant."

"We may be committed to have dinner with Admiral Hickox and General MacArthur, but you will get the word on that and we will check in with you this afternoon. I love Italian food."

Commander Raymer called, advising Homer and Moses that dinner with the General was pushed back to tomorrow night. "I suspect he wants to read the Log tonight. If you are still interested in a great Italian dinner, drive the jeep over to Headquarters at 1600 and we will take my car." Dinner was everything that it was advertised to be.

April 12, 1942

Dinner with General MacArthur was much more formal. Admiral Hickox picked up Homer and Moses dressed in their new dress white Navy uniforms, and had a few words of advice during the ride to the Growings Hotel at Market and George Street.

"The General will probably ask a number of questions but he likes short direct answers. He likes to talk about West Point and will probably recall some Army-Navy football games. Moses, he may want to talk about conditions in Germany, your family, and life in the Krieg's Marine. Mrs. MacArthur is a lovely woman who will want to know personal things about your future plans. You will find that the General has deep feelings for the officer corps traditions in both the Navy and Army. Gentlemen, I think this will be a dinner to remember."

April 13, 1942

Commander Raymer met Homer and Moses at the BOQ for a 37- mile ride to the RAAF Camden Airdrome.

"I want you to meet General MacArthur and Admiral Hickox' pilots. You will be using two Consolidated Liberator C-87 executive transports for your trip to London. The Admiral's C-87 has seats for 25 and the General's aircraft is set up for only sixteen passengers."

When they arrived, Major Tommy Schneider and Lieutenant Commander Frank Lawton were in the maintenance hangar with their crew chiefs. They were in the process of installing six additional fuel tanks holding 2400 gallons of one hundred octane aviation gas.

Major Schneider was saying, "I don't want those damn tanks to leak like they did when I was flying over the hump and nearly passed out."

Commander Raymer waited until they finished this conversation and introduced Homer and Moses.

Commander Lawton shook hands with Homer and said, "Don't worry about leaks. We will be running off these tanks first because they are at our center of gravity where the bomb bay would be."

Major Schneider asked Homer, "How much extra cargo will you be bringing by weight?"

"We will have myself and two armed guards plus about three hundred pounds of classified material. Moses will have the same on his flight."

Commander Lawton said, "That must be really important classified material to commit both of these Liberators."

Commander Raymer said, "It is! Have you been working on your flight plans?"

Commander Lawton spread out charts on a table and weighed the corners down with small wrenches. "We are going to depart RAAF Camden and fly almost due west to Perth on the coast. We will re-fuel and check everything for a long hop over the Indian Ocean to RAF Chennai, India on the southeast coast. Then we will re-fuel and fly northwest to Bombay, then on to Cairo. That will begin the dangerous part of this mission because the Luftwaffe is active all over the Mediterranean."

Major Schneider added, "From Cairo to Gibraltar, we will have the advantage of our high-altitude performance. The four Wright 14-cylinder turbocharged engines will get us up above the service ceiling of any German aircraft. Our cruise speed is 215 miles per hour to get the best fuel economy, but we can crank these babies up to three hundred if we need to evade. Also, the Cairo to Gibraltar leg will be at night, and we can call for a RAF fighter escort when we are close to touch down around dawn. On the last leg to London, we will swing out wide over the Atlantic so the only enemy aircraft that we could run into might be a Focke-Wulf Condor on Naval patrol, and we can easily outrun them."

Commander Lawton added "We will have a co-pilot and an extra pilot so we can take turns getting some rest. We will also have a navigator and a flight engineer along with our crew chief. Any chance either of you," he looked at Homer and Moses, "have any flying experience?"

Homer volunteered, "I kept a DC-3 on course for a few hundred miles between Annapolis and Atlanta but I have no ability when it comes to landing or taking off."

Moses said, "I've only been a passenger."

Commander Raymer said, "We will have everything ready by 1500. We may have one or two extra passengers that need to go to Cairo or London if that is not a problem. When will you be ready to take off?"

Major Schneider said, "Unless we run into a mechanical snag, we should be able to go by 2000. Can you get the BOQ mess to make up sandwiches and plenty of coffee in a marmite can? There will be six of our crew on each plane and three or a few more passengers. Maybe they could add some cold fried chicken. We won't be able to pick up much if anything to eat along the way."

Commander Raymer said, "The Admiral and I will see that you guys don't go hungry."

Homer and Moses flipped a coin to see who would get the luxury flight on General MacArthur's plane with the name Bataan on the nose. Heads up, it was Homer.

They arrived at RAAF Camden at 1900 and carefully loaded the classified packages on each aircraft. At the last minute, they were handed a large mailbag with regular mail that would normally have gone out low priority by ship, and two marmite cans per aircraft, one marked hot and the other cold.

Homer and Moses thanked Commander Raymer, who said, "I almost forgot to give you this personal letter from General MacArthur to Admiral David O'Brien, and another to General Eisenhower in London to be delivered by your hand. I also wrote one to my wife, and I would guess she will get it in less than a week when you drop it in the mail in London. Best of luck to you both."

Navy Lieutenant Alex Vanderwier, the extra co-pilot, helped Moses get settled. Moses was surprised to see windows that were the same size as the Pan Am Clipper, as well as comfortable reclining seats. One accessory that the Clipper didn't have was oxygen equipment for each seat. Overall, Moses wondered how the General's plane could be nicer than this one.

Homer was settled in with the aid of the co-pilot First Lieutenant David Sullivan on the Bataan. Homer thought, 'this aircraft cabin must have been built by the same company that did the interior for the Coca-Cola DC-3, with one addition: the full-size bed back near the tail.'

Major Schneider came on the intercom and said, "Pre-flight checks are complete. Hang on everybody we will use all of the runway. We are heavy with this extra fuel."

The Bataan and the Navy C-87 Liberator Express broke ground at 2000 hours on schedule. After about an hour, Major Schneider came back to the passenger cabin and had a cup of coffee with Homer.

"Homer, call me Tommy, we are going to be together for at least three days or more. We will be covering 14,613 air miles. If you would like to come up to the jump seat, we would be glad to have you. Your sergeants would also be welcome one at a time. We enjoy getting to know our passengers."

"I'd also like to spend some time with your navigator. I'm a naval navigator, but I'm sure there are different procedures that would be interesting."

"Captain Holyfield is most likely the best navigator in the Army Air Corps, or he wouldn't be on the Bataan. We should be in Perth in about ten hours so Holyfield should have plenty of time for you. Besides, this is the easiest leg because we are riding a radio beam."

Homer, Moses, Sergeants Hank Holbrook, and Billy Powell spent four hours on the ground in Perth, while the crew chiefs and RAAF mechanics checked everything for the 3,901-mile flight to RAF Chennai air base on the west coast of India.

Departure Perth, April 14, 1942, 1400 hours

Homer figured that this leg would take about eighteen hours, give or take head winds or tail winds. He also thought that he could give Captain John Holyfield, the navigator a rest for a few hours. He learned that Major Schneider was a navigator before becoming a pilot, and would also be able to offer some relief for Holyfield. It seemed that the Army had things well covered.

The Flight Engineer, Master Sergeant Wayne Hamilton, spent a great deal of time harmonizing the engines and making adjustments on fuel. When it was time for Hamilton to take a nap, he was relieved by the extra co-pilot Second Lieutenant George May.

He told May, "Just don't change nothing. If you think a change is needed, wake me up."

At 1800 hours, Major Schneider asked Homer if he would like to take the Co-Pilot's right seat while Lieutenant Sullivan took a nap. Homer and Tommy Schneider talked for about four hours.

Schneider told Homer about flying General MacArthur and his family out of Mindanao in the Philippians in a worn-out B-17 Flying Fortress.

"I really liked the B-17 because it was more forgiving than this Liberator. You can't relax for a minute here, because this plane doesn't like it. On the plus side it is much faster by about eighty miles per hour on the top end and has a lot more range. By the way, who do you report to in London?"

Homer replied "The CNO Admiral David O'Brian, and then I have no idea. Changing the subject, is there any way you can see how the Navy is doing off our wing without using the radio?"

"Sure, do you know Morse code?"

"We use flashing light signals in the Navy all the time."

"Well, see that switch? It controls our navigation lights, so just use it like one of your flasher lights and they will answer. Ask them for a fuel reading and if everything is okay."

The answer came back:

> /we have 60% in aux tank/ no use reg tanks/ everything
> good/how you/over/

"Tell them we have 62% left in aux tank, and we are on schedule."

"What happens if we lose visual contact?"

"We should be holding the same course long enough to get to better weather, but if we are really separated, we could use a low power radio signal, or hope for the best and navigate independently."

Homer could see a picture of a pretty woman surrounded by three young children taped to an empty spot on the instrument panel and asked, "Is this your family?"

Schneider smiled and said, "That is my Patty, and our three boys. The big one is Jerry, the middle one is David, and the baby is James. They are a handful. I feel guilty leaving her with all of them, but I don't have any choice. How about you Homer, are you married?"

"Not yet, I have a wonderful girl back in Annapolis. Caroline is a registered nurse and her dad is a Navy Captain from The Great War and a professor at the Academy. He thinks I'm not good enough for her, and has been telling her that for four years."

"Well Homer, Caroline is the one with an opinion that counts. The future father-in-law will just have to come around. You have one thing going for you."

"What's that?"

"You are not in the Army. I heard that General MacArthur was going to grab you back in Australia."

"Admiral Hickox talked him into letting me back in the Navy."

"He must have had a powerful reason, because the General rarely changes his mind. Say, would you like to work the shortwave receiver and see if you can get the BBC so we can find out what is going on?" Homer began to run through the five hundred band and the first thing that came in was radio Berlin as if the transmitter was only a mile away.

Homer said, "Would you mind if we listened to this? I'm pretty fluent in German"

"Sure, if you don't mind translating the gist of their propaganda."

After a few minutes, Homer said, "Germany is winning everywhere, Adolph Hitler is a genius, and more bull crap."

They got a weak signal from the BBC and heard bits and pieces of a speech from Churchill.

About that time, the co-pilot and assistant co-pilot came on the flight deck and said, "We're ready to take over so you guys can get something to eat and take a nap."

Homer got up first and George May slid into the co-pilot seat, and then David Sullivan replaced Major Schneider. Homer and the Major went a few steps off the flight deck to a small galley and started to pour some coffee, but Major Schneider said, "I'll pass on the coffee. It will keep me awake and I need four hours so water will have to do."

April 15, 0200 hours

The assistant Co-Pilot, George May, woke both Homer and Major Schneider saying "It is 0200 and you wanted to wake up. Here is some coffee."

Major Schneider said, "Thanks George, I think we should keep you on as a stewardess. Is everything OK up front?"

"Yes Sir, we picked up a 50-mile per hour tail wind for the last four hours. We're almost halfway to India, and ahead of schedule."

"Is the Navy still off your right wing?"

"Yes Sir. On position."

The routine continued for the next 8 hours. Homer was startled at 1000 hours in the jump seat when a pair of Spitfires made a close identification pass.

Major Schneider said, "We must be on their radar, so they sent an escort. If we had been a pair of those Kawasaki flying boats, they would have smoked us."

At 1115 hours, the Bataan landed first, followed by the Navy Liberator. The Chennai RAF base was small but orderly. It showed no signs of ever being bombed. Both Liberators followed a Ford pickup truck with a 'FOLLOW ME' sign to several large maintenance hangers, and shut down their engines.

Homer told his sergeants to stand guard. "I will check things out and come back to relieve you."

Major Schneider, Commander Lawton, and Moses were in operations when Homer arrived. They were offered tea by the friendly British staff.

Commander Lawton said, "They have bunks and a mess for us. I would suggest letting our Chief Engineers get some food and rest before beginning refueling and maintenance. The Brits have offered some security personnel."

Homer agreed, "I'm not opposed to having a couple of Tommie's stand guard, but one of our guys must be with them on each aircraft. Moses and I

167

will take the first shift and then we can rotate depending on how long we are here."

At 1500, engine oil tanks were topped off and the British fuel sergeant pumped one thousand gallons of aviation gas into each Liberator, then told Major Schneider that that was all they could spare.

The sergeant explained, "Anymore and we won't be flying our Spitfires. You only have a short 600-mile hop to Bombay, and they have plenty of fuel."

At 1800, both liberators touched down and topped off their fuel. Then, at 1900, took off for Kinshasa in the Belgian Congo for a 4,231-mile trip from Bombay.

Homer thought to himself, 'If we are going to have a problem it will be in the Congo. From what I have heard these Belgian forces are still loyal even though their country is run by the Nazis. We will have to guard everything and carefully check the fuel even though it is from Royal Dutch Shell.'

April 16, 1942, 1500 hours

Both Liberators touched down and were met by two large fuel trucks. Flight Engineer Wayne Hamilton put on his Army 45 and so did Lieutenant David Sullivan, then they both deplaned and went to inspect the fuel. Hamilton went to a valve at the bottom of each truck and poured out a half gallon of aviation gas checking for water or impurities. It looked okay. Major Schneider went around the aircraft and noticed they were being surrounded by native troops holding a circle perimeter about three hundred feet away from both Liberators.

Commander Lawton and Major Schneider both called into their aircraft, telling the Army Sergeants armed with Tommy guns to come out and help inspect the planes.

This show of force seemed to work. With full tanks, Major Schneider signed for the fuel and taxied toward the circle of troops.

He said, "Either they will start shooting or give way. No matter what, we're going through them if necessary."

When they were back in the air at 1600, everyone heaved a sigh of relief.

Major Schneider came on the intercom and said, "We have 2600 miles to Cairo, which should take about twelve hours. After nine hours we need to be extra alert for enemy aircraft."

As they approached Cairo, they could see two Hawker Hurricane fighters approaching across the north end of the Red Sea. Both Liberators were told by a busy air traffic control to enter a right hand pattern and land on runway 10, running from south to north.

April 17, 1942

When they landed in Cairo at 0400, they could be quickly re-fueled and leave or wait until next evening, taking a chance of being bombed by the Germans or Italians.

Major Schneider asked the fuel trucks to hurry so they could take off quickly for Gibraltar. Captain Holyfield plotted a route up the Mediterranean avoiding areas where the Luftwaffe was most active. He estimated that they would cover 2,158 miles.

Both Liberators took off with full tanks at 0445 which the Brits said was a pit stop record. They climbed at 6,000 feet per minute until they reached 28,000 feet in the cool night air. Before leaving, Commander Lawton and Major Schneider met with their crew chiefs to discuss a fast run at close to max speed to Gibraltar. Fuel would not be a problem.

Major Schneider said, "We should be getting in range for a fighter escort by 1200 or a little before."

At 0800, they spotted an enemy formation of twin-engine bombers about ten thousand feet below probably headed back to Italy.

Two of the bombers were trailing smoke. Homer was in the jump seat and said, "Maybe they ran into our escort."

At 1445, both Liberators touched down on a very short runway on the Rock. The RAF service crews pulled British Petroleum tank trucks up and began fueling. A British pilot with one arm in a sling came up in a small Morris staff car. He brought a mail sack and told Major Schneider that a Royal Navy submarine on picket duty off Italy reported a large flight of both fighters and bombers were headed toward Gibraltar with an ETA of less than an hour.

He said, "You chaps better get out of here before it gets rather nasty."

Major Schneider said, "You don't have to ask us twice. Good Luck."

At 1530, on 17 April, both Liberators began climbing to their 28,000-foot service ceiling and swung wide out into the Atlantic Ocean. The normal air route would have been a little over one thousand miles to London, but Captain Holyfield projected a wide 1500 mile circle that would keep them away from all of the German land planes, except the Focke-Wulf four engine Condors operating out of bases in occupied France.

The Condors were converted 25-seat, long-range passenger airliners that were used for marine patrol. They actually carried a few bombs on hard points under the wings, but couldn't hit the floor with a brick with both eyes open.

While they looked modern, they were underpowered and cruised at only 208 MPH. The Liberators could fly much higher and faster.

Major Schneider got on the intercom and told the crew and passengers, "Unless we have a mechanical problem, we should be landing at RAF Duxford north of London by 2200 or a little earlier."

Homer was happy to see the Navy Liberator tucked in off their right wing. His mind drifted for a while, and he thought to himself, 'What is going to happen to Moses and me when we get there after we report to Naval Headquarters? Then what will happen to Sergeant Powell and Sergeant Holbrook? They are outstanding and I hope they don't get some lousy assignment. I've never been to England. Caroline and I talked about visiting castles someday. I wonder what has happened to Hans. He must be on active duty in the Army. I wonder how Penny and her dad are doing. I'll bet Mr. Ponder is looking out for Aunt Virginia. I wonder how my roommates are doing. Jim and Charles were really great guys. I wonder where they are. They won't believe it if they see me in a Commander's uniform.'

Then Homer closed his eyes and caught a short nap.

The sharp chirp of rubber tires on asphalt brought Homer out of a deep sleep. At 2215 both Liberators shut down their engines at RAF Duxford in front of the fuel trucks.

Major Schneider picked up the intercom and said, "We have flown almost 15,000 miles without a mechanical problem or any enemy bullet holes. I am damn proud of this crew!"

Homer thanked every crew member and helped Sergeants Hank Holbrook and Billy Powell off load their classified material. Moses did the same with the Navy crew. Then, Sergeants Kevin Tate and Frank House helped Moses with their classified load, and then the Sergeants assembled both into one big pile.

Both Liberators were pulled by tugs to a sandbag protected area to wait their turn at maintenance. Homer and Moses went to operations and requested a truck.

The grey-haired Lieutenant behind the counter corrected them, "You mean a lorry. How large, and for what purpose?"

Homer replied, "A deuce and a half would work."

"Need I ask you again? For what purpose?"

"We have classified material for the American Navy headquarters in London. A driver who knows his way around would be very helpful."

"It will need to be a Royal Airforce auxiliary woman driver. All of our men are in combat."

Homer thought to himself, 'Where do you think we have been, old boy?'

April 18, 1942

At 0100, a British truck about the size of a duce and a half rolled up, with a beautiful, eighteen-year-old, short-haired, blue-eyed blond, wearing a baggy uniform.

She flashed a smile and said, "Where do you Yanks need to go?"

Sergeant Billy Powell said, "I'm in love"

Homer told their driver to take them to American Navy headquarters in London, and asked, "How far and how long to get there, Miss?"

She replied, "My name is Patience Periwinkle. It may take one to two hours, depending on the air raids. Sometimes they hold us up for hours on a side road."

Tonight was one of those nights where waves of German bombers kept hitting London until the all clear signal at 0400. During this wait, Billy got to know Patience and secured her phone number.

Hank asked Patience, "Do you have a sister?"

Patience said, "Only an older brother, who is in the Navy. I do have a really good friend who lost her husband on a RAF Lancaster raid, and she has a very nice personality."

When they got back on the road, Billy told Hank, "You know what that nice personality line means? She will weigh over two hundred and fifty pounds."

The lorry pulled up to Naval Headquarters as it was getting light at 0600.

Then two armed Marines came up to Patience and said, "You can't park here!"

Homer got out on the left side of the lorry and came around to the driver's side. Both Marines were holding their rifles at a trail with the butt plates on the pavement, and executed a crisp rifle salute to Homer.

Homer said, "Here is my identification, we are carrying classified material that needs to be secured off the street."

At this time, all four army Sergeants got out of the back of the lorry with their Thompson sub machine guns at sling arms.

The older Marine Sergeant said, "Looks like the Navy needed a little Army security help. Why don't you pull the truck through the gate and I'll get an officer down here."

Patience was impressed that they weren't hassled. She guessed the Navy chap with three stripes on his sleeve must be important.

The night duty officer, a Lieutenant Commander, came down and asked politely "What is all this about?"

Homer replied, "We are here to see Vice Admiral O'Brien, and this is highly classified."

Homer and the duty officer went up to the Admiral's Aide's office and reported to Captain March Miller, the Admiral's aide. Homer said to himself, 'I must be diplomatic.

He explained to Captain Miller that he had a letter from Admiral Hickox, and one from General MacArthur, that he was ordered to deliver personally to Admiral O'Brien.

"Sir, we also have top secret material on the truck inside your compound under Army guard that I am sure Admiral O'Brien will read you in on."

"Commander, he is returning from a meeting with Mr. Churchill and General Eisenhower and should be here any minute. Can we get you some coffee?"

"Thank you, Sir. We have just arrived from Sidney, and the coffee on the plane was three days old."

When the Admiral arrived, Homer reported to him and Captain Miller asked if he should leave.

"No March, please stay. When I was coming in, I saw four Army sergeants with tommy guns and a Navy Lieutenant with a 45 automatic guarding a truck. What is this all about?"

Homer said "Sir, I was ordered to deliver this letter from Admiral Hickox directly to you, and it will explain why we are here."

The Admiral sat at his desk, put his reading glasses on, and used a Fairburn knife to open the well-sealed letter.

After about five minutes of silence, the Admiral said, "March, would you get the Navy Lieutenant out at the truck to bring the ships log up here. Also, would you have them bring me a cup of coffee and a refill for the Commander? While they are gone, Commander Harris, I must say that I have never received a letter from a flag officer that I highly respect like this one. Admiral Hickox says you are the greatest American Naval Hero since John Paul Jones! That is some statement!"

"Sir, I had an awful lot of help from some very brave American soldiers, and a young man named Moses Goldberg who is bringing the Log to your office."

When Moses brought the log in, he reported to Admiral O'Brien. "The Commander has told me a little about your background, Lieutenant Goldberg. I must admit I have never met an officer that served in the German Navy and the American Navy during the same war. This should be interesting."

Admiral O'Brien went through the Log page by page and exclaimed, "I'll be damned!"

When he got to the gunfire stopping the Japanese torpedo, he said, "Why didn't we think of this?" Then he said, "Every merchant ship should have some depth charges to scare the U-Boats off. That was a brilliant idea to make up some."

When he got to the Japanese I-Boat surfacing he said, "It took some guts to turn into the sub to scare him off. Commander Harris, you did exactly what I would do by taking out the radios before they could call for help and training the Army tankers where to place their fire. March, I want to see that the Navy recognizes those Army troops and especially the boarding party that," there was a long pause, "My GOD! You captured the Jap naval codes, cyphers, maps, and recognitions."

"Yes Sir. Admiral Hickox has sent the Japanese intelligence to Pearl on the SS Silverfish."

Then the Admiral said, "I only wish we had that same intelligence information from the Germans."

Homer couldn't resist saying, "Just turn the page, Sir."

The next page of the log explained how an American Liberty ship captured all of the secret German naval codes, cyphers, maps with current minefields, recognition signals and two models of the Enigma code machines. The log also described how the Army boarding parties freed allied prisoners, plus an American citizen radio operator in the Krieg's Marine. Then planted charges in the *Leopard*'s torpedo storage hold that caused the German raider to sink.

Admiral O'Brien wiped his glasses and exclaimed "Gentlemen, this was a more important victory than sinking the Bismarck or any other engagement that I can think of! With this information, we can save thousands of lives and get our supplies where they need to go without the terrible losses that we have had to bear. I am amazed and proud of you, and all of the Navy, Army and Merchant Marine personnel. Lieutenant Goldberg, after I finish reading this log, I want to hear the details about your experience in the German Navy."

There was another five-minute pause. Homer knew that the Admiral was reading about the *Earl Horne* sinking four German U-Boats.

Admiral O'Brien stood up from behind his desk, cleared his voice, and said, "During my 33 years in the Navy I have never had a feeling of emotion like this! Sinking five enemy submarines, the raider, and capturing one of their new submarine oil tankers puts me at a loss for words. What is even more incredible is that you did it without casualties!"

The Admiral asked his aide to contact the Prime Minister for an appointment. Captain Miller came back in the Admirals office and said, "Mr. Churchill will see you as soon as you can get to Number 10 Downing Street."

The Admiral then said, "March, I would like for you to cut orders assigning 0-4 Lieutenant Commander Goldberg as liaison officer to Bletchley Park. You will need to take the intelligence material with you and have them make copies so we can send duplicates to Admiral King. You can also make certain that the right people know how important he is to the war effort and get him settled in over there. Then bring the Army Sergeants back here. When we have finished with Mr. Churchill, we will go to see General Eisenhower. I think we will want to transfer those tank commanders into the Navy. Also, cut orders promoting Commander Harris to 0-6 Captain."

Homer and 3-star Admiral O'Brien got in the back of his 1939 Grey Buick staff car for the short ride across town.

Admiral O'Brien introduced Homer and then told the Prime Minister "Sir, we have a report for you detailing what happened on the American Liberty ship bringing twenty Sherman tanks to General MacArthur in Australia."

Churchill offered the Admiral and Homer a cigar before they began the briefing.

Homer said, "Thank you Sir, but I don't smoke."

"Admiral, you have a smart young man here. This is a nasty habit, a nasty habit."

During the briefing, Churchill asked many questions that Homer answered.

When they finished, the Prime Minister said "As a former naval person, I am overwhelmed with pride. Captain Harris, you have delivered to us the keys to victory! It will be my honor to award the ORDER OF THE BRITISH EMPIRE decoration to you."

At this point, Churchill touched his intercom and asked an aide to bring in an OBE for presentation, and then said, "Put me through on the phone to His Majesty."

After a brief minute, Churchill picked up the phone and said, "Your Highness, as part of my constitutional duty I would like to pass some ultra-high classified information to you and introduce you to an American officer that made it come to pass. When would a meeting be convenient?"

Apparently, King George said right now. Mr. Churchill, Admiral O'Brien and Homer rode to Buckingham Palace in the Prime Minister's Rolls Royce and were ushered immediately to a comfortable library room with heavy leather chairs in a circle facing a Dark brown chair with a high back. King George stood and extended his hand to the Prime Minister and then Admiral O'Brian and Homer.

Churchill began by saying, "Your Highness, this amazingly important, highly classified information has warmed the cockles of my old British heart. I would like for Admiral O'Brien and Captain Harris to begin the briefing, and I must beg your leave and get back to 10 Downing."

When they continued briefing King George, you could see that this was the only good news that he had heard since the British Navy sank the German Battleship Bismarck almost one year ago.

King George was sincere when he stated, "Without American help we could very well have lost Australia by now. Captain Harris, I am awfully glad that you are on our side."

When King George asked Homer about his future plans, he said. "Sir-Your Highness, it is up to the Navy but I have been told I will be going back to the States along with others who have knowledge of this intelligence information so we can't be captured."

"Are you married? If not, I have two lovely daughters, Elizabeth and Margaret, that are about your age who would enjoy meeting you."

Homer replied, "I would enjoy meeting your daughters, however, I am engaged to a wonderful nurse in Annapolis."

The King pushed a button on a side table, and a member of the household staff appeared out of nowhere. The King spoke quietly in the man's ear, then the man left walking backward from the room and returned with a flat leather box with a gold crown pressed into the leather.

King George took the box and asked Homer "Could you stand here by Admiral O'Brien so I may present you with Brittan's highest award for valor The Victoria Cross."

From out of nowhere, a photographer appeared and took one picture of King George and Homer and then the photographer asked the Admiral to stand with the King and Homer for a second picture. After about ten minutes of conversation, the same member of the household staff returned and handed King George a small jewelry box.

The King then said, "Captain Harris, since you are going to be married to this fine girl that you have told me about, my family would like for you to have an engagement ring as a token of our deep appreciation for everything that you have done."

When King George opened the box, Homer and Admiral O'Brien saw a large yellow diamond. "This stone was given to my mother by Sir Cecil Rhodes, the founder of our Rhodesian Colony. We want you to have something to remember our family and England. Perhaps when this war is over, you will come back to the United Kingdom with your wife and stay with us."

"Thank you, Your Highness. You are very kind to offer this beautiful ring for Caroline but I don't know if I am allowed to accept such a fine gift."

Admiral O'Brien said, "Homer, if this is property of the Crown you will have to turn it over to our government but if it is private property, I see no reason why you can't accept this extraordinary gift."

King George said, "It most certainly is family property and we want you to have this token of our appreciation. If however, as some engagements do not culminate in marriage, we would ask you to return the ring to our Embassy and they will send it back here."

Homer put the ring in his pocket and thanked King George again.

King George said, "It is I that owe thanks to you and the Americans who have done so much for us."

Homer and Admiral O'Brien then paid a brief visit with General Eisenhower. It was agreed that the four Army Sergeants could be transferred to the Navy if they were willing. General Eisenhower felt that they should have a choice. Admiral O'Brien explained that they had valuable experience stopping torpedoes.

When they returned to Navy Headquarters, Admiral O'Brien suggested, "Would you like for me to keep the ring in my safe until you are ready to leave?"

Homer replied, "Thank you, Sir. I was wondering what I should do with it."

The Admiral said, "It will take a few days to prepare all of the intelligence information for transport with you. In the meantime, I am going to prepare a letter for you to hand carry to Admiral Ernest King, suggesting that you set up an R&D facility to prefect torpedo interception and any other bright ideas that you come up with. I will ask Captain Miller to help with the transfer papers for your Army personnel. We have a large house near Bletchley Park where we can quarter you and your Sergeants until it is time to catch one of the WASP flights home. Lieutenant Commander Goldberg is quartered there. This will give you time to discuss the transfer with your Sergeants. I would like for you and Captain Miller to decide on an appropriate Navy rank. You could also spend some time with Commander Goldberg and see a little bit of England. There are some excellent tailors on Bond Street where you both can get correct uniforms. If you need a pay advance, Captain Miller can take care of that."

"Sir, thank you!" Homer shook hands, saluted, did an about face, and went to Captain Miller's office.

Homer knocked on the door even though it was open, and Captain Miller looked up and said, "Come in Homer."

"Sir, Admiral O'Brien suggested—"

"Woah, Homer, you don't call me Sir. Remember, we are both Navy Captains. Granted, I have a lot more time in grade than you do, but when we are not in a formal setting just call me March."

"Yes March, it will take some adjustment for me. Admiral O'Brien would like for us to decide on a proper rank to offer my E-6 Staff Sergeants."

"What do you think, since you know them pretty well, Homer?"

"Well, I have heard many of the Army personnel say disparaging things about the enlisted Navy uniforms. You know, calling sailors bell hops and stuff like that."

Miller laughed and said, "The doggies get called much worse by our sailors."

"Seriously March, to get them to transfer, I think Lieutenant JG, equal to First Lieutenant in the Army, would be more acceptable considering their years of service and combat experience. Another consideration is our Navy Senior Chiefs that they would be working alongside. It took those Chiefs many years to earn their rank, and they are already used to nursing junior officers. Also, the khaki uniforms would be more to their liking."

"That makes sense, Homer. Why don't you stay here tonight with your sergeants and have a good meal at our mess then give them the option of a transfer. If they prefer to stay in the Army, we can release them to Army Headquarters for assignment in the morning."

While they were having dinner, a Navy Commander came into the mess and said, "Give me your attention!"

When the room became silent, he said, "Gentlemen, we have just received word that Colonel Jimmy Doolittle with a flight of Army bombers has just bombed Tokyo!"

The mess went wild. The questions started. How did we do it? Was the Navy involved?

The Commander said, "That is all I have for now, but we should be getting details. 18 April will go down in history!"

When the mess cleared, Homer said, over a second cup of coffee, "Sergeant House and Sergeant Powell, Sergeant Holbrook, Sergeant Tate, I know you are tired so I will make this short. Admiral O'Brien and General Eisenhower have authorized your voluntary transfer to the Navy as 0-2 Lieutenants. I have been told that we will be going back to the states to set up R & D torpedo interception testing. I would like for you to accept this commission, but it is definitely voluntary. If you would rather stay with the Army, you will be assigned to Army Headquarters for further assignment. Take a moment and let me know what you want to do."

Sergeant Billy Powell said, "Sir, I want to stay here in the Army."

Hank Holbrook said, "Does Patience Periwinkle have anything to do with this important decision, Billy?"

"It might have a little, but I really like tanks. Also, that time when we all got seasick on the *Earl Horne*, I told myself the Navy wasn't for me."

Hank said, "If Billy stays, we have been together too long to go our separate ways, so I want to stay in the Army."

Kevin Tate said, "Right now the devil you know is better than the devil you don't know, so I want to stay in the Army."

Homer looked at Sergeant House and said, "What about you Frank?"

"Sir, I have a wife and kids in Tombstone, Arizona, and depending on where this R&D facility is set up we could be together, and that would mean a lot to me. So count me in."

"Billy, Hank, and Kevin, I will prepare a report for your 201 file, letting the Army know about your courage, leadership ability, and your fitness for promotion. I expect when we get more tanks over here, they will make you tank platoon leaders. I wish you were going back to the states with me but understand how you feel. Get a good night's rest and tomorrow morning we will get transfer orders cut for you. Frank, you will need to be sworn into the Navy in the morning. I hope they let me have the honor. After that Frank, you, Moses and I will go uniform shopping at a tailor that has been recommended."

"Sir, is it true that they still make officers buy their uniforms?"

"I'm afraid so Frank, but we can get an advance pay from Captain Miller. Just think of it this way, you are getting a big fat pay raise so you will come out much better financially."

April 19, 1942 Naval Headquarters

After breakfast, Homer handed his sergeants their orders, shook hands, and wished them the best. Then Homer performed the oath with Lieutenant Frank House in Captain Miller's office. Their picture was taken by a Navy photographer, who said they would see that Lieutenant House would eventually get a print. Captain Miller handed Lieutenant House his new ID, then gave Homer the equivalent of $500 in British Pounds to purchase uniforms, and the same amount to Lieutenant House.

He said, "Go to the motor pool and give the driver this address of the tailor shop that I have used. You will be leaving in two days, so let him know your uniforms must be ready or he won't get paid. Then head out to Bletchley Park. You can send the driver back here, because they have a motor pool at Bletchley."

Moses was glad to see Homer and offered congratulations to Lieutenant House. Then they went to the mansion that the Navy had taken over for officer quarters.

Lieutenant House looked at their temporary quarters and said, "That saying, 'rank has its privilege,' sure is true here."

Moses arranged for a British lady Corporal to take them by car to her favorite fish and chips place in North Hampton.

The driver arrived in a Morris Oxford four door and asked, "Are you yanks looking for the best fish and chips? My name is Corporal Donna Lewis and I'm from North Hampton, so I should know the best place in my hometown." Donna was in her late thirties and wore a baggy uniform. She liked to talk and asked where Homer, Frank and Moses were from.

When the answers came back—Sparta, New Jersey, Tombstone Arizona, Dusseldorf, Germany—Donna exclaimed, "Dusseldorf! We have been bombing the blazes out of that place. What brings you here dearie?"

Moses said, "I should have added Chicago, because I'm a naturalized U.S. citizen."

"Well that's better, or I would have put you out on the road here and now!"

Homer said, "Donna, would you be our guest for dinner, and we can hear about you and your family?"

"That's very American of you. British officers would never take a Corporal to dinner."

The fish and chips were served in wrapped newspaper and pewter mugs of warm English ale or hot tea were automatically served. The Bucks Head Inn had a restaurant attached to a small hotel. The place was full of Royal Air Force enlisted personnel having a good time, singing around a piano and consuming multiple pints of ale or beer. Donna explained that her husband was a gunner on a Halifax bomber, and this was his favorite pub.

"My husband, John Lewis, won't be here tonight because he is on a mission, but I'd like for you to meet him. I have a 13-year-old son, John Junior, who better be home studying. I have always wanted to visit America, to see what we lost."

Moses asked, "What do you mean by lost?"

"I mean when General Cornwallis surrendered, we lost America. I'm glad you aren't holding that other little problem called the War of 1812 against us now. We would be in a pickle fix if you weren't helping us." Frank House said, "I used to be a sergeant, so I can assure you Donna we are on your side for good!"

Donna dropped her new friends off at the Mansion.

"Hope I get to take you boys somewhere again."

They called in unison, "Thanks Donna."

April 20, 1942

A message was delivered to Homer during breakfast at the mansion that said, 'Return HQ. ASAP with House you are going early/ Miller.'

Homer said, "Finish your bangers and eggs Frank, we need to call the motor pool and ask for a larger car."

After they checked out of the mansion, Homer said, "I'll be, it's Donna, and she is in a Rover Six Saloon."

"Well how nice, it is my American friends! Where are we going, Captain?"

"To Naval Headquarters and then to RAF Polebrook, but I'm not sure if you will take us there or if they have other transportation planned."

"Polebrook, that is a long way from London, possibly 140 miles north. I won't have enough petrol unless we fill up at your Navy motor pool."

While Donna was filling the Rover with petrol, Homer and Lieutenant House went in to see if Captain Miller had anything else for them, and say goodbye.

Miller said, "Everything is set up for you at RAF Polebrook. You will be on a B-17 B with about fifteen WASPS, Women Auxiliary Service Pilots, who deliver the aircraft from the Boeing plant to England. They are holding the departure for you so I will wish you both the best."

Homer said, "Please thank Admiral O'Brien for everything that he has done for us."

When they got back to the Rover, Donna said, "We're ready to go."

After a six hour drive through what Donna called the midlands, with more small towns and villages than you could count, they arrived at RAF Polebrook. After showing their orders and ID to the British Home Guard soldiers at the main gate, they went to operations and said good bye to Donna.

She said, "Please come back and look us up after this war is over," and gave Homer and Frank a note with their address and phone number.

Homer left Lieutenant House with his Thompson and the classified packages and went into operations.

They were met by an Army Master Sergeant who said, "Sir, I'm glad you finally made it. These pilots want to get out of here and they are driving me nuts."

They loaded the classified material in a Dodge pickup truck, and were driven down the flight line to an older model B-17 that did not have any machine guns.

They were greeted by the senior pilot Madelyn "Maddy" Tyson, who said, "Glad you are here. Lets' get you loaded. We've got 2400 miles to RCAF Gander Newfoundland. There were fifteen pilots or flight engineers already on the plane, all women. Homer and Frank were handed bulky insulated flight suits and parachutes. They were helped getting their suits on by a cute red head with an Emelia Earhart haircut.

"My Name is Mia Ellis from Huntsville, Alabama. This is my co-pilot, Terry Mullin. This is our eighth trip. Where are you sailors from?"

Frank answered first, "I'm from Tombstone, Arizona.

Homer answered, "Lake Mohawk, New Jersey."

Terry said, "where is that in relation to New York City?"

"It is fifty miles northwest in the first mountain range at the corner of Pennsylvania and New York State."

Terry pointed to a large pile of arctic sleeping bags up near the cockpit.

"You should go get a couple of them now, because it will get cold as a blue pig when we get up to cruising altitude and there is no heat back here. These suits can be plugged in to heat them up, but they don't help as much as getting in the sleeping bag. You can use the parachute pack for a pillow. It will take about ten hours to make Gander. We will refuel and then we will get off at New York LaGuardia Airport and go commercial back to the Boeing plant. Then we'll do it all over again."

Mia Ellis piped up with a deep southern accent, "Maddy Tyson is going to take you to Washington, because you have classified stuff. I guess that is why you have those sub machine guns."

About five hours into the expected 10-hour trip, Terry brought hot coffee with Spam and cheese sandwiches back to Homer and Frank.

She said, "I'm so tired of spam, but it's not so bad fried for breakfast. Have you been in London for long?"

Homer answered, "Only a few days. This is my first ride on a B-17 however Frank and I have almost fifteen thousand miles in a Liberator."

Terry said, "I'd like to fly one. I hear they are not as forgiving as the B-17, but faster."

April 21, 1942, Gander, Newfoundland

The WASP B-17 landed at 0115 in cold rain.

Terry said, "I hope it doesn't turn to ice or we will get stuck here. We rotate in the cockpit on long flights and I have to fly this thing to New York. It is only 1,100 miles so we should be there in about five hours. Maddy will take over again for your hop to DC."

They were wheels up at 0200 and climbed to eight thousand feet. The engines sounded to Homer that they were running at a higher RPM than before.

"I think Terry is in a hurry and put the pedal to the metal."

Frank said, "It will be nice to step on U.S. soil or concrete!"

When they got to LaGuardia, the WASP pilots got off at 0630.

181

Homer remarked to Frank, "These WASP pilots are an outstanding asset for our country and some of them look pretty sharp, particularly Terry."

"Remember Sir, you are engaged, and I'm happily married."

Since they had more than enough fuel to make the short 214-mile hop to Washington National Maddy, didn't take on any fuel and left as soon as she could get tower clearance. At 0900, Homer and Frank got the classified packages off the B-17, thanked Madelyn Tyson for the ride, and flagged down an Army truck.

Since they were carrying Thompson sub machine guns, the driver was happy to take them wherever they wanted to go.

Chapter 29
The White House

April 21, 1942, 1100 Hours

U.S. Navy Headquarters Washington DC presented the same problem with Marine guards. Four heavily armed Marines were at a gate that led to a secure area. Captain Harris showed his ID, and told the Master Sergeant in charge of the detail that they had classified material that needed to get off the street.

"We don't let no large trucks in, unless they are thoroughly searched. We have to go through all those boxes."

"Sergeant, this material is for eyes only of CNO Admiral Ernest King, so contact his office and ask for his aide and I will talk to him."

When Captain Frank Malle and a Navy Chief came to the gate, Homer identified himself and the material was taken through the gate. Then the Army driver was released with a note signed by Homer, explaining where he had been.

Captain Malle was the Junior Aide to 4-star Admiral Ernest King. Homer explained that he had a letter from Vice Admiral O'Brien that he was ordered to hand deliver to Admiral King. He asked if the Chief could remain with Lieutenant House until the Admiral decides where he wants this material to go.

Captain Malle said, "The Admiral is here, so I will see if he will take a minute to see you."

Homer waited outside the office of the Chief of Naval Operations, holding the log of the SS *Earl Horne* and the letter, until Captain Malle returned and said, "No more than five minutes."

Homer said to himself, 'I hope I don't screw this up. I can't believe I'm about to see the top officer in the United States Navy. Oh well, I made it through Mr. Churchill and the King of England, so here goes.'

Homer entered the office with Captain Malle and reported to Admiral King. "Sir, here is a letter from Admiral O'Brien that will explain why I am here."

The Admiral said, "Have a seat while I read this."

After a couple of minutes, Admiral King said to his Aide, "Frank, will you have this highly classified material brought to my office while I read this ship's log; then come back in. Also, cancel the staff meeting. We will re-schedule."

Admiral King took the log from Homer and went through it carefully, page by page. When Captain Malle returned Admiral King said, "Frank, get Admiral DeVito and ask him to come here ASAP."

Rear Admiral (upper level 2-star) Stephen DeVito, the CNO's senior Aide, arrived and Admiral King handled the introductions then said, "Have a seat, Steve. You are about to hear one of the best things that has happened for us since the Pearl Harbor disaster. This very young Navy Captain took over command of a Liberty ship transporting tanks to MacArthur in Australia. He trained the Army tankers in a technique that he did a research paper on at the Academy to use large caliber gun fire to intercept torpedoes and dammed if it didn't work. They blew up a Jap torpedo before it could strike their hull. Then the I-Boat captain decided to surface and sink the Liberty ship with his deck gun. Captain Harris turned into the sub and when it surfaced, they fired several hundred main gun tank rounds knocking out the radio antennae and filling the I-Boat with holes above the water line. Then an Army boarding party secured all of the JN-25 Naval codes, cyphers, maps covering all mine fields in the Pacific and a lot more. Then they planted satchel charges in the sub's deck gun ammo storage, cracked the hull wide open and sent it to the bottom."

Admiral DeVito exclaimed, "Thank God, that is the edge we need. We can ambush them and cut them down to size!"

Homer added, "Sir, Admiral Hickox sent copies of everything to Pearl on the Silverfish. It should be arriving in a few days."

Admiral King continued, "Steve, you can read details in the log of the SS *Earl Horne* about the next victory. They were attacked by that German commerce raider, the *Leopard*, and they disabled it with tank fire. Then the Army boarding parties captured all of the German codes, cyphers, charts, radio equipment and maps for every Nazi mine field. They also rescued British personnel being held prisoner on the *Leopard* and then set charges sinking the raider. They also rescued a Jewish American who was trying to get his parents out of Germany when Hitler declared war on us. His name is Moses Goldberg, a radio expert who joined the Krieg's Marine and served on the *Leopard* as a radio operator with fake documents to avoid a Nazi firing squad. Captain Harris verified Goldberg with the FBI and then set up an elaborate scheme to bring four German U-Boats in for replenishment and sunk all four. Admiral O'Brien commissioned Goldberg as a Lieutenant Commander and he is serving at Bletchley Park breaking codes. If this wasn't enough, three days out from Sidney, they captured one of the new Nazi submarine oil tankers along with their full crew. Captain Harris made the decision to place an American crew augmented by several rescued British seamen on the prize and bring it on the surface behind the *Earl Horne* into Sidney. The Australians pumped off enough oil to supply our Navy and theirs for a month. The amazing thing is that they did this with no casualties during any of the engagements."

Admiral DeVito and Captain Malle both congratulated Homer who said, "I could not have pulled this off without great help from the Army tankers and Moses Goldberg."

Admiral King said, "Admiral O'Brien, in his letter to me, suggested establishment of a Naval O&D (Offensive & Defensive) Testing Laboratory for Captain Harris to run. Do you feel up to that type of assignment Captain Harris?"

"Yes Sir. I would need to select a site where we would have naval support, probably Norfolk or Jacksonville. I will prepare a detailed table of organization report and with your approval assemble a small staff."

Admiral King stood up from his desk and shook hands with Homer then said, "It gives me great pride to have a fellow Naval Academy officer who graduated 41 years after me join the ranks of those that will never be forgotten. Frank, will you bring me a Navy Cross so I may have the honor of awarding it to him? Then, Captain Harris, we will go see the President."

At 1600 Homer and Admiral King entered the oval office. Admiral King and Homer saluted the President.

President Roosevelt said, "It is always good to see you Ernest. I hope you and this young officer have something good for me."

"Mr. President, this young Captain is Homer Harris, a recent Naval Academy graduate who assumed command of a Liberty ship carrying twenty Sherman tanks to General MacArthur in Australia. We have a classified copy of the log of the *Earl Horne* so you will be able to read the many details, but the bottom line is Captain Harris has achieved amazing American Naval victories that will place him in the company of John Paul Jones."

The President said, "Please have a seat. I want to hear all about this."

Mrs. Roosevelt entered the office and said, "I hope I am not interrupting. How nice to see you, Ernest."

The President said, "Please join us, Eleanor. This young Captain is Homer Harris, and he has something important that we should know."

Admiral King began by explaining, "Captain Harris had showed the Army tankers how to stop an inbound torpedo saving their Liberty ship. He then attacked the Japanese sub that fired on them, filling it full of holes. Then, he sent an Army boarding party over to the sub and captured all of the intelligence. This highly classified information will give us a major advantage in the Pacific.

Later, our Liberty ship was engaged by the dangerously successful German raider, the *Leopard*. Using deception, he brought the raider broadside and opened fire. After hundreds of tank rounds, the raider was turned into a shattered wreck. Two army boarding parties recovered all of the German codes and cyphers and their Enigma code machine. They freed a number of British prisoners and an American. When our personnel were off the raider, Master Sergeant Frank House placed charges and barely got off the raider before all of the torpedoes that were intended to supply a four U-Boat Pacific wolf pack blew the raider apart. A rescued American turned out to be a naturalized Jewish citizen from Chicago that was a radio company co-owner. He went to Dusseldorf to try to help his family out of Germany when Hitler declared war on us. He joined the German Navy as a radioman using fake papers and was assigned to the raider. Captain Harris used the FBI to verify that Moses Goldberg was legitimate. Then, Moses and Homer put together a ruse that allowed them to bring all four U-Boats to our ship for replenishment and sink them. Then they captured a new Nazi submarine oil tanker before reaching Sidney. The remarkable thing is that they did all this with no casualties."

President Roosevelt said, "Let's see, that would be five enemy submarines sunk and one captured plus the raider. The most important thing, however, is capturing both the Japanese and German Naval codes, not to mention developing a way to stop torpedoes."

"Mr. President, with your approval I would like to set up a R&D Lab for Captain Harris to perfect stopping torpedoes."

"That is a fine idea Ernest, but I would like to ensure that higher ups cannot manage away this young officer's creativity so I propose that we promote him to Rear Admiral lower level."

"Mr. President, that is a very good idea. I will take care of the details."

Mrs. Roosevelt asked Admiral King, "Could you both stay for dinner?"

"Thank you, but I have a staff meeting that is holding for my return, however I could leave Captain Harris."

The President said, "I would like that."

Mrs. Roosevelt smiled and said, "Homer, you could even stay over and join us for breakfast."

At this point Homer's jaw dropped. He couldn't believe that he was going to be an Admiral, have dinner and breakfast with the Roosevelts and get to set up a R&D facility.

Admiral King said, "That would be fine, I will have his B-4 bag with his uniforms brought to our tailor unit that can make the uniform changes and have them delivered by morning. Homer, you can contact my aide Admiral DeVito and get back together with him next week for assignment."

Mrs. Roosevelt and the President said goodbye to Admiral King.

Then the President said, "He is the finest!"

Mrs. Roosevelt told Homer that a staff person would show him to the Lincoln bedroom, where he could freshen up for a casual dinner at six o'clock.

At dinner, the President said "Homer, I want to hear the details that were left out this afternoon."

Mrs. Roosevelt addressed Homer as if he was one of her boys and said, "I want to know about you. We are so proud to have you with us."

By the time the President finished his before- dinner libation and Homer had a Coca-Cola, Mrs. Roosevelt learned about the loss of his parents and the legal problems with his uncle.

When she asked, "Are there any young ladies in your life," Homer first talked about Penny and her dad, Douglas Ponder.

The President commented, "I've met Doug Ponder, who I believe is now President of Coca-Cola. As a Republican, he is a pretty good fellow."

Mrs. Roosevelt asked, "Are you serious about Miss. Ponder?"

"Yes ma'am, but I am also serious about a nurse who I began to spend time with during my Plebe year at the Academy. She has said she wanted to marry me. Of course, Midshipmen can't be married, so after I was commissioned and assigned to a Liberty ship, I didn't want Caroline to be a widow so things are on hold. When King George asked me about marriage plans, I told him about Caroline, and he gave me this engagement ring."

Homer reached into his pocket and showed the ring to the President and Mrs. Roosevelt.

The President reacted with surprise. "That is a huge canary diamond."

Mrs. Roosevelt said, "Oh my goodness!"

Homer explained that the ring was given to Queen Victoria by Sir Cecil Rhodes. "The King said he wanted to thank me for what we had done for England and his family. He assured Admiral O'Brien and me that the ring was family property."

The President said, "I'm no diamond expert, but a good friend of mine is." He picked up the phone and asked the White House operator, "Please put a call in to Harry Winston in New York."

"Hello?"

"Is this Mr. Harry Winston?"

"Yes, it is."

"Please hold for the President."

"Harry, this is Franklin. I have a young naval officer spending the night with us who was given a remarkably large yellow diamond by King George for an engagement ring. He was told that it is the Rhodesian Sun diamond that was given to his mother by Sir Cecil Rhodes. Do you know anything about it?"

"Do I know anything about it! That is the most perfect canary diamond that has ever been discovered. It is worth at least ten million or more at auction. That girl can't wear it in public without at least two armed bodyguards. What did he do to warrant such a gift?"

"Harry, I wish I could tell you, but it is classified. I can say that it may just be the thing to save England."

"Franklin, I am going to send an appropriate engagement ring down by currier. You should have it in the morning."

"Harry just put it on my account."

"I'll do none of the sort. If this young man has done something this significant, the ring is on the house."

"That is very kind of you. His name is Homer Harris and we are about to make him the youngest Admiral in the United States Navy. I am sure he will be in touch to thank you. You may get to meet him. Eleanor has offered to host the wedding at the White House."

"Just let me know, I would really like to meet him. Good evening, Franklin."

"Thanks, Harry."

The President turned to Homer and offered to keep the ring in his safe.

April 22, 1942, The White House

In the morning, Homer joined the President, Mrs. Roosevelt, and Senior Advisor Harry Hopkins for breakfast. The three-carat diamond solitaire engagement ring from Harry Winston had been delivered.

The President explained to Harry Hopkins, "This young officer will be setting up an offensive and defensive R&D laboratory to perfect stopping enemy torpedoes and several other projects. He may need your help with red tape, funding, and getting a priority staff. I don't want anyone to get in his way. Harry, we can't release this because it is classified, but for your ears only, as Captain of a Liberty ship transporting tanks to Australia, he sank five enemy subs and the German raider the *Leopard*. He also captured a new German submarine oil tanker. General MacArthur has recommended the Medal of Honor and I would like to see that move quickly through congressional approval."

After breakfast, Homer asked if it would be possible for him to go to Annapolis.

Mrs. Roosevelt said, "Certainly Homer. We will send you down in a White House car after you check in at Naval Headquarters with Admiral DeVito."

Following completion of a pile of paperwork, Homer went to the tailor shop with Captain Malle and tried on his new jacket, complete with the appropriate ribbons.

Captain Malle said, "The Navy Cross, Silver Star, and Bronze Star were no problem. We had to get help from the British Embassy for the OBE and the Victoria Cross. So far, we have not located the Order of Australia, but their Embassy said they will get back to us. Admiral King wants you to have your picture taken in uniform for a press release as our youngest Admiral. We can go over to the photographer after lunch. They are closed between 1200 and 1300. Your orders are here for a 7-day liberty however if you begin your search for an R&D location, we will extend to whatever you need."

"I really appreciate your help, Captain Malle."

"It would be advisable to check in at least once a day at our office. You will need to let us know who you would like for an Aide or we can just assign one."

"I would like Lieutenant Frank House. He is the one that fired the shot that stopped the Jap torpedo. He went to Arizona to see his family and I have his phone number. He has already said he would like to stay with the R&D project. I just need to figure out a good place to set up shop."

Captain Malle suggested three locations: Groton, Connecticut, Norfolk, Virginia, and Jacksonville, Florida.

"I would check them all out."

Chapter 30
Return to Annapolis

The White House limo picked up Homer with his B-4 bag at Naval Headquarters for the 40-mile ride to Annapolis. There was a 1-star flag on the left front fender of a black 1941 Cadillac. When they arrived at the heavily guarded entrance to the Academy, the shore patrol carefully checked Homer's ID and asked if they needed directions.

"No, we are going to Captain Dugas' quarters and I know my way." Homer returned a sharp solute.

When they reached the address, there was nobody home, so Homer told the driver "I'll just wait on the porch. They should be home soon. You can head back to DC."

Homer sat on the porch swing that he had been on many times and thought about what he was going to say to Caroline. The cherry blossoms were out but it was beginning to get a little chilly when a Packard convertible pulled up in front of the quarters.

Homer saw a man and a woman that looked like Caroline locked in a long kiss. Then some conversation, and another kiss before the passenger door opened and Caroline headed to the front door with her key out. Homer just sat in the swing, stunned.

As she was turning the key, Caroline saw Homer. She went across the porch and said, "Why didn't you call?"

Homer paused and then said, "I'm glad that I didn't call. What is going on Caroline?"

She said, "Come inside. I didn't think you were ever coming back, and Doctor Barnes took me to dinner, and it just went on from there. He is really a nice guy."

"Has he tried to get in your pants?"

"Yes, but not successfully. I am so embarrassed."

Then Caroline started to cry. Homer reached in his pocket and gave her a handkerchief.

"Daddy will be home soon and I'm sure he will be glad to see you."

Homer thought, 'I really doubt that.'

Caroline said "Please help me fix dinner. This is fried spam and eggs night if you don't mind. I want to hear about where you have been. Please stay."

Homer took off his coat and jacket and placed them on a straight chair in the living room, then went back to help Caroline.

"After we left Jacksonville, Florida, the Captain passed away from natural causes so as the first mate, I took command and made it to Australia. Then from there to London where I got to meet Mr. Churchill and King George. Then back to the states and I spent last night at the White House. I've been promoted several times. I was really looking forward to seeing you, but right now the spark just isn't there. I'll always be your friend, and I hope things work out with the Doctor."

Caroline heard the front door and said, "Daddy is home. Daddy, we're back in the kitchen."

Captain Dugas came in the kitchen, expecting to see Dr. Barnes, who he fully approved of, and instead saw Homer. "Oh, you are back I see."

"Yes, Caroline wanted me to stay for spam and eggs, but I really should go."

"What brings you back to the Academy?"

"I have a week liberty and wanted to see your daughter."

Caroline said, "Please stay Homer, I have fixed a plate for all three of us. Daddy, Homer has been to Australia and London where he saw Mr. Churchill and the King. Then he spent last night at the White House."

Captain Dugas said, "That is interesting."

When he went back to the living room closet to hang up his coat, Captain Dugas spotted Homer's uniform jacket hanging on the straight chair, then went upstairs to a phone by his bed and called the Shore Patrol to advise them that there is a class of 1942 Ensign wearing the uniform impersonating an Admiral. "Come to my quarters and pick him up."

Caroline served scrambled eggs, fried spam, toast, and coffee. Before they were finished, two shore patrol personnel arrived and took Homer to the Brig. Homer showed the SP's his ID, but they assumed it was forged.

After they left, Captain Dugas said "I have just done a huge favor for you young lady. That guy was never any good from the beginning. Did you see his uniform? He had the audacity to come in my quarters and impersonate an Admiral."

"Daddy, Homer has never told me a lie."

"Don't be naïve, Caroline. He just graduated last February, and you think he is really an Admiral? Wake up!"

Caroline piled the dishes in the sink, went to her room, and shut the door.

She said to herself, 'I know he isn't lying. Daddy shouldn't have had him arrested. He probably saw me kiss Doctor Barnes and that killed it after all of these years. I wish today had never happened. I'll never get him back now.'

Caroline laid down on her bed in her nurse uniform, pulled a blanket up to her chin and fell asleep. Her pillow was wet with tears.

April 23, 1942, Naval Academy Brig

Homer was treated with suspicion that he was a wacko by the Chief Petty Officer during processing into the completely empty Naval Academy brig. After emptying his pockets, he was led to a clean cell with fresh sheets and a grey Navy blanket. Homer requested and was given a receipt for the diamond ring. He actually got a decent nights' rest and was served a tray of mush and coffee for breakfast.

After breakfast he asked the seaman who picked up his tray "Don't I get to make a phone call?" A third-class Petty Officer came and helped Homer with his phone call. Homer realized that he had Mrs. Roosevelt's secretary's card with her phone number, so he called the White House.

When he told the secretary that they had locked him up in the brig, she said, "Hold please for Mrs. Roosevelt."

Mrs. Roosevelt was upset that they had locked Homer in the brig for no reason other than they didn't believe he was an Admiral.

She handed the phone to the President who asked, "What happened to your ID, Homer?"

"Mr. President, they thought it was forged and called me a wacko." "You just stay on the line and I will be back to you shortly."

The President went to another phone and told the White House operator to please get the Superintendent at the Naval Academy on the line.

"Admiral Westfield. Mr. President, how may I be of service?"

"I'd like to know what kind of protocol you used for locking up flag officers in your brig for no damn reason?"

"Sir, I'm not aware of any such thing."

"Then you don't know what the hell is going on under your nose! You happen to have the greatest American naval hero since John Paul Jones disgracefully placed behind bars, Admiral. I am going to give you ten minutes to correct this incompetence, or you can pack your bags because there will be a new Superintendent by this afternoon."

"Yes Mr. President, right away, Sir! Anything else, Sir?"

"No! Just do your job!"

Mrs. Roosevelt came on the line and said "Homer, I'm sorry for this embarrassing situation. You will be out of there very soon. Please call me back to let us know you are OK."

"Yes ma'am, thank you!"

The next call went from Admiral Westfield to the brig. "Give me the Duty Officer, this is Admiral Westfield."

"Sir, this is CPO Grigsby. What can I do for you Sir?"

"Who requested the shore patrol pick up Admiral Homer Harris and incarcerate him last night?"

"Sir, that was Captain Dugas. He said he was a wacko impersonating an Admiral, Sir."

"Well, he is an Admiral. Make him as comfortable as possible and I will be right there."

The next call went to Captain Dugas quarters. Since it was Saturday morning, he didn't have a class. "Captain Dugas, I have just been chewed out by the President of The United States because of your stupidity. You get to the brig in five minutes or you will be reduced in rank and retired immediately."

"Yes, Sir," Captain Dugas said. He thought, 'I'll bet that former boyfriend of Caroline's has done something really shameful. Impersonating an Admiral!'

When Captain Dugas got to the brig, Admiral Westfield was in the office, and put Homer on the phone with President Roosevelt.

"Mr. President, it was a mistake, and all I got was a good nights' rest. No harm done. Thank you, Sir, for getting me out."

"Give Mrs. Roosevelt a call when you have your plans finalized." "Thank you again, Mr. President."

Admiral Westfield glared at Captain Dugas. "Dugas, you almost got me kicked out of the Navy. You owe Admiral Harris an apology. The President told me he is the greatest American Naval Hero since John Paul Jones."

"I am very sorry Homer; I should have listened to Caroline. I made a terrible mistake and I hope you will forgive me, Sir."

"Captain Dugas, no harm was done. Admiral Westfield has a nice, clean, and quiet brig, and I got a good night's rest. So, I suggest we just forget that this has happened. Admiral Westfield, I appreciate getting a fine education here at the academy. No hard feelings."

"Admiral Harris, can we take you to the club for lunch?"

"Thank you, but I need to get up to Groton. I would appreciate a lift to the train station."

"Let me send you with my driver up to Groton. You can keep him as long as you need him."

"Thank you, Sir. You could do me a favor and call the commander at the Groton Subbase and tell him that I will be looking for a R&D location." "I'll be glad to do that, Admiral."

Chapter 31
Becoming Operational

April 24, 1942, Groton Submarine Base

When Homer arrived at the Groton Subbase, he was escorted to the VIP quarters. Upon check in he was handed a note from Captain George Stone.

'Admiral Peter Gannon would like to invite you for dinner at the Officers Club at 1700. Please have your aide call me to confirm.'

Homer asked the front desk Petty Officer, "Please call Captain Stone for me."

Homer was handed the phone. "Captain Stone, this is Admiral Harris. I don't have an aide assigned to me yet, so I would like to accept Admiral Gannon's invitation and I will be there at 1700."

Homer asked the Petty Officer at the desk to arrange accommodations for his driver then went to his room to freshen up.

Admiral Gannon asked his aide, George Stone to join them for dinner.

Homer began the conversation by thanking Admiral Gannon for the courtesies extended. "I received a call from Admiral Westfield at the Academy saying that the President has you evaluating locations for a R&D facility."

"That is true. There is a classified project that I will be running to intercept torpedoes before they can strike our ships. I have had one successful demonstration with a Japanese long lance torpedo, but that is a long way from a proven system. I plan to also look at Norfolk and Jacksonville as possible locations."

Admiral Gannon said, "George, my aide, will be able to show you everything we have at this base in the morning. We have constant submarine training, so if this involves live testing, Groton seems like a logical choice."

"I've been here before, when I had my third-year summer cruise on the SS *Perch SS176*."

Captain Stone laughed and said, "That old Porpoise-class boat is still leaking and continues separating the Midshipmen that really want to be submariners from the faint at heart."

In the morning Homer and Captain Stone used Admiral Westfield's car and drove all over the streets named after famous submarines. When they returned to Captain Stone's office Homer asked if they could check on any Navy flights to either Norfolk, Atlanta or Jacksonville. There were none.

"Please thank Admiral Gannon for a fine dinner and your assistance. I guess my best option will be to return Admiral Westfield's car and get dropped at Washington National. There are always Navy flights, or I can go commercial."

"Best wishes! Please feel free to call me if I can be of assistance."

"Thank you, Captain Stone."

On the drive to Washington, Homer wrote notes to himself on Groton. It was getting dark when they arrived, so Homer told Admiral Westfield's driver, "Just drop me off at the Willard Hotel, and you can head back to the Academy. Thank you for your help."

In the morning, Homer put on his freshly pressed uniform and called Naval Flight operations.

They had an R4D leaving for Norfolk in one hour, but said, "We will hold the flight for you Admiral."

When Homer arrived in Norfolk, he thought, "I really need an aide to make arrangements so they will take me seriously. I don't even know who the commanding officer is."

That question was solved when Homer saw pictures of the chain of command on the wall in operations. He went to a phone and asked to speak with Admiral Flynn's aide.

"This is Captain Woolbert."

"This is Admiral Homer Harris. Please send a car over to flight operations and take me to your office so I can explain why I am here."

"Certainly Sir, my driver will bring you right over."

Homer explained his project to Captain Woolbert, who said "Let's take a ride. I will be glad to show you the base and we can schedule a meeting with Admiral Flynn at a later time."

Norfolk was very busy and there did not seem to be any area that was not being used for something. Homer had checked with operations before leaving on the tour and learned that there was a Catalina leaving for NAS Atlanta at 1800.

Captain Woolbert said, "Lets' go by the club and get something for you to eat then I will drop you at the airfield."

Homer said, "I really appreciate your assistance and I'll contact you if a follow up visit is needed."

The 4-hour flight on the slow Catalina PBY-4 amphibian was uneventful, and gave Homer time to think about Penny and her dad.

"When I check into Admiral King's office by phone in the morning, I will tell Admiral DeVito that I have visited Groton and Norfolk and, after visiting friends and family in Atlanta, I will check out Jacksonville."

Chapter 32
Penny

Homer took a Navy sedan from NAS Atlanta to the Biltmore Hotel and arrived at 2345. The bellman helped him with his B-4 bag following him to the front desk.

The night manager greeted Homer and said, "Do you have a reservation Sir?"

Homer replied, "No, but I have stayed with you many times."

"Sir, I am sorry to say the house is full."

Homer then asked, "Is there anyone in the Coca-Cola suite?"

The manager replied, "Yes, Mr. Ponder is here."

"Well, please call him and tell him Homer Harris is here, and needs a place to sleep."

"I can't disturb him. He is the President of Coca-Cola and it is almost midnight."

"Trust me, it will be okay, I'm family."

"Mr. Ponder, this is the front desk, and there is a gentleman who says he is family and insisted that I disturb you. His name is Homer Harris. Mr. Ponder said to send you right up."

April 27, 1942, 0005 hours, Biltmore Hotel Atlanta

Doug Ponder greeted Homer at the door of the Coca-Cola suite. They first shook hands, then Doug Ponder gave Homer a hug.

"It is so good to see you. Penny shared the letter that you sent from the Panama Canal, and then you dropped off the face of the earth. What kind of uniform are you wearing? I thought you were in the Merchant Marines."

"Sir, I was, but I was transferred by General MacArthur into the Army as a Major, and then Admiral Hickox talked General MacArthur into releasing me back to the Navy."

"Hold that thought while I order a pot of coffee. Are you hungry?"

"No Sir, I had something to eat in Norfolk."

"So Homer, what are you now? I don't understand Navy rank very well."

"It is hard to believe but I am a 1-star Admiral."

"What are all of these ribbons for?"

"This one is the Navy Cross, then the Silver Star and the Bronze Star. Then Mr. Churchill awarded the Order of the British Empire and King George gave me the Victoria Cross. I don't have the ribbon for the Order of Australia, but they are sending it to their Embassy. President Roosevelt told me that General MacArthur recommended me for the Medal of Honor but it has to be voted on in Congress."

"Homer, I knew from the first day I met you out at the farm that you were special. Now a lot of people have reached the same conclusion. I am so proud of you! In fact, I couldn't be prouder if you were actually my son."

The coffee arrived and Doug Ponder poured a steaming hot cup for Homer and one for himself.

"I know you must be tired. Why don't you get into a robe and PJ's over in the spare bedroom, and by that time the coffee will be cool enough to drink?"

When Homer returned to the living room, Doug Ponder said, "I will understand if you can't tell me what happened since you left the Academy."

"Sir—"

"Please call me Doug."

"Yes, Doug, a great deal is highly classified top secret and everything that we can discuss is classified confidential. I will fill in some of the spaces with this understanding. After leaving Jacksonville on the Liberty Ship SS *Earl Horne* with twenty Sherman tanks and Army crew, the Captain passed away from natural causes and I assumed command. In the Pacific, we stopped a torpedo using a term paper idea that I wrote at the Academy then sank the Jap sub, then the German Raider the *Leopard*, and four U-Boats. Finally, we captured a new Nazi underwater submarine oil tanker. There is a lot more but even this is not being released to the public. I know you will not discuss this with anyone. I have been asked by Admiral King and the President to set up a R&D testing lab to develop offensive and defensive tactics and equipment. I have just looked at Groton, Connecticut and Norfolk as possible locations and then I will go to Jacksonville. I wanted to stop here and see you and Penny and my Aunt Virginia and my cousin Sandy."

"I am so glad that you are here Homer. I have wanted to talk with you about Penny. She finished at Emory and is working as a paralegal with the Spaulding Law firm. She is studying for the Georgia Bar Exam. On a personal note, I can tell she is not really happy. The boyfriend that you met had no ambition and she dumped him. Then there was this young lawyer that tried to sweep her off her feet and actually gave her an engagement ring. He didn't sit well with me, but I stayed out of it. Penny finally saw through him and gave the ring back to him. Penny and I have been close since her mother died, and she talks to me. The bottom line is that Penny compares every young man that she ever meets to you and they don't measure up."

"Well, Mr. Ponder…Doug, I don't know what to say. Penny is a wonderful girl and I have always cared for her."

"She thought you were tied up with the nurse in Annapolis, so she didn't make her feelings known."

"Well, the nurse is history. She is involved with a doctor and I am not involved with her."

"As a father, I would like to suggest that you and Penny spend some time together and see what happens. Oh, my! It's two in the morning. Lets' get some rest and call Penny over here in the morning."

"Great idea. Good night."

April 28, 1942, 0730 Hours

"Homer, I've changed my mind. During breakfast, we can listen to the news and then you can drop me off at the office, and go over to the Spaulding Law firm to surprise Penny. Then you can both go out to the farm and I will meet you there for dinner. You may want to swing by the bottling plant on Spring Street and see your Aunt Virginia. She is now the secretary to the plant manager. I am not sure if Penny has met her, so you could take her in with you and introduce them."

When Homer arrived at Spaulding Law on Peachtree Street, he went to the reception desk on the ground floor then asked the receptionist to call Penny Ponder, and request she come down to greet a visitor. When Penny stepped off the elevator, she saw Homer and ran across the lobby nearly knocking him over when she threw her arms around his neck.

"Oh Homer, I have prayed for you every night. I just knew your Liberty ship would be sunk. Then we didn't hear from you and that made it worse. This is the happiest day of my life!"

"Penny, I've always adored you. Your dad suggested we go out to the farm and he would meet us for dinner. Can you leave?"

"I am working for Ned MacNeely so I will need to clear it with him. You know him of course, so why don't you come up with me?"

When they walked through the office with Penny on Homer's arm, some of her co-workers started to buzz, 'He looks like an Admiral. Look how young he is.'

Ned MacNeely was pleased to see Homer and asked, "What rank are you, Homer?"

"I'm a 1-star Admiral."

Penny said, "An Admiral! I thought you were in the Merchant Marine."

"It is a long story, but during war time promotions can come quickly."

Ned MacNeely said, "Penny, we will get along without you. Just give me a call and let me know when you can come back."

"Thank you, Mr. MacNeely."

"Congratulations, Homer, I'm glad I got to see you."

Penny and Homer stopped at the bottling plant and saw Aunt Virginia. She was delighted to see Homer, and enjoyed meeting Penny.

"Your dad has been very kind to me, and most likely put in a good word for me when I was hired for the typing pool."

After saying goodbye, they picked up Homer's bag at the Biltmore. When they reached the farm in Penny's Jaguar, they parked in the back and went in through the kitchen.

Mary Lee Wells saw Homer and put her arms around him. "Mr. Homer, I'm so happy to see you. You have always been my favorite! I hope you can stay for dinner."

"That sounds wonderful, Mary Lee."

"Mr. Homer, that shore is a pretty uniform. You must still be in the Navy."

"I am."

Penny suggested that they go upstairs and change into some casual clothes and go see the horses.

Homer said, "I don't have any casual clothes with me."

"Well you are the same size as daddy, we will just borrow something. You do have a pair of your boots that I put away in the tack room. Say, why don't we take a ride before dinner?"

"Penny, I have only been on a horse once in the last four years at the Academy."

"Homer, you don't forget. It is like riding a bicycle. We still have the Babe, and I have a new thoroughbred."

After a gentle ride for an hour, they dismounted and let their horses have a drink from a pond at the back of the farm.

"Penny, this is like being in a different world. I have thought about you almost every day. When you were seeing that doggie up at Lake Burton, I was jealous and fought hard to keep it from showing. When you wrote me the note that you put in my bag with a sandwich, I wanted to tell you I felt the same about you. Then I told myself that all a Midshipmen can have is a friend relationship. The nurse that I was seeing up in Annapolis is tied up with a doctor and that doesn't bother me a bit."

"Homer, I dumped Pick because he turned down going to Fort Jackson to take over a rifle company so he could stay behind a desk measuring oil and gasoline tanks. He had no ambition. I guess this is tell all time. After Pick, I had one of the lawyers at the law firm force an engagement ring on my finger. He lacked character and trust. After a week of thinking about a life with him, I gave the ring back. Every time somebody makes a pass at me, I compare him to you. I just don't want to settle for second or third best. So, there it is Homer, I am available. I hope you love me, because I love you."

Homer took a deep breath, reached in his pocket and then got down on his knee and said, "Penny, I hope you want to marry me as much as I want to marry you."

Then Homer opened the box and put the 3-carat diamond on Penny's ring finger.

Penny knelt down and put her arms around Homer, kissed him and said "Yes, yes!"

Homer was holding the Babe by her reins and the Babe put her head down and gave Homer a nudge knocking Homer and Penny over.

Penny laughed and said, "Well I guess the Babe approves."

They both sat on the ground and just looked at each other.

Penny said, "I have prayed for you, and for this to happen."

Homer said "This is the happiest day of my life. Penny, would you like to get married at the White House? Mrs. Roosevelt said they would like to have a happy event, and the President said he would be honored to be my best man. Unless you would rather have a church wedding, or we could elope. The President said he knows and likes your dad. Speaking of your dad, I need to ask for his blessing."

"Don't worry about Daddy. He has compared every young man that I have crossed paths with to you, and he will be thrilled."

That night, Penny asked Mary Lee to set a place at the table for four.

"Who else is coming, Miss Penny?"

"Nobody, we want you with us for a very important announcement."

Before dinner, Homer and his future father-in-law had their talk.

Doug Ponder said, "You didn't waste any time Homer, but I can assure you, you have my blessing."

At dinner, Mary Lee said, "This must be important, because I've had dinner with you, Mr. Ponder, and with you, Miss Penny, when we were alone, but never with the family."

Doug Ponder said, "If you would raise your glass for a toast to the future bride and groom."

Mary Lee let out a whoop! "Hallelujah, praise God! I've been praying for this, Miss Penny. Mr. Homer, you were the one I always wanted for Miss Penny. I am so glad you will be a part of the family."

Penny said, "President and Mrs. Roosevelt have asked if we would like to have the wedding at the White House so, Mary Lee, you will be going as a member of our family along with Homer's Aunt Virginia and his cousin Sandy."

Homer said, "Penny, you will need to go meet with Mrs. Roosevelt to work out all the details and set a date. I need to go to Jacksonville tomorrow to evaluate the Mayport Naval Station for a research lab location. Then we can go to Washington."

"Homer, can I go with you to Jacksonville? We have friends with a beautiful place on the St. Johns River called Epping Forrest. If the DuPont's aren't using it, I am sure they would be happy for us to stay there."

Doug Ponder said, "I will call my friend Mike DuPont."

"Penny, if you go with me to Jacksonville, I would need to leave you with the DuPont's when I go out to Mayport, and we might be there for a couple of days. Normally, I would fly down on a Navy plane, but if Penny and I go together I would need to borrow a car. It wouldn't look right for me to drive up to the Admiral's headquarters in Penny's Jaguar."

"Sure, Homer, you can take my Cadillac."

"I need to find out who is the base commander so I can call his aide and set up the visit."

Penny said, "No problem, I have a friend from Emory who is a reporter at the Florida Times Union. I'll give Brittany a call. She will know who the base commander is."

Brittany told Penny that Captain Gaspard was the C.O. at Mayport, and if she was coming to Jacksonville they must get together. In the Morning, Homer called Captain Gaspard's deputy, Commander Bill Hopeman, and arranged for a visit.

"We can discuss the reason for the visit in person. I look forward to seeing you on the first of May."

April 29, 1942, Jacksonville, Florida

Penny and Homer arrived at Epping Forrest in the late afternoon and were greeted by the housekeeper and butler. None of the DuPont family were there, but arrangements had been made. Penny had called Brittany, who was a college friend but not a sorority sister, and she insisted on taking them to an excellent seafood restaurant called Corkey Bells.

"I can't wait to meet your fiancé."

They had a great shrimp dinner, with the best coleslaw and hushpuppies that Homer had ever tasted.

Brittany wanted to know why Homer was going to Mayport and he politely responded, "It is a classified naval project."

Brittany was a nice girl who had majored in journalism at Emory and this was her first paying job. During dinner, Homer felt that he was being interviewed for a story, so he was nice but vague. Penny explained that they went to high school together in Roswell, but they stayed in contact while Homer was at Annapolis.

When Brittany asked, "What rank were you?" Homer explained that all Midshipmen are commissioned Ensigns upon graduation.

Brittany responded with, "That's nice."

Penny told Brittany, "There is a possibility that we may move here after the wedding."

"You will love it here. We have a nice beach and St. Augustine is the oldest city in America. The Coast Guard has taken over St. Augustine for a training base. But it is still a very interesting place to visit. There is so much to do. We go motor boating and sailing on the three hundred and 23-mile-long St. Johns River. You know it is the only big river in the world that flows from south to north other, than the Nile?"

Penny asked Brittany if there were some nice houses for sale. Homer joined the conversation, saying, "Penny, we may be living in Navy housing."

"That is okay, as long as we are together." Brittany turned to Penny.

"You are so lucky! Does Homer have a brother?"

"No, but he had some really nice roommates at Annapolis."

On April 30th, Homer drove around Jacksonville with Penny, looking at the docks and getting the lay of the land. In the evening, he took Penny and Brittany for dinner at the Naval Air Station Jacksonville Officer's Club on the St. Johns. He called ahead for reservations and requested no honors.

When they picked up Brittany, Homer was in uniform, and Brittany said, "I thought you said you were an Ensign. It looks like you are an Admiral."

Homer replied, "I was an Ensign."

Penny said "This is the second time I have been to an officer's club. The food is so much better here than the food at Fort MacPherson in Atlanta."

Homer said, "I guess that's why I picked the Navy."

May 1, 1942, Mayport Naval Station
(Prior to station commissioning)

Homer arrived at the front gate and showed his ID to the Marine guards and was given directions to Captain Gaspard's office. Homer parked the Cadillac and walked to the front door where he was met by Commander Hopeman.

After a salute, Commander Hopeman said, "Captain Gaspard is looking forward to your visit."

After the formalities, a cup of strong Navy coffee was offered, and Homer proceeded to explain why he was at Mayport.

Captain Gaspard was relieved that he wasn't being replaced with an Admiral, and said, "We have a great deal of open space for a research facility because we are still under construction. Another reason to pick Mayport is that it is more secluded than Groton or certainly Norfolk. I can promise you full support from this base. And by the way, we have better weather."

After driving all over the Naval Station, Homer told Captain Gaspard, "Mayport looks like the best choice."

Captain Gaspard replied, "I'm glad to hear your choice, Sir."

"When we are together, my name is Homer. I hope you don't mind if I call you George. I realize that you have much more active duty experience than me, and I look forward to your advice and counsel."

When Homer returned to Epping Forrest, he wrote a report for Admiral King explaining the advantages of Mayport, and Penny typed it up for him. Homer called NAS Jacksonville and asked if they had a flight to Washington. Then he had second thoughts.

'I have Doug Ponder's car, which should be returned, and Penny and I could fly commercial to Washington so she could meet Mrs. Roosevelt to plan the wedding, and I could present the report to Admiral King in person.'

May 3, 1942, Washington DC

Homer and Penny went to the White House for a 10 a.m. appointment with Mrs. Roosevelt.

"I'm nervous, Homer. I've never been to the White House. I hope I say the right things to Mrs. Roosevelt. Do you think they know Daddy is a Republican?"

"They know your dad is a Republican, and the President said he was a good fellow."

Mrs. Roosevelt immediately put Penny at ease. "We are so proud of your husband-to-be. Homer has told me so many good things about you. I knew you would be as nice as you are."

Homer said, "I hope you will excuse me, Mrs. Roosevelt. I have an appointment with Admiral King at 1100. Whatever you and Penny decide about the wedding will be all right with me."

"We will be sending out wedding invitations for you, and we will need your list of people that you and Penny would like to invite. By the way, where are you staying?"

Penny replied, "We have separate rooms on separate floors at the Willard."

Mrs. Roosevelt said, "We can have your things moved over here and you can have dinner with Franklin and me." Penny said "That would be very nice. In fact, that will be an honor."

Homer said, "I will meet you at the Willard after the meeting and we can get our things together. Mrs. Roosevelt, you are so kind to extend this invitation. Thank you."

Homer met with Captain Malle and Vice Admiral DeVito.

Admiral DeVito said, "Admiral King has delegated your R&D lab project to me. He wants to be kept in the loop but as you can imagine he is up to his neck with immediate operations. The classified information you secured for us has helped to reveal important details about a big Jap operation for Admiral King."

"Sir, I will really appreciate all the help and guidance that you can give me on the lab project. With your approval, I have selected Mayport for the lab. Here is the report that I prepared showing the advantages over Groton and Norfolk. There is plenty of room for a separate dock in the Mayport basin and they have plenty of contractors putting up buildings. We should be operational before long."

Captain Malle said, "I want to send you a good finance officer and a senior personnel chief. As of today, you will be designated the Naval O&D Laboratory Mayport. You will be able to cut orders and transfer people, and most important, get them paid."

Admiral DeVito asked, "Have you decided on an aide?"

"I would like to bring in Lieutenant Frank House."

Captain Malle said, "I have looked at his record, and he is certainly acceptable. However, you are entitled to a higher rank officer, and I thought House would be more effective as head of operational testing, rather than being a dog robber. I hate to admit it, but there are officers in the Navy that will listen to a Commander or Lieutenant Commander but blow off a Lieutenant J.G. Aide."

"You make a good point. When House was Master Sergeant, he fired the shot that stopped the Jap torpedo, and was the best gunnery trainer. If you have an aide in mind, I would like to get him on board ASAP."

Captain Malle said, "We will set up an interview with Lieutenant Commander Bob Jones Jr. for tomorrow at 1000 at my office. He has been recuperating at Bethesda Naval Hospital and is about to be discharged. Jones was Admiral Kimmel's junior aide and was injured during the bombing at Pearl. He is a good guy, class of 1937."

"Do you think he will have a problem serving with a class of 1942?"

Admiral DeVito said, "Not when he sees your record. He is a real down to earth, common sense guy, who got a bad final fitness report from Admiral Kimmel because he suggested a number of things that Kimmel chose not to do that might have saved our butts."

"I look forward to meeting Commander Jones, and thank you for your suggestions."

Homer met Penny at the Willard and found that she had packed up both of their rooms, and the Willard staff was transferring their bags to the White House. Penny was happy to see Homer, and executed a PDA (Public Display of Affection) in the lobby.

Penny said, "Mrs. Roosevelt was so nice to me. She knew a lot about me. That my mother had died from cancer, and that I had graduated with honors from Emory. She also had some very nice things to say about you. She offered to be my matron of honor, and I accepted. She said the President was going to put on his braces so he could stand beside you as your best man. Homer, this brought tears to my eyes. I felt such pride, I was afraid I was going to pop open. What is amazing is that they know daddy and I are Republicans."

"Penny, they know that we are all Americans."

Dinner was in the small dining room in the family quarters. They served southern fried chicken, crackling cornbread and southern style green beans.

Penny said, "This meal makes me feel like I am right at home."

President Roosevelt quipped, "That is the idea. My chef from Warm Springs knows how to do it right."

Penny added, "When we were planning the wedding list, I mentioned to Mrs. Roosevelt that I wanted to bring our housekeeper Mary Lee Wells, who practically raised me. She would enjoy meeting your chef and compare recipes."

The President said, "Mary Lee must be black, if she knows how to do great fried chicken. You know we would love to have her."

Penny and Mrs. Roosevelt settled on Saturday, June 6th for the wedding, at 2 in the afternoon.

President Roosevelt said, "Homer, I am ordering you to take a one week of your leave for your honeymoon. Now tell me how the R&D lab project is coming along. And don't forget to use Harry Hopkins to help with corporate red tape."

"Mr. President, after looking at Groton and Norfolk, I found that the new Naval Station Mayport would be the best choice since it is under construction and hasn't been commissioned. They have plenty of room and the other bases are crowded. Another advantage is good year round weather and very good security. Admiral King asked Admiral DeVito to oversee the project and keep him in the loop. They have already been most helpful."

"I want you to keep me in the loop as well. When you have the torpedo stopping project perfected, I would like to come down for a demonstration."

"It will be an honor to have you, Mr. President."

Chapter 33
The Plank Owners

May 4, 1942, 1100 Hours

The next morning, Homer took Penny to Washington National for a flight to Atlanta, and Homer went to Naval Headquarters to begin interviews with his new staff. He placed a call to Lieutenant Frank House, who was with his family in Tombstone.

"Frank, we will be setting up the O&D lab at Mayport near Jacksonville. I have been in conference with Admiral DeVito, and it has been decided that you are too valuable to be a dog robber (Admiral's Aide). With your experience, you will be head of operational testing. I can probably get you promoted more quickly from that position, and finding someone to be an aide is easy. Orders will be cut for a PCS (Permanent Change of Station) for you and your family to the Jacksonville area. You will need to report ASAP, and let your family follow when you have a place for them. If you have never been here, this area is really nice."

At 1100, Lieutenant Commander Bob Jones Jr. knocked on the side of Homer's temporary office, and was invited in. Earlier, Captain Malle had met with Commander Jones and briefed him on Admiral Harris's record, and was certain that there was no problem.

Jones said, "I can't wait to meet him. I've heard a little scuttlebutt about him, and it is all favorable."

Homer began the interview by explaining the mission to develop a reliable method of intercepting torpedoes.

Homer said, "I haven't been on active duty long enough to know how to avoid the rocks and shoals. This is a two-way street, so if you decide to accept this assignment, I will need your advice and counsel and I promise to listen carefully. We have stopped one Jap torpedo with 75- millimeter, armor piercing tank fire, but that is a long way from a proven system. We have been made operational as the Naval O&D Laboratory Mayport. The new base has not been commissioned, but will be soon. We need to hit the ground running and will have strong support from the top down. Now tell me about yourself and if this job is attractive."

"Sir, let me assure you that the time on active duty and rank does not cause any problem for me. The word is out that you sank five submarines and the German raider, then captured another oil tanker sub with no casualties as captain of a Liberty ship. You mentioned a two-way street, and I'm looking forward to learning from you as well. I want you to know that I got a really bad fitness report from Admiral Kimmel."

Homer laughed and said, "Kimmel's fitness report would make yours look like a Presidential citation, so put that behind you."

"We are in a hurry, because every ship of ours that gets sunk extends the time to finish this war. Do you have a family that will need to move to Jacksonville?"

"No Sir, I'm single, and they plan to discharge me from Bethesda tomorrow."

"Could you stay and join me for two more interviews with a Finance Officer that has been recommended by Captain Malle, and a Senior Chief Personnel man? I would like for you to take the lead in the interviews and bring me in if they ask a question that you would rather I answer."

The Finance Officer was Lieutenant Thomas Lipick, a University of Florida ROTC graduate with a B.S. in Accounting.

When Lipick learned that the assignment was in Jacksonville he said, "That is terrific! I have been counting rivets at the ice-cold Bath Iron Works in Maine for almost three years."

Commander Jones gave Lipick an in-depth interview and asked him to wait in the outer office.

Homer asked Commander Jones, "What do you think?"

"I think he will do just fine."

"So do I. Please call him back in when we finish the next interview."

The Senior Personnel Chief, Michael McKenna, had held almost every enlisted job in the Navy except deep sea diver during his 25 years on active duty. Homer and Commander Jones agreed that Mckenna would know the ropes, and they liked his can-do attitude.

Homer said, "Chief, we have given you the picture. Do you want this job?"

"Sir, I'd like nothing better than to put together a crew that can stop torpedoes from sinking our ships."

Commander Jones called Lieutenant Lipick back in the office.

Homer said, "Gentlemen, the four of us are the plank holders of the Naval O&D Laboratory Mayport. I look forward to working with you. We have one more member who is going to join us in a few days. You will meet Lieutenant

Frank House, who actually stopped a Jap torpedo. He is a gunnery expert that we transferred from the Army. Please give Commander Jones your contact information and your best estimate of a reporting date. We have a lot to do so I look forward to seeing you in Jacksonville."

May 4, 1942 Atlanta

Penny was picked up at Candler Field by her dad, and she had a lot to say.

"Daddy, I know Homer is right for me. I guess I've known it all along. You never tried to push any of the young men that I have known up or down, but I could see it in your eyes with Homer. He is the only one that I kept measuring everybody else against."

"Now that things are decided, daughter, Homer is the only one I could be really proud to have in our family. I won't be here forever and knowing that your husband has character, judgment, strength, and kindness gives me confidence that you will be good for each other."

"Daddy, Mrs. Roosevelt was so nice to me. We spent the night at the White House and Homer told me that the Roosevelts knew we were both Republicans. You can tell the President thinks Homer is something special, and offered to be Homer's best man. Mrs. Roosevelt offered to be my matron of honor and I accepted with thanks. Of course, you are the father of the bride. Now, I need to get the invitation list to Mrs. Roosevelt and buy a dress from Homer's best friend's mother Mrs. Schmidt in New Jersey. Mrs. Roosevelt said they would handle the music, the reception, and send out the invitations. The White House is a beautiful place for a wedding. Will my sorority sisters ever be excited when they are invited to the White House! Now Homer and I have to decide who will marry us. He suggested Dr. Porter from the Sparta Presbyterian Church, or we could have the Chaplain from Annapolis."

"I remember Dr. Porter when we brought him to Georgia for the lawsuit. It is up to you and Homer, but our minister is new, and we don't really know him, so I would vote for Dr. Porter. Penny, the Roosevelts have extended an honor that is really exceptional. Whoever you choose to marry you will be fine."

"I know, Daddy. I can't wait for the 6th of June to get here."

Chapter 34
Epping Forrest

Homer called Penny that evening and told her that he had four key members of the team signed up, and he was going to catch a flight to Jacksonville in the morning.

"I have a really good aide coming down day after tomorrow and a Finance Officer coming from Maine in a few days. We also have a Senior Chief for personnel, and Frank House is going to be the Director of Operational Testing. I need to find some place to set up temporary shop and find quarters for everyone including you and me. I'll call you when I get to Jacksonville. I love you."

May 5, 1942, Jacksonville
Homer checked in to the partially complete Navy Lodge Mayport and then went to Captain Gaspard's office.

"George, it is good to see you. I need to start collecting favors."

"Good to see you Sir, what do you need?"

"I need a desk, a phone, and a locking filing cabinet."

"That is no problem. How did it go in DC?"

"We are operational as the Naval O&D Laboratory Mayport. I have a Lieutenant Commander Aide who is being discharged from Bethesda today, a Finance Lieutenant who was at the Bath Iron Works, a Senior Chief Personnel Man and a Lieutenant JG who will be the Director of Operational Testing."

"You don't let any barnacles grow on you!"

"I'm going to need quarters for them. The Senior Chief and the JG have families and I'm getting married on June six."

"Congratulations! I will get Brown and Root Contractors to give you plans for a BOQ right by the planned officers club. We have a consolidated galley for now, so meals won't be a problem. There are no family quarters in the budget for now, so I'm afraid you will need to find civilian housing."

"I really appreciate your help, George."

Homer was set up in a small interior office that was a former storage closet. Captain Gaspard had offered his office to Homer, but the offer was refused with thanks. The first phone call from his office was to Penny.

After the hello and I love you, Penny said, "Daddy talked with Mike DuPont and you can have the whole Epping Forrest place for the duration if you need it, for one dollar per year."

"Wow! That solves an immediate problem. What a patriotic gesture! I was going to find civilian family housing and something temporary on base for my two bachelors. We can put the Senior Chief's family in one of the separate guest houses, and the JG's family in the other. There is an owner's suite for you and me, unless we need to move ourselves to a bedroom and turn the suite into group quarters. If I remember correctly there are eight or ten large bedrooms. I'm going to see if we can retain the current DuPont staff and add some Navy help in the galley. That is the kitchen, Penny."

"Daddy told me that the staff will stay on the DuPont payroll, at no cost to the Navy."

"It just keeps getting better. I can't wait to see the reaction that our staff and the families have when they see the most beautiful accommodations that they will probably ever live in. Please tell your dad to thank Mr. DuPont. If you will get his address, I will write him a letter."

During the next week, the staff arrived and could hardly believe that Epping Forrest, a 58- acre property with a 15,000 square foot mansion with 25 spectacular rooms, would be their new Navy quarters.

Senior Chief McKenna's three boys were enrolled at the Bolles Navy Military Academy on the Saint Johns River, and Homer quietly paid their tuition with the agreement that the Chief would be told that the school had a program for military families. Bolles had the reputation for the best advance placement program and held the best Florida athletic program award for 21 years. Lieutenant House enrolled his three girls at the public Duval County Loretta Elementary School, which was founded in 1893 and enjoyed an excellent reputation.

Mrs. June Mckenna and Mrs. Rosalie House became immediate friends when June McKenna found out that both husbands wore E-7 stripes, and Rosalie's husband had just been recently promoted from the Army into the Navy. The only bad news that came in during the week was the loss of the aircraft carrier *Lexington*, during the battle of the Corral Sea on May 8th.

Homer thought to himself, 'Thank goodness Jim Coriello is on the *Hornet*.'

May 10, 1942, Naval Air Station Jacksonville

Lieutenant Commander Bob Jones and Lieutenant Tom Lipick arrived together on a Catalina amphibian flying boat at 1400, and landed on the St. Johns River. Homer and Lieutenant House drove to NAS JAX to pick them up in Doug Ponder's borrowed Cadillac.

When they arrived at Epping Forrest, Bob Jones said, "Admiral, you have got to be kidding! First a Cadillac and then a Mansion. This can't be Navy quarters."

Homer explained the generous offer from the DuPont family.

Lieutenant Lipick said, "Compared to where I was living at the Bath Iron Works, this is paradise!"

"I'm glad you gentlemen are pleased, but we have much to do in a short time. We are having a meet and greet shrimp dinner tonight and at 0800 tomorrow it is all business. We will begin with a staff meeting at breakfast."

Just before dinner, a taxi arrived at Epping Forrest. It was Penny. She had decided to surprise Homer and meet everyone.

"Why didn't you call me, so I could pick you up at the airport?"

"Then it wouldn't have been a surprise."

"In the future, please call. I could have gone somewhere"

"Yes dear. You still love me?"

"Forever, Penny!"

"I'm glad, because I have to go back to Atlanta tomorrow. We are going to court on a very interesting case, and Ned MacNeely needs me."

During the next three weeks, a dock was built in the Mayport Basin and a thirty thousand square foot warehouse with an electric crane for loading torpedoes was installed. The O&D Laboratory received a shipment of twenty practice torpedoes and the USS *Pike* to fire them.

The *Pike*, SS173, was an earlier Porpoise class boat almost identical to the USS *Perch* that Homer had taken his summer training cruise on during his second year at the Naval Academy. Getting a Liberty ship became difficult, because immediately after their shakedown cruise high priority cargos were on their way to a critical area.

A message came from Captain Malle that an Italian cargo ship had been captured before it could leave Baltimore when war was declared, and it was available to be used as a target. The message informed the O&D Lab that they would need to bring it to Mayport. Commander Jones volunteered to Captain the ship. Chief McKenna put together a crew and went with Commander Jones as First Mate. Lieutenant House had been working on an electrically powered gun platform with the engineers at Ford Motor Company who were turning out Sherman tanks. Lieutenant Lepick had been seeing that the bills were paid. He also secured 2 jeeps, a three-quarter ton Dodge truck, and a new 1941 Plymouth staff car. Arrangements were made to return Doug Ponder's Cadillac.

Offices at Epping Forrest were set up with secure encryption teletype. Lieutenant Lepick set up a second office at the Mayport warehouse. Chief McKenna and Lieutenant Lepick Got a junior cook and a Filipino steward transferred to work under the DuPont head chef at Epping Forrest. Lieutenant Lepick suggested that they take two thousand feet of the warehouse and set up quarters for the USS *Pike* and the Italian freighter American crew.

Lieutenant Commander Jim Vanderwier, Captain of the Pike, was all for the idea, and assigned part of his crew to assist in the carpentry work since they didn't have the Italian target ship to conduct testing.

Chapter 35
The Wedding

On June 4th, Homer took a R4D from NAS JAX to Washington. Penny and her dad had checked in at the Willard across the street from the White House. After dinner, they went over the RSVP list.

On Homer's list, he had Fred and Frida Schmidt, Christine Costello, Aunt Virginia, Cousin Sandy Harris, Mr. and Mrs. Arthur Haviland, Mr. and Mrs. Larry Cohen, Mr. and Mrs. Sam Cornelius, Mr. and Mrs. Ned Mac Neely, and Mr. and Mrs. Israel Iseman. Army Second Lieutenant Hans Schmidt sent regrets, as did both of his Annapolis Roommates Ensigns Jim Coriello and Charles Forrest.

Hans explained that they transferred him from the Armor School at Fort Knox to the OSS due to his flawless ability to speak and read German, and he was on his way to England. Hans also told Homer that he and Lizzy were engaged.

Charles Forrest wrote that he was almost finished with Jump School at Fort Benning as a Marine Second Lieutenant, and they wouldn't give him even one day off. Jim Coriello wrote that he and Emily Derieux were engaged.

'Emily will be at the wedding, but I'm on the *Lexington* and we are about to put to sea again.'

Jim's letter was posted from the FPO at Pearl Harbor. Homer thought to himself, 'Dear God, they transferred Jim from the *Hornet* to the *Lexington*. Please keep Jim safe. I guess no news is good news.'

Penny's RSVP list included Mary Lee Wells, Emily Derieux, Elizabeth Montgomery, three other Phi Mu sorority sisters, and Mr. and Mrs. Ned MacNeely. Dr. and Mrs. Porter were on the invitation list, even though Dr. Porter would be marrying them.

President and Mrs. Roosevelt invited their friend Harry Winston and Mrs. Winston, Henry and Mrs. Ford, Admiral and Mrs. King, Admiral and Mrs. Devito, Admiral Westfield from Annapolis, Captain and Mrs. Malle, Bob

Hope and his wife. The total, 36 guests, was below the number that Mrs. Roosevelt said they would be comfortable with.

June 5, 1942, Naval Headquarters Washington

Homer reported to Admiral Devito and was joined by Captain Malle. His report covered the work at Mayport and the success that Lieutenant House was having with the engineers at Ford designing the gun platform.

Captain Malle and Admiral Devito knew about the Italian cargo ship that Commander Jones was presently bringing to Mayport. Homer told Admiral Devito and Captain Malle that Commander Bob Jones was an excellent selection.

"He has been invaluable!" He went on to say, "Lieutenant Lepick was an excellent scrounger and administrator and a perfect fit for the job that he is doing. Senior Chief McKenna has handled the personnel requirements with ease, but he has the ability to organize and lead that far exceeds his rank. When we prove that we can stop these torpedoes, I'd like to promote all four of these outstanding officers."

Admiral Devito paused and said, "We will see how everything works out."

"Also, Sir, when Commander Goldberg can be released from Bletchley Park, I would like to have him transferred to the Lab so that we can work on an idea that I discussed with him using radio controlled anti-aircraft fire. There is another project that we could explore; making depth charges follow the magnetism coming from a sub's hull, and have a propellant system that would allow the charge to move the explosive to the sub."

Admiral DeVito said, "Those are interesting ideas, I will let Admiral King know that the lab may be taking on projects after the torpedoes. My wife and I are looking forward to meeting your bride at the wedding tomorrow. Homer, thank you for all that you have done and continue to do. We are going to win this war!"

That evening Homer took Doug Ponder, Penny, Mary Lee, and the bridesmaids Emily and Lizzy for dinner in a private dining room at the Willard. All of the other out of town guests were arriving in the morning.

After dinner, Homer called Lieutenant Lepick to see how things were going. "Have you heard from Commander Jones?"

"Yes Sir, he was held up at Savannah due to U-Boat activity. They are sending an escort up from Mayport tomorrow."

"Thanks, keep me advised."

Then Homer called Frank House at his hotel in Detroit. "What is the latest on the gun platform?"

"Sir, Ford says they are ready to ship a prototype to Mayport."

"That is good news. Were you impressed by any of the engineers?" "They were all good, but one was outstanding. He is a mechanical engineer from Georgia Tech named Emory Taylor. I would like to bring him down with me."

"We are in luck. You know tomorrow I'm getting married at the White House, and Henry Ford is on the President's guest list. I will ask Mr. Ford to let us have Mr. Taylor."

June 6, 1942, The White House

Doug Ponder hosted a brunch at the Willard for all of the out of town guests on Penny and Homer's list. Then, Penny and her bridesmaids went to her suite to get ready for the wedding.

Homer and his future father-in-law stayed with the group for another hour before they went to their rooms to get dressed. The wedding party and Dr. Porter were driven across the street for a rehearsal at 1 p.m.

Mrs. Roosevelt had everything in order. The flowers were beautiful, American flags were on their stands, an organ had been brought into the west wing meeting room, and Captain Malle had lined up six Ensigns from Naval Headquarters to form a saber arch when the bride and groom left the White House.

Just before the organist began playing, "Here Comes the Bride," Mrs. Roosevelt kissed Penny on the cheek and whispered, "Today, my dear, you are America's daughter."

Penny placed her arm on her dad's arm, and they walked through the door toward Homer and President Roosevelt. Admiral King was standing by the President to steady him.

Homer said to himself, "Penny is the most beautiful girl in the world."

When everyone was in place, President Roosevelt said, "Before we proceed, I have an official duty that I am honored to administer."

Admiral King handed the President the Medal of Honor and assisted him in placing it around Homer's neck, and then read the citation.

When he finished, the President said, "This is the second Medal of Honor in the Harris family. I wish Homer's father, Bob Harris, and his mother, Mildred Harris, could be here to see their son receive this honor."

Dr. Porter began by saying, "Who brings this woman?"

Douglas Ponder responded, "Her father," then he stepped aside.

"By the grace of God, we are gathered here today to join these two wonderful young people in the bond of holy matrimony. To love and to cherish, in sickness and in health, until death do you part. Do you, Homer, take Penny as your lawfully wedded wife?"

"I do."

"Do you, Penny, take Homer as your lawfully wedded husband?"

"I do."

"If anyone knows why these two should not be married, let them speak now."

There was silence.

"As an ordained minister of the Presbyterian Church, I now pronounce you man and wife. You may kiss the bride."

After a photographer took two pictures with Homer, Penny, President Roosevelt, Mrs. Roosevelt, Admiral King, Lizzy, Emily, and Doug Ponder, then a second with just Homer and Penny.

President Roosevelt said, "We have prepared some refreshments for you all."

Homer thanked Harry Winston for the beautiful rings.

Winston asked Homer, "What have you decided to do with the Rhodesian sun ring from King George?"

Homer replied, "This may sound crazy but until now I have forgotten all about it after we put it in the President's safe. I will have to ask his guidance about the ring."

Penny asked, "What ring?"

"I'll tell you all about it later."

Henry Ford was introduced to Homer and Penny by Admiral King. "Mr. Ford, I want to thank you for the excellent cooperation on the classified project that your staff is helping us with."

"Son, I know all about the project and what earned you the Medal. We are terribly proud of you."

"Sir, I would also like to compliment Ford on the Liberator Express that I took a 12000-mile ride on recently."

"I know all about that, too. I also know that you don't own a car. So, we found an almost complete maroon 1942 Deluxe Convertible sitting on the assembly line without chrome bumpers. That car now has aluminum painted wood bumpers, and we had it shipped to my friend Bob Wade at Wade Ford in Atlanta. You can pick it up and drive to the Cloister at Sea Island. I even know that is where you and your beautiful bride are going for your honeymoon."

"Mr. Ford, I can't thank you enough for my second Ford. The first was a 1929 Model A pickup truck that I gave to my favorite teacher, Mr. Iseman, when I left for the Naval Academy. He is right over there with his wife. I know he would like to meet you. Oh, I have a favor to ask Mr. Ford. Would it be possible for you to send Emory Taylor, a mechanical engineer, who has been most helpful on the classified project down to Mayport for instillation and testing?"

"I'll try to remember, but call my secretary and she will have him report to you."

When they were about to leave, Homer thanked everyone, and especially President Roosevelt and Mrs. Roosevelt. Penny hugged Mrs. Roosevelt. They were both surprised by the saber arch when they left the White House.

The photographer got a picture with Penny and Homer ducking under the sabers.

The End, and the Beginning.

Please leave a review for BROADSIDE on Amazon Books and mention that you are a member of the St. Augustine, Fl. Library. The story is in consideration for a miniseries and reviews are helpful.